MOONGARDEN

PLOTTING
❧ THE ❧
STARS

MOONGARDEN

MICHELLE A. BARRY

PIXEL✛INK

*To Julia and Jensen, for bringing extraordinary
magic into my everyday life.*

*And to Jared. When I get lost in daydreams or city streets (which is
often), you are forever my compass and home.*
—M.A.B.

PIXEL✛INK

Text copyright © 2022 by Michelle A. Barry
Jacket illustration copyright © 2022 by TGM Development Corp.
Jacket illustration by Sarah J. Coleman
All rights reserved

Pixel+Ink is an imprint of TGM Development Corp.
www.pixelandinkbooks.com
Printed and bound in September 2022 at Lake Book Manufacturing, Melrose Park, IL, U.S.A.
Jacket design by Sammy Yuen and Jay Colvin
Book design by Jay Colvin

Library of Congress Cataloging-in-Publication Data
Names: Barry, Michelle A., author.
Title: Moongarden / Michelle A. Barry.
Description: First edition. | New York : Pixel+Ink, 2022. | Series: Plotting the stars ; 1 | Audience: Grades
4-6. | Summary: Crumbling under the pressure at her elite school on the moon, misfit Myra Hodger
discovers a lab full of toxic plants and uses her botanical magic to weed out its secrets, but quickly
discovers some will do anything to take those secrets to the grave.
Identifiers: LCCN 2022021313 (print) | LCCN 2022021314 (ebook) | ISBN 9781645951261
(hardcover) | ISBN 9781645951285 (paperback) | ISBN 9781645951278 (epub)
Subjects: CYAC: Magic—Fiction. | Gardens—Fiction. | Poisonous Plants—Fiction. | Conspiracies—
Fiction. | Moon—Fiction. | Schools—Fiction. | Science fiction. | LCGFT: Novels. | Science fiction.
Classification: LCC PZ7.1.B37277 Mo 2022 (print) | LCC PZ7.1.B37277 (ebook) | DDC [Fic]—dc23
LC record available at https://lccn.loc.gov/2022021313
LC ebook record available at https://lccn.loc.gov/2022021314

Hardcover ISBN: 978-1-64595-126-1
E-book ISBN: 978-1-64595-127-8

First Edition

1 3 5 7 9 10 8 6 4 2

CHAPTER ONE

Second Month, 2448

I PEER THROUGH THE DOOR AT THE LONE empty seat in the classroom—my empty seat. When most kids cut class, they get as far away as possible, and I will, too. But first I like to check and see if they notice I'm missing. Or listen to what the other kids say when I'm not there.

A chime pings through invisible speakers embedded in the walls. I crouch just out of sight. Our teacher, a Number Whisperer like my parents, glances around the class. Light from one of the overhead panels glints off the pin clasped to her chest, mirroring the flash in her eyes as they settle on the one empty workstation in the rows and rows of seats.

"Has anyone seen Myra Hodger today?" Ms. Goble's dark braid whips off her shoulder as she scans the room, looking for the flicker of a hand.

There isn't one. I knew there wouldn't be.

"She's probably off inventing some new algorithm to teleport us all back to the Old World," some round-faced, curly-haired boy calls. Other kids snicker, and I roll my eyes.

"We don't need to teleport back, genius," I whisper. We have ships that could take us from the Lunar Colony to the Old World. That's not the problem. It's the fact that we can't *breathe* the air there anymore.

Ms. Goble waits for another moment, then makes an entry on the school-issued pendant hanging around her neck. Walking to the front of the class, she twists her braid into a tight bun beneath her ear and settles into the lesson. The laughter dies away. The class watches in a mixture of awe and envy as she swipes her hand through the air, leaving a trail of complicated-looking formulas glowing in its wake.

I quickly decipher the theory outlined in the misty, floating numbers. *Contouring decimal equations.* Easy stuff for most of the class, an assortment of twelve-year-old wannabe Number Whisperers. They're called that because hundreds of years ago, before we knew about the fusion of magic and science, people used to say the numbers whispered to a chosen few, telling them their secrets.

Convinced no more questions about my absence are looming, I back away from the door and set off down the hall with my head held high and my steps brisk but not rushed. Rule Number One of cutting class is to always act like you know exactly where you're going.

I don't. I never do.

I pass a closet, a darkened lab, and an abandoned teacher's lounge. I've used them all before, so they're off limits. Rule Number Two for cutting class is never go to the same place twice. If you get caught somewhere more than once, it's a lot harder to say you were there by accident.

My reflection gleams off the polished, silver walls as I stroll down the hall, and I glance sideways at the girl prowling beside me. She brushes dark hair out of her eyes, staring back. She looks confident. Like she belongs here. *Good. At least one of us does.*

I turn a corner, and the floor slopes up. My reflection morphs as the wall twists upward, too. The Scientific Lunar Academy of Magic, S.L.A.M. for short, is shaped like a corkscrew, twirling up six levels. The school, the best on the Moon and exclusively for those gifted with science-fueled magic, is plenty big enough to disappear into for a class period or two. A shortage of hiding places hasn't proven to be a problem. Not yet, anyway. School's only been in session for one rotation around the Old World, but give it another Moon cycle and I'll have to start repeating hiding spots.

If I'm still here then.

I turn into an unfamiliar corridor. I don't have any classes in this hall, and it seems deserted. There are a series of doorways, but all the rooms beyond them are dark and perfect for hiding.

Bzzzz! Bzzzz! Bzzzz!

I jump, spinning in a quick circle, before I realize the buzzing is coming from the pendant hanging against my chest. MANDATORY SCHOOL ASSEMBLY flashes up at me, and I groan. If I scan my pendant on the auditorium entryway but don't sit with my assigned class, I'm caught. And if I don't scan in at all, then I'm super-caught. With few other options and even less time, I turn and lightspeed it back the way I came, skidding into the Anti-Grav Chamber and slapping the activation button.

Immediately, I regret it. I usually avoid the Anti-Grav Chamber at all costs, even though most of my classmates think it's as fun as a hover coaster. (For the record, I don't like those, either). My feet float in midair as the floor falls away and I drift downward, pressure from the roof of the chamber propelling me toward the lower level. My stomach in my throat and my elbows sore from jostling the sides of the chamber, I tumble out at Level One and run down the hall toward my classroom, arriving just as the last kid files out and into the hallway. I jump to the end of the line, trying to stay out of sight, but a flick of Ms. Goble's head followed by a heated glare mean I'll be hearing from her later.

Soon after, we reach the Fiona A. Weathers Memorial Auditorium, named for the school director's wife. She died years ago in a shuttle crash. Space accidents are rare with computers running all flights, but every once in a while, you hear about some sort of glitch. Given that she was unlucky enough to be in a malfunctioning shuttle, naming a room after her seems like the least the school could do.

I scan my pendant on the doorway, following my class inside and onto a lift. A platform rises up and up and up to a row of seats at the very top of the auditorium, only a few yards lower than the ceiling. Bench-style seats wind around and around the circular room, a single podium hovering in the middle. Classes are seated by grade, with the first-years sitting at the very top, second-years in the row below us, third-years below them, and so on. The row of sixth-years is nearly level with the podium.

As we settle into our row, the boy seated beside me glances my way, then turns around to the girl on his other side. I put my chin on my hand and lean forward, waiting for the assembly to start and wishing on every lucky meteor that it takes the whole class period.

The lights dim, and conversations fade. Then Director Weathers appears at the floating podium as if out of thin air. He might be considered handsome, for an old guy anyway, if his expression wasn't so stony and cold. Wrinkles frame his eyes, his glare as hard as Mercurian ore. But with his dark-blond hair and athletic build, he still reminds me of the covers of the *Men's Biometrics* e-magazine Dad reads.

"Good afternoon, S.L.A.M. scholars," Director Weathers says, and his gaze flashes around the room like a strobe light. He regards us all silently for a moment, ensuring every last whisper has dissolved, then adjusts the Creer pin on his chest. The tiny symbol of an atom glints silver in the spotlight. I can't see it—he's much too far away—but everyone knows Director Weathers is a Chemic, the Creer that controls chemical compounds and mixtures. "I'll keep this brief," he finally says, "as I don't want to take more time away from your studies than is necessary. As you are all well aware, the more knowledge you cultivate and the more you sharpen your skills, the more expansive your magic will grow."

I force myself not to roll my eyes. My parents have given me this same lecture for as long as I can remember. I could probably give this speech myself by now.

"Learn as much as you can here at the Scientific Lunar Academy of Magic, and when you graduate, you will be well positioned to pursue the career of your choosing." He punctuates his statement with a wink, which might as well be a period at the end of a chapter as he switches gears entirely. "But that's not why we're here today. I wanted to alert you to a new and exciting development in the school cafeteria. Or, more precisely, to the cafeteria's menu."

Most of the kids around me murmur with excitement, but I raise an eyebrow. A school-wide assembly just to tell us about a menu change? This cannot be good. Plus, the forced quality of his "new and exciting" reminds me of the way my parents try to convince me that memorizing duplication tables will be a thrilling adventure.

Spoiler signal: it's not.

"S.L.A.M.'s nutrition vendor recently patented a cutting-edge food cloning technology, and we're lucky enough to be part of their pilot program. Our food will still taste the same—better, actually—and even *more* exciting is its modernized appearance."

And there it is.

"Many people don't realize that our food choices often have nothing to do with flavor," he continues as if reading a transcript from a commercial. "Other factors, such as scent, sight, and texture, play a much larger role in our dietary preferences. This new product neutralizes those obstacles, but the appearance of the food may . . . take some getting used to."

Whispers buzz through the auditorium and Director Weathers holds up his hands.

"Now, now," he says firmly. "As you are all young scientists, you should understand that appearances are hardly conclusive. It's nothing to be alarmed about. The food will simply have a certain . . . uniformity to it. We'll hardly even notice the difference after a few meals, I'm sure."

I'm not, but there's nothing I can do about it. And based on the grumpy murmurs still buzzing around the auditorium, I'm not alone.

I tune out as Director Weathers drones on about the science behind the new food-production process, vaguely hoping people ask enough questions to keep him talking for the rest of the period. The unexplored hallway I found pulls at my thoughts. I cross and uncross my ankles, my feet itching to investigate. The darkened classrooms lining the corridor are perfect candidates for my next week of hiding spots.

A loud crackling jolts me out of my planning and halts the director's monologue abruptly. I glance down at Director Weathers. His mouth hangs open, clearly midsentence, and his eyes dart around the room, searching for the source of the sound.

Something hisses over my head, and I duck. I'm not the only one. Multicolored flashes zoom from one side of the room to the other. *Lightning pulses.* It only takes me a nanosecond to find the source.

As most of the students gasp and dive behind their seats,

across the auditorium from me a group of Electors in JV hoverball uniforms try unsuccessfully to stifle their laughter. I recognize the blond-haired boy in the center, Canter Weathers, the director's son. He's a year older than me, and the captain of the JV hoverball team. I don't know him, but having seen him around school I can tell his ego is big enough to have its own gravitational field.

As the boys double over, the colorful currents get more erratic. One whizzes down from the ceiling and crashes into the podium, prompting screams from the sixth-year students seated up front. A whine shrieks from the voice amplifier, consuming any tirade Director Weathers would have shouted into it. The current of electricity must travel through the auditorium's power grid, because a moment later everything goes black.

Thuds and yelps echo around the auditorium as kids scramble in the dark. The boy next to me somehow manages to step on my elbow, obviously mistaking my seat for the stairs. Director Weathers shouts, trying to be heard over the confusion, but I can't make out what he's saying. Even so, I get the gist of it. With the assembly clearly over and plenty of class time left, there's no chance Director Weathers will just dismiss us for the rest of the period.

I quickly compute how long it will take Ms. Goble to thread her way through the confusion to collect her students, simultaneously calculating the pros and cons of cutting her class twice in one day.

The tally clear (numbers never lie—only humans do), I climb carefully down the rows and slip out the auditorium door.

CHAPTER TWO

I HURRY THROUGH THE EMPTY HALLWAYS, which are sure to be flooded with students at any moment, and head back toward the darkened corridor I'd discovered before the assembly. It takes me a while to retrace my steps, but after a few wrong turns and dead ends I find it.

Unfortunately, I'm not the only one. Voices drift toward me as I approach. I peek around the corner and spot the backs of two kids. They're both in T-shirts and jeans, same as me. First-years are allowed to wear what we want at school, but once you take the practical magic test at the end of your first year and are accepted into your Creer, you wear your Creer's color. That, or you don't pass and go home.

I tug on my sleeves, wrapping the hems around my palm as I turn to leave.

As I pull back, the boy drops into a crouch, like he's trying to block someone playing hoverball, and the girl giggles. With a start, I realize there's a third person in the hallway—an adult. For a moment I tense, ready to bolt the other way, but my eyes catch on her gray uniform and I feel the tightness melt away. "Just a Rep," I mutter under my breath. The kids are intentionally blocking the hall so she can't get by. They know there isn't much a Rep can do about it.

Heat creeps down my neck and through my arms as I clench my fists, still frozen in place.

Don't say anything, Myra. Rule Number Three of cutting class is *never talk to anyone.* If they hear your voice, they'll remember your face.

I backpedal one step, then another. I can duck around the corner and disappear in an instant. Even if the kids caught a glimpse of me, there's no way they'd know where I was going.

Sidestepping into the connecting hall, I twist my backpack straps in my hands. I need to leave, and fast, but my feet stick to the ground like it's silver quicksand. Around the corner, sneakers squeak and a loud burst of laughter cuts through the silence.

Don't do it, Myra! Rule Number Three!

"Blast it!" I whisper, and peek my head back around

the wall. "You guys better cut it out," I bark, and the kids jump. "Director Weathers is coming this way."

The Rep woman uses their moment of distraction to hurry around them. She passes by without a glance in my direction, then disappears into the Anti-Grav Chamber.

"Thanks!" the girl whispers, her eyes wide. The boy nods his appreciation, and they both take off in the other direction.

Director Weathers is nowhere in sight, obviously. If he were, I'd be gone even faster than they were. I scowl after them, listening as their footsteps echo farther and farther away. Once the sound fades altogether, I drift down the hall, trailing my fingers in front of the sensor panels on the doors as I pass. Finally, one glows green. I pivot as it slides open and vanish from the hallway as if by magic.

If only it were real magic; then I wouldn't need to cut class at all.

It takes my eyes a few moments to adjust to the darkness. Workstations form neat rows opposite a teacher's desk. Judging by the excessive number of buttons on the student workstations and the bulkiness of the teacher's, the room must not have been in use for some time. Desks now are shaped more like teardrops and most of the buttons have been replaced by a retractable control panel.

I plop down on the floor behind the teacher's workstation, scooting over so I'm in the empty space of the *U*-shaped interior, which, like the student desks, is lined with little buttons, drawers, and sensor pads. I don't dare touch any of them. *Leave behind no evidence*—that's the Fourth Rule of cutting class. If you start messing with things, people start wondering who was there, and then they start looking for who wasn't where they were supposed to be.

I lean back against the wall and fiddle with the engraved design in the tile instead. The door to the classroom flies open so suddenly that I jam my finger in the crease where the tile meets the display board. Wincing as I squeeze the injured fingertip in my fist, I pull my legs up to my chest, trying to become one with the wall.

"You can take as many of these desks as you need," a scratchy voice drawls, the words punctuated by a crackle of electricity. I don't need to see her face to know it must be the Elector professor, Ms. Curie. A careful peek around the corner of the desk confirms my suspicions. In the dimly lit classroom, sparks illuminate long, pale fingers wrapped in a tangle of wires. I scoot back even farther behind the desk, out of sight.

"No one's using this classroom anymore"—Ms. Curie barks a quick laugh that's more like a hiccup—"but somehow, it's still here."

14

I cock my head to the side. Ms. Curie is by far my strangest professor, and that's saying something.

A few seconds later, I hear her footsteps click away from the classroom, but I'm not safe yet. A storm of thundering steps from what must be a legion of Reps is punctuated by the scrape of student workstations across the floor as they're dragged away.

I don't move. I don't even dare to breathe. I'm not afraid of Reps, obviously, but they report to Director Weathers, and I know if they spot me, there would be nothing I could say to convince them not to turn me in. Instead, I huddle behind the workstation and wait for them to finish, pushing my glasses up my nose like I do a hundred times a day. When I'm older, a Mender can heal my eyesight in a nanosecond. Until then, I'm stuck shuffling lenses around my face.

As the last Rep leaves and the door swooshes shut, I risk another peek around the classroom. Half the desks are gone, a grid of dust and empty squares the only thing marking where they sat for who knows how many years. Something glints on the ground where the front row had been moments before. I glance quickly at the door. The hall's still empty. *Good.* On my hands and knees, I crawl across the floor to snag the long, shiny object, before scurrying back to my hiding spot faster than you can say "shooting stars."

I wrap the long piece of wire around my fingers the way Ms. Curie had, willing myself to feel a shiver of magic, the ghost of a spark. I imagine what it would be like to be an Elector, one of the most envied Creers of magic. I picture myself in a dull lecture, casually short-circuiting the power to the room, ending class early. Or being called upon by the director to restore electricity to the auditorium after a group of mischievous students wreaked havoc on the grid, like today. As I daydream, I feel a strange tingle in my hand and gasp, but quickly realize the wire is just wrapped too tight and cutting off circulation to my fingers.

Sighing, I unwind the wire and stuff it into my pocket. *Maybe I'll give it another try later.*

Leaning back against the wall, I count the minutes until the next bell, dreading it at the same time. I shouldn't skip more than one class in a day. It's too risky. Besides, I can get by in my other classes, even though I'll never be a Novice in any of them. But unlike with Number Whispering, no one expects me to be.

My fingertips trace the wall engravings again, the surface cold against my skin. Cold and gray like the rest of the moon.

I slide my hand over to the curvy triangle carved into the tile, covering it with my palm. Warmth rushes through me from my hands to my feet. My hair ruffles as a blast of hot air escapes through the seam in the wall. Before I can even blink, the wall shivers then disappears, and I tumble backward into who knows what, watching in horror as the wall reappears in front of me, sealing me in.

CHAPTER THREE

GOOSE BUMPS COVER MY SKIN, EVEN THOUGH the room is sweltering. My hands paw desperately at the wall in front of me—*the one I was just in front of*—but there's no way out.

Holding my breath, I turn around. The room slowly comes into focus. I climb uneasily to my feet, hands hovering in front of me, ready to fend off an attack from whatever monster calls this place home.

Humm!

I jump and spin in a circle, looking for the source of the sound. For a moment, nothing happens. Then the humming sounds again, and the overhead lights flick on.

"It's some sort of lab," I say aloud, then immediately wish I hadn't as my voice echoes in the large room.

I walk slowly to a rectangular countertop dissecting the

space in two. The surface is covered with a variety of tools and instruments, some I recognize, some I don't. Magnifiers are scattered across the smooth white counter, each with a streak of something on its observation disc. I stand on my tiptoes and peer closer, not daring to touch any of it. Each slide has what looks like a pinch of gritty dirt covering it, which isn't all that remarkable—I've studied moondust enough times to recognize the stuff when I see it. What *is* remarkable is the range of hues. A few are smeared with a brilliant green. Another is a rich red. Two have what looks like golden sand under the microscope lens, and another slide has a splatter of purple across it.

My eyes soak in the colors. They're so bright and beautiful, it almost makes my eyes water. Here in the Lunar Settlement, and on the Mars and Venus Settlements, too, Chemics manufacture our colors in labs, just like our food. There are no wild plants in the Settlements to supply things like dyes or nutrients. The only true plants in existence are back on the Old World, and those turned poisonous long ago, leaching toxins into the atmosphere. That's the whole reason our ancestors had to leave.

But the colors on these slides are nothing like the pigments the Chemics concoct for our clothes and inks. Those seem cheap compared to these. Fake, even, like cartoon versions. I reach out and carefully pluck a green-smeared slide from beneath a magnifier and hold it up to my eye.

There must be a hundred different shades of green on this tiny piece of glass, no bigger than the size of my thumbnail.

"This is amazing," I whisper.

"Beep, beep, boop!"

I stumble backward and jam my hip into the edge of the counter. "Ow!"

A rustling on the floor behind me makes me forget the pain flaring in my hip as I jump up onto the countertop.

I peer past my dangling feet to the floor, where a small robot resembling a metal shoebox with wheels is sliding back and forth, its squealing and beeping reminding me strongly of my neighbor's dog back home waiting for someone to throw it a ball.

"Um, hello?"

"Beep ber whooo beep!" I've never seen a machine so excited. I didn't even know machines could *get* excited.

"If I jump down, you're not going to eat my feet or anything, are you?"

As if in response, the robot spins in a circle, merrily chirping away. She makes a sound like a toddler blowing a raspberry, and I can't help giggling.

"Do you have a name?" I guess I've committed myself to talking to a machine. I kneel down next to her. The robot nudges gently against my knee, and I run my hands over her smooth metal hull. "Where do I press to turn on your identifier?" I ask when no buttons glow in response to my touch.

The robot stops moving and keels over sideways.

"Oh no! Did I break—"

Before I can finish, a panel flips open on the robot's underside. I peer at the data etched there. "A manual panel? I thought they did away with those decades ago. Oh wait, they did." I squint. "'Made in 2350.' That's almost a hundred years ago! No wonder you don't talk." Being that old, it's amazing she even moves.

I peer closer. MODEL NUMBER B-I-N-R-0-6-1-7-3-5-2-9 is stamped across the back of the panel.

"Hmm, that's too long." I pet the top of her like a dog. "How about I call you Bin-ro?"

She chirps in response, flips right side up, and spins in three circles.

"I guess you like that," I say with a grin, climbing to my feet. "My name's Myra. Not that you can say that."

She blows another raspberry and I giggle, then glance back at the counter, where the magnifiers have toppled over in a heap. I must have knocked into them when I jumped up. "Does anyone still use this lab?" I ask. "Beep once for yes, twice for no."

Bin-ro shakes her metal body back and forth a few times, chirping twice.

"Good, because I don't know if I can fix these. What's this place for anyway?"

Bin-ro erupts into a series of beeps and chirps that seem to go on forever.

"Long story, huh?"

She whistles.

I walk around the room, trailing my fingers over the sleek white walls, then open and close the drawers of the island at the room's center. They're all empty. Still, I can't shake the feeling that there's more to this place than meets the eye.

"Well, if this lab really is abandoned, I think I've found my new favorite hiding spot." Coming back here again might mean breaking a few rules (mine, not the school's), but this place is so secret, so well hidden, I'm not sure I'll be able to resist. And Bin-ro being here is an added bonus. "As long as you don't mind me visiting now and then," I add quickly.

Bin-ro emits enough whistles and bells, the noise could be mistaken for a circus vid-stream.

I laugh and make my way back over to the wall I came in through. The bell must be about to chime. As if on cue, the pendant hanging around my neck buzzes, signaling the end of class. After a few more moments of searching, I find a small button the same size and shape as the triangular engraving on the classroom tile. I press it. The wall in front of me fades, like when I change the filter on one of my photos.

"I'll be back soon, Bin-ro!" I call over my shoulder, then take a deep breath and walk through the wall. Something pulls at me as I leave, a feeling like I've forgotten something. I pat my pockets and check my pendant, but nothing is missing. Still, the urge to go back floods through me. I try and ignore it as I slip back into the classroom.

The space feels eerie now that most of the workstations have been hauled away. Thankfully, the Reps haven't come back for the rest. I cross the room to the door and throw it open, stepping into the hall.

"Hey, watch it now!" a voice snaps, and I freeze.

An older Rep man with pale skin and gray hair hovers over me, a dust blaster tucked under one arm.

"You—you watch it!" I stammer, then straighten up. "Watch where I'm going!"

"I'm going to have to"—he sniffs—"since it sure seems like you can't."

My mouth falls open. I've never heard a Rep talk to a student like that before.

"What were you doing in there, anyway?" he continues, peering over my shoulder into the empty classroom. "That room's unoccupied."

If he reports me, I'll have to explain why I was lurking in a classroom that just happens to hold a hidden lab.

And if that place is secret, it must be for a reason, and I'm guessing the school doesn't want anyone stumbling upon it, especially a kid.

"Reps aren't allowed to question students," I snap, brushing past him. I sound like a total jerk, and I know it—but if the spacesuit fits, right?

"Students aren't allowed to poke around in there," he replies, his eyes narrowing.

"I had permission." Even though I haven't been to a Worship Center in years, I say a small prayer my bluff works.

"From whom?"

"From a *teacher*. How about you worry about what you're doing," I say, pointing my chin at his dust blaster, "and I'll worry about myself." I step around him and walk boldly down the hall, refusing to look back, hoping he doesn't bother mentioning our encounter to anyone.

Still, I feel bad. *Repetitions are clones,* I remind myself. They're grown in a lab, and they don't have feelings like regular humans.

I hope they don't have long memories, either.

CHAPTER FOUR

THAT AFTERNOON, I SIT IN MY ELECTOR THEORY class, waiting for Ms. Curie to begin her lesson, wishing on every lucky meteor, moon, and star that I could be anywhere else. But my double-skip of Ms. Goble's class this morning looms over me, so I sigh and power on my workstation.

At least I'm allowed to do that. Just hit a button and *poof*, all the little knobs and dials and control panels light up. The kids on the Elector track aren't so lucky. Their On/Off sensors were removed from their workstations week one. Now if they want to power up, they have to use their magic, and some of them are more successful than others.

"You can do it, Jack," the girl sitting in front of me says to the boy beside her. "Just find your own electrical current and let it wash off you into the machine."

Jack tries to follow her directions. He scrunches up his face and taps the top of his desk. There's an audible *zap* and he jerks away. "It shocked me," he whispers as his workstation powers on.

The girl smiles. "You get used to it. I kind of like it now."

"Ahem!" Ms. Curie pushes off her desk an instant before the bell rings, eyes lasered in on the pair. "Mr. Antone, you won't always have Miss Darcy whispering instructions in your ear. You need to find your voltage on your own."

"Yes, Ms. Curie," Jack murmurs. The girl studies her workstation silently.

Ms. Curie gives a curt nod, then turns to address the entire class. "Now, all those here for theory, swipe to page fifty-nine in your textbook. And my Elector students." She narrows her dark eyes so they almost become pinpricks below her equally dark hair. "Please use your own power to turn to the correct page."

There's no sound, but I can practically hear the internal groans. The girl in front of me, Something-or-other Darcy, hovers her hand over her book projection, and I watch as the pages whiz by, then stop. It must be on page fifty-nine, because she beams. Jack isn't so lucky. When he holds his hand out and screws up his face, either a solitary page flutters by or all the pages scroll to the end. He shakes his head and keeps trying.

I flick my fingers on the projected pages of my book

until I reach the correct section, then settle in to wait. From the furrowed brows of most of the Elector students, it's going to be a while before we actually begin the lesson.

Ms. Curie strolls between the rows of desks, checking progress. Silver and black Inscriptions cover her skin, creeping up from under her collar to encircle her throat like a necklace made of smoke. The tangle of wire she had in the deserted classroom is wound around her wrist, emitting random sparks as she moves about the room.

"No talking and no devices while you're waiting."

The girl beside me looks up, nods solemnly, then ducks her head back to the messenger on her lap. A smirk tugs at the edge of her mouth as she taps away. I roll my eyes. I'm no Elector, but I understand the basics of the Creer. Holding your messenger out of sight isn't going to make a bit of difference to an Elector professor. Ms. Curie doesn't need to see the girl tapping away on her screen to know she's doing it.

As if to prove my point, Ms. Curie freezes a few rows over, her eyes already zeroed in on the electricity-powered distraction. My neighbor, of course, is oblivious. She grins as she reads something, then quickly replies. An instant later, a shriek pierces the classroom's silence as the girl jumps and her device clatters to the floor. She looks up at Ms. Curie, horrified.

Our teacher nods at the messenger now resting near my

foot, its screen dark.

"It's dead," the girl moans as she leans over to pick it up.

"Powered off," Ms. Curie corrects. "And the next time I detect it on in my class, I'll short-circuit it so fast, you won't even feel the surge."

The girl tucks her messenger in her bag, then leans back in her seat, her arms crossed.

I smirk as I return my focus to my book. Serves her right.

In front of me, Something-or-other Darcy's hand flies into the air like a shuttle shooting through the atmosphere.

"You have a question, Miss Darcy?"

"Yes. I mean, no. I mean, *look!*"

She's whispering, like she's trying not to attract attention, but it has the opposite effect as everyone in the room leans toward her to see what's so important.

Ms. Curie strolls over to her desk, a rare smile pulling at her lips. "Very nice. Is it your first?"

I peer over and can just make out something gray etched across her forearm. An Inscription. Of course. I turn back to my textbook, but no matter how many times I read and reread the words glowing in front of me, I can't seem to focus on what they say.

Out of the corner of my eye, I see her nodding eagerly. "I've been waiting and waiting to get one. Don't they always start out on people's arms?"

"Typically, but not always," Ms. Curie says. "My first Inscription appeared on my left ankle when I was a bit younger than you."

Something-or-other Darcy's eyes widen as she looks up at Ms. Curie. "You mean you got one before you even started school? I thought you had to study loads of magical and scientific theory before that happened."

Ms. Curie pauses. The whole class is hanging on her every word, clearly hoping to learn a trick for getting more of their own. I'm no exception. "That's the usual path for most, but no one knows exactly how or why Inscriptions form. When you consider the greater galaxy around us, however, the opportunity for a magical education is everywhere. For instance, electricity is constantly present around us in our tools, our technology, our environment . . . Even back on the Old World, plants emitted a form of electricity." She hiccups a laugh, and I cock my head to the side, amazed by the sheer boldness of her strangeness. "Or they were said to, anyway."

I fight the urge to groan. My parents are practically legends when it comes to Number Whispering magic, and because of that, everyone assumes I've got loads of Inscriptions already. It doesn't matter that most people— the majority of the galaxy—never get any at all. And even though Creers aren't the norm, my parents think if you don't have a Creer, you don't matter. Period.

I reflexively tug my sleeves down over my wrists. Since I got to S.L.A.M., I've been careful to keep my arms well hidden from all the prying eyes, or else they'd know that I haven't got *any*.

Not even a freckle.

And then they'd know what a hack I am.

"My point," Ms. Curie continues, jarring me out of my thoughts, "is if you immerse yourself in the magic around you, whether in your textbooks, your practical lessons, or in the school Rec hall, the Inscriptions will come."

I've been telling myself that very thing for weeks. *The magic will come.* It has to. I've studied mathematical theory for as long as I can remember. I can recite formulas better than any of the students my mom teaches at the Lunar University.

And yet, the numbers have never whispered to me.

The fact that they haven't isn't what scares me the most, though.

It's that deep, deep down . . . I don't care. Not about number whispering, anyway. I wish I could say the same about my parents' inevitable disappointment, but I'll just have to try to avoid that for as long as I can.

My best friend, Hannah, was the only person I ever told how I truly felt about numbers. Back before our friendship went supernova.

I try and pay attention as Ms. Curie begins her lecture—everyone must have finally gotten their books to the correct page—but old worries keep taking the place of new voltages.

There's still a chance my magic will appear, I tell myself again. A small one. I don't need Number Whisperer abilities to know that the odds of that are going to keep getting smaller.

Just like my days at S.L.A.M. if my magic doesn't show up soon.

CHAPTER FIVE

HOURS AFTER CLASSES HAVE ENDED FOR THE day, and well past the dinner bell, I walk into a nearly empty cafeteria. *Perfect.* Out of the rows and rows of tables, only the one in the far corner is occupied. A few older kids dressed in Chemic-purple jumpsuits are huddled around a tiny glass vial set at the center of the table, their empty dinner trays piled on the floor and forgotten. Blue steam pours out of the cup, swirling into a miniature vortex. It must be a powerful concoction—the spiraling mist whips the Chemic girl's ponytail round and round like a lasso.

Turning away from them and their homework, I slip into the dinner station and peer into the bin. I wrinkle my nose as I extract a rubbery beige square with a pair of tongs, holding it at eye level. It glistens under the cafeteria lights as if coated in a thin layer of slime.

"What is this?" I ask a Rep who's clearing empty bins at the end of the station.

She doesn't look up. "Tuesdays are tacos."

"*This* is a taco? It looks like a Chemic experiment gone wrong."

The Rep doesn't answer, not that I expected her to.

With a shudder, I drop the shiny square onto my tray. It gives a little bounce as it settles. "Will all the food look like this now?" Director Weathers had said something about *uniformity* at the assembly this morning, but I never imagined anything like this.

The Rep nods, then hurries away, a large pile of bins weighing down her arms.

There is no way on the Moon this will taste like a real taco, much less better.

With a sigh, I plop myself and my tray down at an empty table, trying my best to ignore the jiggling of the taco square. Gritting my teeth, I dissect it into six perfectly even pieces, then pop one into my mouth. The texture is terrible—slippery and wet. After I choke it down, a vague hint of corn chips and salsa lingers on my tongue, like someone dipped the square into the real thing, then wiped it off. I pinch my nose and skewer another slice.

"Hey, Canter," a deep voice thunders behind me. "Looks like that first-year saved our table for us."

I glance back over my shoulder and wince. The JV

hoverball team files into the cafeteria. It's the same group of boys who interrupted the assembly with their Elector magic. It looks like they've just left practice.

I turn back around and eat faster, hardly even chewing the taco squares before launching them down my throat.

Canter Weathers saunters past my table. He pauses when he's right in front of me, crossing his bare arms across his jersey. Like most of the other JV hoverball boys', they're covered in Inscriptions.

I force my gaze away from the gray markings winding around Canter's arms and stare him directly in the eyes.

He waits, maybe expecting me to apologize for taking his seat, maybe just waiting for me to move. *Hope he has a few light-years, because neither of those things are happening.* I force down another bite.

"You heard Marco," he finally says. "We always sit here."

I lean back against the table, propping my legs up on the bench seat, then pick up my cup and take a long, loud drink from the straw. "Until today."

"She's really not going to move?" Marco asks as he crosses the room, stopping at Canter's side.

"Apparently not." Canter continues watching me, and I stare right back. After a few more seconds, he smirks and elbows Marco. "Maybe she wants to sit with us."

Marco guffaws. "Can't blame her. We *are* the junior galactic hoverball champions."

"It's okay, newbie," Canter says, still grinning. "You can stay."

Heat rushes into my cheeks, but I keep my narrowed eyes lasered in on Canter. "Go spark yourself, Weathers."

The two boys double over laughing, then go join the rest of the team at the food station. When they're out of sight, I push off the table and slip out the door.

The housing-section hallways are filled with kids milling around, visiting friends or heading off to the modulab to study. Every door in the hall is decorated. Some are completely covered with designs and photos and friendship visuals, clearly the result of hours spent programming the doors with the silliest pictures they could find, jokes that only made sense to the occupants.

I reach my now-familiar door, which, like the rest in the hall, is covered in pictures and swirling, glittering names. *Lila, Sloane,* and *Bethany* flash from various corners, with *Myra* written in a quick scrawl squeezed between two pictures. It clearly doesn't belong on the door, which is fitting, because I don't belong inside.

I scan the hall for a blank door—one that might have been meant for Hannah and me—but they're all flashing with designs and signatures. Whichever one was supposed to be ours has been erased. Just like our friendship.

I sigh and turn back to my dorm room, scanning my pendant on the security panel. The door slides open and the gaggle of voices quickly dissolve into silence.

"Hey, Myra."

I glance up at Lila, who's leaning back on her bed, her dark, curly hair cascading over her shoulders. Sloane and Bethany are clustered on either side of her. There are four full-sized ergo-engineered beds in the room, but my roommates always seem to try and squeeze onto one.

"Hey," I say quickly, then make my way over to my dresser, shimmying between the bed frames to reach it. When I arrived at school room-less and friendless, some school administrator had the brilliant idea to add a bed and dresser to a triple. "Now it's bursting with fun," they'd said. It's bursting with something, but *fun* isn't the word I'd use.

"So, er, what'd you guys do in class today?" Lila asks the two blondes perched beside her. It took me forever to remember who was who, and sometimes I still forget.

"Um, just, you know, stupid lessons," Blondie One answers from behind me. Bethany, I think. I'm eighty percent sure.

Whenever I walk in and hear my roommates' awkward attempts at conversation, I know they were just talking about me. I wish they'd just keep going. I'd rather hear the chatter about me than get their opinions in the snippets I catch before they notice I'm in the room. That's why I listen in on my classmates before skipping class—I couldn't care less that they gossip, but I can't stand not knowing what they're saying.

Blondie Two, Sloane, groans and squeezes the pillow clutched in her arms. "I don't know how we're expected to get Inscriptions when most of the teachers don't start the practical lessons until midyear."

"Most kids don't get Inscriptions until the end of their first year," I reply before I can stop myself.

"Easy for you to say," Bethany mutters under her breath. "I heard you've got a dozen already."

"What are you complaining about?" I retort, rounding on her, the hems of my sleeves clenched in my fists. "Aren't you Elector-tracked? Ms. Curie's one of the only teachers who does practical magic in the first term."

"Only because she's *weird*." Bethany rolls her eyes and flips her hair in a perfectly choreographed rhythm. "Just like *you*."

I ignore her and pull out my bookpod from my desk, clutching it in my fist. A wave of homesickness crashes over me. I miss my quiet, non-twelve-year-old-girl-infested bedroom.

"I'm not really worried about my Mender classes," Lila says, mercifully breaking the tense silence. "I've got one

Mender Inscription already, at least. It's my other classes that are stressing me out."

"I know," Sloane says behind me. "I wish the administration would just let us stick with our Creers. They almost never change from what's shown on our aptitude tests."

After ducking into the bathroom to pull on my pajamas, I throw myself into bed, powering on my bookpod so the projection of the pages shields my face.

The year before last, we'd all taken our aptitude tests. The exams don't matter, not really. They just show what Creer you *might* have an affinity for, what field you *could* develop magic in. It's not proven science. That's why in our first year at S.L.A.M we have to learn the theory *and* the practical magic of every Creer. The test isn't perfect, and every experiment has its deviations. Some people even switch Creers over time, though that's pretty rare.

At home, I'd had a whole group of friends—CHARM: Celeste, Hannah, Audrey, Rylin, and Myra. But after we all took the test, it was like someone flipped a switch. All anyone cared about was what Creer someone was assigned, if they were assigned one at all. Suddenly, the would-be Menders only hung out with the other would-be Menders. Supposed Chemics only sat with the other supposed Chemics.

My test had indicated a likely magical talent for math,

but the Number Whisperers were the last group I wanted to hang out with. I got enough math theory at home. At school I wanted to hear about the funny video loops Celeste saw on the open network or how to unlock the secret levels in Audrey's hologames. Instead, CHARM splintered and no one wanted to hang out anymore. No one but Hannah. She wanted things to stay the way they'd been, too. And for us, they did for a while. But then I had to go and mess that up. . . .

"I'm okay in all my classes except Goble's Number Whispering," Lila complains, jolting me out of my memories. "I'm drowning in the formulas. My homework's a galactic mess."

"Hey, Myra," Sloane says, and I jump. I'm not used to them talking *to* me, only *about* me. I can't really blame them. I'd probably have done the same thing if the school squeezed some random kid into my room.

"Yeah?" I ask, peeking up over the top of my book projection.

"Can you help Lila with her Number Whispering theory homework? It'll probably take you three minutes to whiz through it all."

I frown. I *could* help her with the theory—it's just formulas and calculation patterns—but if I show her that, it could lead to more questions. Maybe she'd even want me to show her practical magic. . . . I shake my head. "How will she learn, then?"

Lila sighs. "She didn't mean *do it for me*, but it's okay. I'll just ask Ms. Goble for a tutor. Thanks, anyway."

"For nothing," one of the others says.

Bethany, I'm eighty percent sure.

CHAPTER SIX

THE NEXT MORNING, I WAKE UP TANGLED IN MY sheets and trip over my shoes when I try to get out of bed, prompting a snicker from Bethany. *Today is not off to a good start.* I fidget with my long-sleeved nightgown while I wait for the others to clear out before heading to the shower. Thankfully, they like to leave early so they can get a table in the cafeteria that overlooks the low-grav hoverball court. The varsity team usually practices there before breakfast.

As I finish dressing and head into the hall (it's late enough now that most of the breakfast crowd will have been and gone), I start running through the classes I've skipped lately, weighing which I can afford to miss today without punishment. Goble's is definitely out. I'm sure she's still fuming over yesterday. I'll have to come up with an excuse for why I didn't return to class after the assembly. I know I probably should wait a few days before skipping anything else, but I want to go back to the secret lab to see Bin-ro. With more time to explore, I might be able to figure out who the lab belongs to and what it's for.

When I turn the corner toward the cafeteria, I skid to a stop. Ms. Goble is in the hall outside her classroom. Maybe I'm actually not that hungry.

Pivoting, I manage a step back the way I came, when I hear, "Miss Hodger, a word."

I freeze, then rotate slowly back around like a planet spinning on its axis. "Ms. Goble," I say in the sweetest voice I can muster. "I was going to try to catch you before class today to explain about yesterday. You see—"

She crosses her arms and walks toward me. Her Creer pin—a shape merging the addition, subtraction, multiplication, and division symbols—sparkles on her collar beneath the glow of the overhead lights. "It's hardly the first time you've been inexplicably absent, Miss Hodger. I've been checking with your other teachers."

I twist my backpack straps between my fingers. "I know, but yesterday was . . . different. I ate the new food, and I don't think it agreed with me."

Ms. Goble peers down her nose at me. "Really? How odd since the new menu was not implemented until *after* the assembly."

For comet's sake, Myra! "Oh . . . oh was it? It must have

been the usual breakfast then. Director Weathers did say the change was to improve on the old food, right? Maybe because it was making people sick. That's—that's why I've been missing so many classes lately, actually. The food seems to be messing with my stomach and—"

Ms. Goble presses her lips into a tight line. "I don't want to hear a galactic space ballad, Miss Hodger. None of it adds up to a plausible explanation."

My mouth falls open. "But, Ms. Goble, I—"

She lifts an Inscription-covered hand to silence me, and I can't help but be distracted by the elaborate patterns etched onto her dark skin like star formations scattered across the night sky. "I don't have time to hear your tall tales, and you don't have time to tell them. You've got an appointment in Director Weathers's office"—she lifts the pendant hanging around her neck to check the screen—"now."

I open my mouth, then shut it. There's no point arguing. Instead, I nod and turn, trudging back the way I came. I take my time, but in what seems like two nanoseconds, I'm in the vestibule outside Director Weathers's office. An older boy, maybe a third-year, with a Chemic-purple jumpsuit and an unfortunate cowlick looks up as I approach.

"Name?" he says by way of greeting.

"Myra Hodger." I glance down at his desk while he minimizes one screen (apparently I interrupted a very important level of *Space Pirates IV*) and pulls up the scheduler.

"The director's last appointment is running long. He'll be with you in a bit. Scan your pendant here." The boy juts his chin at a panel on his desk, then nods toward a bench pushed up against the far wall. "Then you can wait over there."

I lean over and wave my pendant over the panel until I hear a soft beep, before I flop onto the bench, throwing my bag beside me. "Pretty early to already have a meeting running long," I mutter. It's not even the end of the breakfast block yet. If Cowlick hears, he ignores me, instead smoothing invisible wrinkles in his jumpsuit before returning to his game.

Minutes tick by with no sign of Director Weathers and no movement from Cowlick apart from an occasional groan or fist pump, usually followed by the sound of a muffled explosion coming from his screen.

I push off the bench and wander around the vestibule, waiting to see if I'm scolded. I'm not, so I continue my stroll, which quickly shifts into pacing. Maybe I can convince Director Weathers I was cutting class to study advanced Number Whispering theory. Or maybe I'll say I was working on proposing a communications exchange program with students at a school in the Martian colony or on Venus. Teachers always eat that stuff up. Or maybe—

Voices interrupt the stream of excuses I'm spinning. I realize I've strayed close to Director Weathers's office door, which is slightly ajar. Through the gap, I see a burly man standing with his back to me, his hand gripping the doorframe. Cosmic cuff links that must have cost a small fortune glitter beneath the overhead lights as he runs his other hand through auburn-and-silver-streaked hair.

"I told you, Rob, we've got it under control," he says as I creep closer, careful to stay out of sight. "They'll hardly notice the difference."

"These are kids you're talking about, Jake," Director Weathers says, his voice drifting out into the waiting area. "Their two main activities are eating and sleeping. Of course they'll notice. They already have. I've got an in-box full of complaints, and the number keeps growing. By lunch, the parents will be messaging me, I guarantee it."

"The flavor was tested at a ninety-six-point-four percent equivalent," the man—Jake—replies.

Director Weathers barks a laugh. I can't see his face from where I'm standing, but I can tell he doesn't find anything about this conversation funny. "Are you kidding? Have you even tried your own product? It looks like squares of engine sealant."

"But the *taste*—"

"Crashing comets, Jake! The stuff tastes like engine sealant, too. Engine sealant sprinkled with freeze-dried remnants of real food."

"Accurate," I mutter under my breath.

Jake takes a step back into the director's office. I edge closer, tilting my head toward them, trying to catch every word.

"We don't have another option, Rob. Not now, anyway."

Director Weathers sighs, and I imagine him rubbing his temples the way my dad does when he can't get his calculations to line up the way he wants. "When?"

"Soon," Jake says. "We'll get the formulas fixed in no time. Then you can just return to the normal food and call it Phase Two of the menu redesign."

"And in the meantime?"

"Just talk about the nutritional content, like we discussed."

"That won't help. The kids are already claiming we're trying to poison them." Tapping echoes from inside the office. Director Weathers must be drumming his fingers on his desktop. "I just don't understand how so many of the food cloning formulas could break at once."

"We'll get them fixed soon," Jake says again.

"Yeah, but what about the next time? I had to cover for three broken food cloning formulas last year."

My eyebrows ping up so high my glasses skid down my nose. I've never heard anything about the food cloning formulas not working.

"We're only a month into the term, and the only formula still functioning is the broccoli one. I don't think

I need to tell you that normal broccoli served with this new garbage is not going to help our situation. And if the Governing Council gets word that we've been covering this up . . ."

My head jerks up. My dad is on the Lunar Governing Council, the panel that oversees the day-to-day workings of the Settlement. Dad's the Number Whispering representative for the Lunar Colony. He oversees a bunch of boring stuff like the population census, resource distribution, budget tracking . . . I try not to pay too much attention.

I take a step closer to the door and catch a glimpse of Jake clapping Director Weathers on the shoulder. "Well, I can personally guarantee that the Chemic representative isn't going to mention it to anyone, seeing as that's me."

My eyes widen. *He's* the Chemic rep on the Council? And he's covering up problems with the food cloning formulas?

"We just better get this squared away soon," Director Weathers grumbles.

"We'll have it cleared up before anyone from the Council catches so much as a whisper of a complaint," Jake says as he turns on his heel and steps into the hall. "And if for some reason we can't, I've got some contingency plans tucked away."

"And if things spiral even further?" Director Weathers asks.

What does that mean? It sounds like more than just the code for broccoli breaking.

"I told you," Jake says, pausing, though he doesn't turn around. "I've got plans for that, too. Don't worry about a thing." He walks down the hall, and I scurry out of the way. Thankfully, he doesn't spot me as he turns and disappears around the corner.

A moment later, Director Weathers steps into the hall and calls to his assistant, "Who's my next appointment?"

"Myra Hodger, sir. Per Ms. Goble's request."

"When's she due?"

"Sir? She's here now." Cowlick gestures toward the bench, and both their eyes bulge for a moment when they realize it's empty. I didn't have time to make it far from the door before Jake passed into the vestibule, and now my feet are glued to the spot . . . a spot that is far too close to Director Weathers's office door. But the look on the director's face when he turns around and finds me standing right behind him is almost worth being in trouble.

He blinks a few times, collecting himself, then motions me into his office. I grab my bag from the bench and hurry after him. The door clicks shut behind me.

He sits behind his desk and I settle into the chair across from him, waiting for the imminent lecture. But he ignores me. He's absorbed in his computer, tapping frantically on the screens on his desk. Director Weathers has never seemed like the nervous type to me, but right now, he is definitely squirming.

After a few minutes, he powers off the screens and meets my gaze, as if sizing me up before beginning the interrogation. At first, math seems like the last thing he wants to talk about. He asks how my parents are, what they're working on. Tells me how thrilled he is to have their daughter at his school. Fifteen minutes in, and Ms. Goble hasn't come up once.

Finally, he sighs and settles back in his chair.

I sit up straighter. Waiting. Preparing. This is a negotiation. I don't know exactly how important the conversation I overheard was, but I know for sure Director Weathers didn't want me to hear it.

"So it seems you've been missing quite a few classes lately," he says, folding his hands on his desk.

"It's really not *that* many." I wring my hands, doing my best to look both nervous and repentant. The former isn't that difficult, but the latter . . .

"S.L.A.M. protocol requires me to let parents know when their child is sent to me for disciplinary reasons," Director Weathers says slowly, "but I'd hate to take up your parents' precious time with something relatively minor, especially with all your father's Governing Council duties and responsibilities." The director studies me. If this is a test, it's one I have no intention of flunking (for once).

"Speaking of the Governing Council," I say carefully, determined not to lose my nerve, "I thought I heard the man in your office mention the Chemic representative. Does he know him? I was wondering if he might know my dad, too."

Director Weathers's jaw muscles twitch. "The man from my office *is* the Chemic rep on the Council."

"Oh," I say, feigning sweetness. "I guess he does then."

Director Weathers doesn't say anything more, and neither do I. Sweat beads on the back of my neck, but I don't move, don't blink, don't do anything that could signal weakness.

Director Weathers breaks first. "Well, then." Tiny wrinkles fan out around his eyes. "Back to the matter at hand. I can't imagine a girl with parents as successful as yours would voluntarily jeopardize her education." He pauses. "So what have you been doing when you're not in class?"

He's looking for a way to let me out of this. "Reading the mathematical theory journals on the school network," I lie.

Director Weathers actually cracks a smile, though it doesn't reach his eyes. "I can't say I'm surprised. Still, I really can't have you doing that during class time, impressive though it may be."

"I understand, sir."

Silence stretches between us, and I hold my breath,

waiting to see what punishment he has in mind for me . . . or what the catch will be for not having one.

"I suppose I can't penalize you for being gifted," he finally says, sighing. "If you can maintain a good attendance record from here on out, I see no reason to note your previous, er, *weaknesses* on the academia network."

Jupiter Jackpot! "I'd appreciate that, sir. My parents use the network to check on my grades and progress reports, and I know they wouldn't like me missing class. Even if it's to read advanced mathematical journals," I add hastily.

"Well, it sounds like we have a deal."

I nod. "It won't happen again, Director Weathers." *Sorry, Bin-ro. Our visit is going to have to wait.*

"Good, good," he says, bobbing his head with each word. "I'll check in on you in a few weeks. If we get this cleared up, then I think we can forget about today's meeting." He looks me dead in the eye, making sure I catch his meaning. "All of it. Am I clear?"

I nod. "I was never here."

CHAPTER SEVEN

ON FRIDAY NIGHT, I SIT IN MY DORM ROOM amid a Martian sandstorm of color. Clothes, headbands, and shoes fly in all directions as my roommates prepare for a trip to the nearest Lunar city, Apolloton.

Obviously, I'm staying behind. Not that I mind. I rarely get the room all to myself for a night, and I'm looking forward to an evening free from snickers and side-eye.

"Hurry up, you guys!" Bethany barks, pulling some sort of sparkling monstrosity out of a drawer and looping it around her neck. "If we don't hurry, we won't get the seats at the back of the transport. That's where the JV hoverball team sits."

"I'm almost ready," Lila says with a laugh, slipping into a sleeveless shirt that shows off an Inscription looping up her forearm. The pale markings seem to glow on her golden-brown skin, illuminating what looks like a partial diagram of the bones in a human leg.

It must be new. I catch Lila angling it in front of the mirror more than once as I settle into my seat, powering on my bookpod.

The girls exit the room in a cloud of perfume and glitter.

"Finally," I mutter, just as the door slides back open.

"Hey, Myra," Lila says, poking her head in again.

My breath catches as I realize she might ask me to join them. A million excuses bubble up inside my chest. "Yeah?" I choke out.

"We might go hang with the hoverball team after we get back to school, just for a little while. They know how to get past the curfew trackers and said they'd show us. But if anyone comes by for a dorm check, can you tell them we're in the bathroom or something?"

"Uh, sure." I watch her, and she watches me. Just as she opens her mouth to say something else, I blurt out, "Are you sure it'll work?" From what I've heard, the curfew trackers are no joke. There are sensors all over the hallways that activate when we're supposed to be in our rooms for the night. No one knows where they are or what they look like, but everyone knows they are nearly impossible to get past. Almost everyone, anyway. Every couple weeks, you hear about a kid in detention because they decided to test their luck.

"They said they've done it before. Guess we'll find out, right?"

I nod.

She stares at me another moment and opens her mouth again. Maybe she really *was* going to invite me.

"Lila, let's go!" one of the other girls bellows from the hallway.

"See you," I say softly.

Lila hesitates another moment, then gives me a quick wave and she's gone.

I sit staring at my book projection for a minute or two, then reach out and power it off, grab my pendant, and leave the room, too.

The hallways are so eerily quiet, it almost feels like I'm the one breaking curfew. I fight the urge to tiptoe as I move from the dormitory corridors to the academic hallways. *I wonder if I'm the only one still here.* There must be at least a teacher or two to oversee any stragglers.

After what feels like light-years, I wave my hand in front of the deserted classroom's sensor. The panel slides open with a *whoosh*, and I slip inside, then trot toward the teacher workstation.

The room buzzes with energy. I can practically feel the vibration of it in the floor. It's probably just that I'm excited to finally see Bin-ro again.

Bending down, I carefully press my palm against the triangular carving etched into the wall. As warm air billows over me, a strange feeling rushes through my chest—a mixture of excitement and anticipation, like the moment you reach the top of a hover coaster and for a pair of heartbeats, all you see is the first drop.

I take two steps forward, passing into the darkness.

The lights flick on and I'm greeted by a blast of bells and whistles so loud, I wouldn't be surprised if my classmates heard it in Apolloton. "Hi, Bin-ro," I say with a laugh as she spins around my ankles. "Miss me?"

She squeals, and I giggle.

"I missed you, too!" I turn in a slow circle, taking in the lab. It looks exactly the way I left it: a few magnifiers knocked astray on the counter, the others still set in a neat line. The rest of the room is empty, but for some reason my eyes keep darting around, as if expecting someone to pop out from a secret hideaway. The hair on the back of my neck prickles.

"I wish I knew what this place was for. There's got to be a reason it's so well hidden." Something nags at me as I walk the perimeter of the room, like there's a clue hidden on the walls, but it's written in invisible ink. I smile down at my little robot friend. "Too bad you can't tell me. I'm sure you know all about it. Bet it'd take forever for you to beep it out."

"*Beep!*" Bin-ro agrees.

"This is going to sound silly," I say, trailing my hands along the sleek walls as I make another loop around the lab, "but since I know you can't share this with anyone, can I tell you something?"

She chirps a yes, and I continue my circle.

I pause next to a section of wall opposite the entrance to the classroom and lay both hands on it, then press my ear against the cool metal. "I feel like there's something in here, something I can't see. It's almost like . . . like feeling a heartbeat, except without the pulse or the sound. I know it's strange, but I feel like there's something . . . something *alive* in here." I shrug. "I don't know how to explain it."

Bin-ro's quiet for a moment. A blue light flashes slowly from somewhere in her metal shell, and then she takes off like a rocket. "*Beep, chirp, beep!*" Bin-ro spins around my feet again before shooting off across the lab, hurtling into the counter in the center of the room.

"Crashing comets, Bin-ro! Are you okay?"

She skids toward me, then back toward the counter, knocking into it again, this time more gently.

"Is there something you want to show me over there?"

She blows a raspberry, clearly saying, *No, Myra. I just like crashing into things.*

I hurry over, my eyes scouring the rectangular counter sitting in the center of the room like a metal island. I clear off the magnifiers, piling them against the wall, then return to the counter, where I run my hands up and down it, pulling out every drawer, feeling around inside each one. Nothing. No unusual ridge, no seam out of place, no decorative engravings. I shake my head. "I don't see anything, Bin-ro."

She squeals like an emergency transport.

"Okay, okay! I'll look again." This time, I take a step back. Then to the side. Then I sit on the ground and look up. That's when I see it. One of the overhead lights glints off the metal countertop. The shape of the reflection is the same shape as the symbol carved into the classroom wall outside this lab.

I stare at the triangle of light, memorizing its location, and climb slowly to my feet. When I move, I lose the angle of the beam and the shape disappears, but I know where it was. I lift my hand slowly to the spot and press my palm to it. A shiver rushes through me, or maybe it's the room shuddering.

A moment later, the countertop retracts into itself as if the metal is being tucked into an invisible pocket. Then the sides drop away, too, melting into the floor, leaving behind a rectangular-shaped hole where the counter was seconds before. I peer inside. A chute like a child's slide slopes downward into darkness.

"What's down there, Bin-ro?"

The robot doesn't answer. Instead, she whistles a tune and rolls up to the edge, as if to check it out. But instead of stopping, she slips over the side and disappears.

"Bin-ro!" I dip my head into the darkness but can't see anything. Not Bin-ro's flashing lights. Not the bottom. Nothing.

Gripping the sides of the opening, I lower myself in, holding tight so I don't slip down. "Bin-ro!" I call again, my voice echoing. In the distance, a soft beep sounds, and I wince, still clinging to the metal sides.

She's just a robot, Myra. Don't do it. Don't do it. Don't—

"Blast it," I whisper. And then I let go.

CHAPTER EIGHT

WARM, DAMP AIR RUSHES BY ME AS I WHIP down the slide into total darkness. I open my mouth to scream, but nothing comes out. After what feels like forever, I land with a crunch. Stiff objects snap under my weight, poking into my skin, and strange textures graze my hands as I paw around, trying to get my bearings.

"Bin-ro?" I croak as I heave myself to my feet, squinting in the dim light. Something glows above me—first red, then orange, then finally pale yellow—before overhead lights flicker on, illuminating the room. I *must* be dreaming, or maybe I hit my head on my way down. There's no way that this can be real.

I blink, then rub my eyes, trying to clear away the green haze. I've never seen a green that's so . . . green, like I'm finally seeing the real version of the color after twelve years of looking at poor, lab-manufactured substitutes. I soak in every detail, every leaf, every stem, every bit of pigment in the room—in the *garden*—surrounding me.

But moons don't have gardens. At least, I didn't think they did.

"This is wild," I murmur, wandering around in a daze as my feet stir up plumes of chalky moondust, and another realization sinks in.

I'm outside!

In a sudden panic, I rip off my sweatshirt and wrap it around my face. *Can I breathe?* I must have been breathing, right? So I must still be within the air and gravity enclosures of the school. Pushing the material down a little, I carefully sniff the air. Smells normal. Actually, better than normal. Somehow cleaner. I move the sweatshirt away altogether, and a new worry nudges its way into my mind. The air may have oxygen, but the plants could still make this place dangerous. How long did it take for the deadly plants to poison people back on the Old World? I don't know. I can't remember. Quickly, I rewrap my sweatshirt around my nose and mouth.

Bin-ro comes bursting out of a clump of green to my right, spinning in circles and churning up a thick cloud of moondust. She skids to a stop at my feet. *"Beep boop?"* The question in her tone is obvious.

"Bin-ro, these plants could be toxic! You've got to

help me get out of here. Can I climb back up that chute?"

I was expecting a one-beep-yes, two-beeps-no answer, but instead, Bin-ro hums what sounds like a game show tune and lazily drifts from one patch of green to the next.

"Does that mean these things are safe?" I ask through the fabric.

"*Beep*," she chirps.

"Are you *sure*?"

"*Beep!*"

"Absolutely positive?"

"*BEEP!*"

"Okay, okay," I say, slowly peeling the fabric away again. Somehow, even before I had Bin-ro's confirmation, I could *feel* that the plants were safe. "This place is amazing." Trees and bushes are clustered so thick I can't see more than ten feet in any direction. I look up through the branches stretching overhead and take in stars and stars and stars. Dark glass glints back at me. I've seen that type of glass before. We have it in our living room ceiling back home. It's reflective—you can only see out, not in—which means this garden is invisible to anyone not inside it.

Through the dome, the arcs and panels of S.L.A.M.'s spiral design stretch high, and in the very middle, something dark and circular. *I must be in the open space at the center of the school, below the Anti-Grav Chamber.*

Tiny lights line the thin metal panels weaving the glass together, but most of them are out. Some even dangle on wires. Clearly, they haven't been functional for a long time.

"How did all this grow?"

Bin-ro erupts into a medley of beeps, chirps, and whistles.

"It's complicated. I get it." I rotate on the spot, mesmerized by the lushness surrounding me. Tree limbs twist this way and that, clusters of leaves creating lopsided walls and bushy borders. The soft, winding curves of their frames are a stark contrast to the precise lines and angles I'm used to seeing in the Lunar Settlement. As I wander, other colors grab my attention. Bits of brown, hints of red, blips of yellow, all tucked within the leafy green like hidden treasure. "Who made this?"

Bin-ro gives a soft, mournful whistle.

"I sure wish you could talk, buddy," I say as I walk carefully through the room—through the *garden*—trailing my fingers along the foliage. The plants almost crackle with energy. Maybe I'm imagining it, but they seem to lean toward me as I pass.

I explore every corner, marveling at the variety—the shapes of the leaves and the wiry vines knitting the garden into what looks like an enormous, cozy nest. I can't help but run my hand over every nearby trunk, brushing the dry, rough bark and tracing the veins of the slick, smooth leaves. I find myself patting each bush as if it's an animal, not even minding when I catch the occasional thorn, like a pet giving my fingers a playful nip. Taking in all of the colors, I realize my eyes are watering. It's as though someone suddenly turned on a light in a darkened room and my vision can't quite adjust to the new vibrancy. "I could stay here all night," I tell Bin-ro. "If I didn't have a curfew, that is."

Oh no! The curfew trackers! Reflexively, I pat my chest, looking for my pendant to check the time . . . except there's nothing there. "My pendant!" I shriek, dropping to my knees and scouring the ground. Luckily, I find it tangled in a thorny plant, not too far from where I landed when I tumbled down the tunnel. Unluckily, I forgot to charge it; it's dead.

"I'd better go," I tell Bin-ro. "It's got to be late and the curfew trackers are no joke."

"Boop, boooop."

"I know," I say, patting her hull. "But I'll be back. Promise." I take one last look at the plants weaving around me, forming a sort of green tapestry. "Galloping Moon gargoyles couldn't keep me away." I hunch and peer into the dark chute. "Looks like a long way back up. Do I have to climb, or is there another way out?"

Bin-ro rolls over to the bottom of the slide, and a suction-cup contraption extends out of a panel in her hull.

Inch by inch, she sticks, pulls, and rolls her way slowly back up the slide.

"I guess that's my answer," I mutter, scooping her into my arms before beginning the long journey.

My thighs are burning as we emerge into the gleaming white lab.

I hesitate, staring at the gaping hole in the floor. "How do I, um, put it back?"

Bin-ro chirps and rolls over to a nondescript section of flooring. Extending the suction cup again, she sticks it to the floor and then retracts it with a sharp *pop*! An instant later, the sides of the counter sprout up out of the floor. When they've reached their original height, the counter-top rolls back out, and everything appears exactly as it was before.

"I'll be back soon, buddy."

I slip out of the lab, and then the classroom, emerging into the hall daydreaming about when I can visit the garden again, who put it there, and why. I'm so wrapped up in my thoughts that I turn the corner right into something solid and gray. A yelp and shuffling of feet make my stomach drop. "Sorr—oh. You again."

The older Rep man, the same one from before, back-pedals out of my path. "I might say the same thing. I told you, no students are allowed—" He stops suddenly, his eyes examining me like I'm a science experiment, getting wider and wider the longer he looks.

With a sickening jolt, I realize I've got bits of plant all over me from my tumble into the garden. I tense, preparing to run, when he grabs my arm.

Startled, I look up. His grip on my elbow is firm, but not overly tight, as he steers me back inside the classroom.

"You can't be walking around here like that!" he says, carefully plucking bits of brown and green from my sleeves. "Don't they teach you history here? Anyone catches you wearing leaves and brambles like they're some sort of absurd coat and you'll be on the first shuttle home. Or worse."

"I know— I didn't mean— Thank you," I stammer, picking debris from my shoulders. A small green-and-brown pile forms around me like a halo. "Wait, aren't you wondering where all this came from?"

"Nope," he says, using a brush he has clipped to his belt to sweep the twigs and leaves into a pile.

"How do—"

"But I will tell you that you would be smart not to go back. To *wherever* it came from." He scoops the fragments into a small pan. "I'll put this back inside. Can't just toss it into the reprocessing bins. People might notice. You go on back to your room. And don't come back here. Ever."

I shift, blocking his path toward the teacher workstation. "How do you know about the garden?"

"Doesn't matter. What matters is you forget about it."

"But—"

"Scoot," he says gruffly, stepping around me and pressing his palm to the wall. "I don't know how you found it, but so long as you forget it, I don't care." He disappears into the lab.

I wait, staring at the wall, but he doesn't reappear. Still in a sort of trance, I back toward the hall, disappearing, too.

CHAPTER NINE

I DON'T EVEN REMEMBER RUNNING BACK TO my dormitory hall, but before I know it, I'm standing outside my room. Still in a daze, I scan my pendant on the panel, then walk promptly into the door.

"Ow!" I rub my probably-bruised shoulder and scan my pendant again. Nothing happens. "Blast it! What's wrong with this thing." I give the door a swift kick, but it still doesn't slide open. Taking in my pendant's darkened screen, I remember the problem has nothing to do with the door.

With a dead pendant and my roommates still in Apolloton, I'm officially locked out. And Lila said they were going to be late. Post-curfew late.

As I'm trying to work out what to do, a familiar high-pitched clamor reaches my ears. It cuts off, per usual, as soon as my roommates catch sight of me.

"Um, hey, Myra," Lila says, her brow furrowing. "What are you doing?"

"My pendant died," I reply, nodding at the security panel.

"Oh." She scans her own pendant on the door, and the three girls tromp inside, me trailing behind them.

"I thought you were going to scam the curfew trackers tonight," I say as the door whizzes shut.

"Shh!" Bethany hisses. "A teacher could have heard you!"

I don't bother saying that there were no teachers in sight. "The JV team didn't know how to hack them?"

"They did," Lila says, tucking something shiny into her dresser drawer. "We were going to the Rec hall so they could show us how to put them on, but Ms. Goble saw us and sent us back to our rooms."

Put what on? I don't ask, and they don't share.

After a few awkward seconds of silence, the girls start buzzing about how much fun they had in Apolloton, and I tune out. After a while, they head to the bathroom to get ready for bed. I peek out the door to make sure they're gone, glad to find the hall empty.

Stepping in front of the mirror, I inspect my hair and clothes for stray plant bits. I'm twisting around, peering at the back of my hair, when the door slides back open and I jump, smacking my elbow into the mirror.

"Er, sorry," Lila says, eyeing me curiously.

"It's fine." I walk around her and drop my pendant onto its charging station.

"What happened to your hands?" she asks.

Startled, I look down, half expecting to see vines and leaves wrapped around them. Instead, there are a collection of scrapes and cuts from when I skidded from the slide into the garden.

"Um, I don't know."

Lila just stares at the scratches like they're sparkling jewels.

"Are you okay?" I finally ask, tugging on my sleeves so they're past my knuckles.

"Uh, yeah, sorry." She giggles nervously. "Just running through my Mender theory for fixing you up."

"Oh." Cogs and levers start whirring in my head. If anyone ever needed an off-the-record Mender scan, it's the girl who just stumbled into a secret (and potentially toxic) moongarden. "Do you want to fix them?" I blurt out.

"Seriously?" Lila gasps. "You'd let me do that?"

I shrug. "You seem like you know what you're doing. You've got Inscriptions and everything."

She beams, and her eyes reflexively flick to my covered arms.

"You could do a scan, too, if you want," I add quickly.

She looks back up at me, her eyes wide. "Wow, that'd be great, Myra!" She shuffles her feet. "We're not supposed to practice on real people until we're second-years, though. You can't tell anyone. Not even Bethany or Sloane."

"No problem."

She glances back toward the door. "We'd better hurry, then. They were already hydro-drying their hair when I left."

I hold out my hands and try not to shudder as Lila presses them between her own and closes her eyes. My hands tingle like they've fallen asleep. A few seconds later, Lila's eyes flutter open and she flips my hands over. All the scratches and scrapes are gone.

"Wow," I whisper. "Thanks a lot!"

"Thank *you*," she says with a grin. "It's great practice."

"The texts make a lot more sense once you start actually using the magic."

"Right." She hesitates. "Is it the same with Number Whispering?"

I wouldn't know, I think as I nod.

"Okay, quick scan then?" she asks, her eyes hopeful.

"Sure," I say. "What do you want me to do?"

"Just stand still." Lila takes a step back, then her eyes flick back and forth as she examines me like there's a book printed over my entire body and she's reading it. She reaches my feet, and her face melts into a grin. "All set."

"Nothing?" I ask, trying to keep the hope and worry out of my voice.

"Nope. Not even a cold brewing. Perfectly healthy."

A sigh of relief escapes my lips, and Lila frowns.

"Are you—"

Before she can finish, the door flies open and Sloane and Bethany skip inside. I've never been so happy to see them.

"Thanks," I say quietly as I shift around them to my dresser.

Lila shoots me a small smile, then turns to listen to something Sloane's saying.

I change in the bathroom, then scoot back into the room, settling under my bedcovers. I'm still lying there awake long after the other girls have fallen asleep. A mantra echoes through my brain like it's stuck in a broadcast loop: *You're not dying. Your scan was clean.* That should be comforting, but for some reason, it isn't. Even though Lila didn't find any trace of the plants in my body, I feel like their toxins might have leeched into my brain because I can't stop thinking about them.

When I finally fall asleep, my dreams take me back to the garden. I'm running again, bouncing off branches and bushes as I rush through the tangled web of greenery. Something's chasing me. Ghosts? Monsters? I don't know. I never see them. I duck behind a tree, trying to hide behind its thick limbs. A rustling creeps up behind me, closer and closer.

I should turn around—I *want* to turn around—but I

can't. Then the tree wraps itself around me, its branches squeezing me tighter and tighter, pressing me against its rough, dry bark, until I'm inside it. No, not inside. I *am* the tree. My arms stretch out a dozen times over, branches reaching and forking and extending away from my dense, stiff core. I try to break free—to walk, to run—but I'm frozen in place, my feet plunging deep into the dusty ground.

A dark figure approaches from the shadows. Whatever it is, it's small and covered head to toe in foliage. As it nears, I can make out a pair of eyes staring at me from behind a dense green mask across its face.

The figure leans closer and the mask falls away, bits of leaf and stem fluttering to the ground. She smiles as she sits beside me, and I recognize her just before I wake up.

Blinking in the dark quiet of my dorm room, I try to forget the dream, to forget the garden, to forget the face— the face that was mine.

CHAPTER TEN

I WAKE UP TO THE SOUNDS OF SATURDAY sleeping-in roommates. Rubbing the tiredness from my eyes, I slide out of bed and make my way over to my desk. My computer beeps a reminder at me, and I smack my forehead. I completely forgot that I'm supposed to be on a video call with my parents.

Who schedules a call this early on a Saturday? Oh right, my math-obsessed parents. They've probably already been working for hours. I pluck my pendant off its charging station and frown. It's still dead.

"What's wrong with this thing?" I murmur, holding it up to my eye for a closer look. My stomach free-falls like it's in a zero-gravity field.

This is not my pendant.

It looks a lot like it, but the fob in my hand is clearly

older. The screen is shaped differently, with boxier edges, and the sides are scuffed from much more use than the month and a half I've had mine. My heartbeat echoes in my ears so loudly I wonder if it will wake my roommates. This means my pendant—my easily-traced-by-the-school-network pendant—is still in the very secret and, if the Rep is to be believed, very dangerous garden.

One of the girls rolls over and I jump, accidentally tossing the pendant so it skids across my desk and falls somewhere behind it. *It's not like anyone would be able to tell from the other side of the room that it's not yours, genius.*

I force my breathing to settle back into a normal rhythm. *Think, Myra.* All I have to do is go back to the garden and get my pendant. Easy.

My computer beeps again.

Blast it. I've got to log in to the video pod to access the system, and if I skip the call, my parents *could* contact the school to alert me. If they do that, the administration could trace my pendant to see where I am, since we're supposed to wear them at all times. . . . My palms start to sweat again. *That can't happen.*

I glance at my roommates, glad to see they're still sound asleep. It's early—really early—and they might not be up for hours. My eyes wander over to the charging station on Lila's desk. Her pendant is resting there, probably fully powered.

My parents never want to talk for long. I could check in with them, scoot over to the moongarden to retrieve my pendant, then be back to return Lila's before she even wakes up.

I creep over to her desk and tuck her pendant in my pocket, then tiptoe to the door. The hallways are completely deserted as I make my way to the modulab. With a minute to spare, I slide into one of the video pods. As I settle into the teardrop-shaped capsule, the pendant logs me into Lila's account. Her academia network homepage glows on the screen in front of me. Before I can minimize it, a message pops up. It's a photo from a contact labeled *H♥me.*

I wince and move to close the message so I can access the video network, trying not to worry about what Lila will think when she's sees a "new" message no longer marked as "new" in her log.

But before I tap away the photo, I scan the image. Those must be Lila's parents staring back at me, with a young, dark-haired boy between them holding up a sign that reads WE MISS YOU, LILA in little-kid scrawl.

I tear my gaze away from the sign, and my eyes automatically crawl over the arms and hands of her parents, looking for Inscriptions. Lila's mom's arms are covered in them, but they're too small for me to make out what Creer she is. My eyes flick to her dad's arms, then widen. They're as blank as mine.

Chewing my lip, I close the message and activate a call, manually typing in my home address so I can ping the video pod linked to the residence.

Eight minutes later, I'm left wondering why I even bothered. I'm still waiting. Scowling, I mute the music and glare at the screen. "I should just go if you're so busy."

The screen encircling me doesn't answer, continuing its slow blink of *Hold Please*.

Even the screen is politer than my parents.

At the twenty-four-minute mark, the screen dissolves into an image of two distracted-looking people. Mom's dark hair is pulled up in a bun, and the top of a stiff white shirt peeks over the bottom of the screen—her classic *working-don't-bother-me* look. Dad keeps glancing to the side, even before he says hello. He's got numbers glowing in the air just out of sight. I'd bet my pendant on it.

"Hi." I make sure my voice is flat and bored. They don't notice.

"Hi, sweetie," Mom says with a quick, clumsy smile. "Sorry we're a little late."

Behind his glasses, Dad's eyes dart to the bottom of their screen. He has no idea they're late. He flashes me his own manufactured grin, the kind he uses when his mind is somewhere else.

When the numbers are whispering to him.

"What are you working on, Dad?"

He raises his eyebrows. Apparently, he thinks he's as good an actor as he is a master of math. He shouldn't quit his day job.

"Oh, it's something really neat, actually. You'd love it." He removes his glasses as he talks, polishing them on his shirt. A Mender corrected his vision ages ago, but he had his eyes set back to how they were not long after. He said he missed having his glasses to fiddle with while he worked. That it helped him think. "We've discovered a reverse underpattern in the way the numbers communicate with one another. It's quite remarkable. They seem to have a sort of unspoken language beneath their obvious equations."

I tune out for the next seven minutes while he drawls on. I stopped trying to follow his never-ending math monologues when I was six. You'd think after so many years of me pretending to listen, he'd have caught on, but even with his big brain processing its big numbers, he still can't put two and two together to figure out that math isn't my thing.

I rest my temple on my hand and reopen Lila's picture message, not even pretending to listen. Zooming in on Lila's dad, I squint and lean closer to the screen. Nope, not a single mark. It's not unusual to be a non-Creer, but most of the kids here have parents that not only have Creers, but are at the top of their fields.

"So, how's school, Myra?" Dad finally asks, like I'm sitting across the breakfast table from them as they go through their empty ritual of stupid questions instead of hundreds of miles away.

"Fine," I reply, waiting for one of them to ask me what I learned recently.

"What did you learn this week?" It's my mother's turn, apparently.

"The healing process for open wounds," I lie. They may be number masters, but they have absolutely no idea about other Creers. Still, as long as I offer up something about some other trade, they can't quiz me on my progress as a Novice Number Whisperer.

"Oh, that's very interesting." Now it's Dad's turn to lie.

"My roommate is a Novice Mender," I announce. My less-than-subtle way of reminding them that they don't know a thing about my life at school.

"Oh, that's right!" Mom tries to act like she knew this already. I don't know why I care; it's not like they paid much more attention to me when I was home. At least then, they'd hover over me while I did my homework, making sure everything was correct. When I got to S.L.A.M., I half expected them to still call or buzz my messenger every night to check my equations. But they haven't—not once. My eyes flick back to the enlarged image of Lila's dad in the corner of my screen. *Her family actually looks like they miss her.* I press my lips together and wait silently for the rest of Mom's cover-up.

"So, what about the facilities?" she tries. "Tell me about your room and the school." Her eyes get a starry, faraway look. "It's been a long time since I was a student at S.L.A.M. I'm sure a lot has changed."

I shrug, hoping to fend off a stroll down memory lane. "Everything's fine."

"Oh, I wanted to ask you," Mom says, sitting up straighter. "How do you like the dining options? I just found out today the university is going to be offering a new menu, and the director told me it's the same one being offered at S.L.A.M."

My eyebrows rise, but I try to cover up my surprise with a dramatic eye roll as my meeting-that-never-happened with Director Weathers flashes in my mind. "It's . . . school food, Mom. Don't expect much."

First S.L.A.M. and now the Lunar University . . . I file the menu news away to mull over later.

Mom looks at me like she wants to ask something more, but Dad jumps in before she can. "Tell us more about your roommates. One's a Mender, but what are the others?"

"Sloane's a Chemic," I say, "and Bethany is an Elector. Her parents are Electors in the capital."

Dad's ears perk up. "What's her family name?" With his position on the Creer Governing Council, he knows just about everyone that matters in the capital, or at least he thinks he does.

I shrug. "You don't know them."

"Oh," Dad replies, disappointed. "So a Mender, a Chemic, and an Elector. Very diverse."

There's a pause, and I open my mouth to end the call.

"How are your classes?" Mom asks.

I groan silently. When either of my parents mention *classes* there's only one subject that matters to them.

"Fine," I reply, hoping it's enough. Of course it's not.

"How do you like Ms. Goble?" Mom asks, her voice tight. "She and I grew up together, you know."

My mouth falls open at this bit of news. "You didn't tell me that."

"I'm sure I did." Mom brushes away a stray strand of hair. "You don't look like you care for her." Her eyes sparkle like they do when she's grading homework and her students score higher than she expected.

"She's just . . . strict."

"That's not surprising." Mom sniffs. "Val—I mean, Ms. Goble—became a bit stuffy when we were at S.L.A.M. It's one of the reasons we grew apart over the years."

"What topics have you covered so far in her class?" Dad

asks, and for once, his eyes are trained on the screen. I have their full attention. Lucky me.

"Algorithms."

"Oh, wonderful," Mom replies. "Which ones? Deviation models? Transitional decimals?"

"Yup, those. Look, I've got a lot of homework. I've gotta go."

"Okay, honey," Dad says, and he looks as relieved as I feel. His eyes are staring off-screen again, instead of anxiously looking back and forth. He's checked out. *Perfect.*

A door whooshes open somewhere behind me. Someone else is entering the modulab.

"We love you," Mom adds, and Dad absently nods his agreement.

"You too." I reach for the End button as footsteps approach my corner of the room.

"Oh, wait, honey. I forgot. What tests do you have coming up? I wanted to check in with—"

I end the call just as Lila arrives at my station. She snags the pendant out of the dock, immediately logging me out of her account. "Next time," she says, "try asking—"

The screen flashes the last images generated from her pendant, the *Call ended* message, and the enlarged photo of her dad, before fading to black.

Cheeks scarlet, Lila glares at me, her pendant clutched beneath white knuckles.

I know I should say something. Tell her I'm sorry, and I don't care that her dad's a non-Creer. Promise her I won't tell anyone. But I don't. I just stare back until she storms away, eyes flashing with hatred and brimming with tears.

I let her go. I let her hate me. It's easier that way. For everyone.

CHAPTER ELEVEN

AFTER LILA STORMS OUT, I SIT AND WAIT FOR A while just to be sure she's gone. I don't want anyone, especially one of my roommates, following me to the deserted classroom. If I didn't have a choice about going back to the moongarden before, I definitely don't now. I picture myself standing outside my dorm-room door, knocking and knocking and knocking. . . .

Sure she's not coming back, I slide out from the video pod, cross the modulab, and make my way through the halls, still empty at such an early hour. Before I know it, I'm back in the hidden lab.

Bin-ro chirps at me.

"Hi, there. I need your help," I say, and she emits a high-pitched whistle like a question. "I left my pendant in the garden. Can you help me find it?"

A quick beep and two spins are my answer.

I smile for the first time in a while, then take a deep breath. "Okay, let's do this." Making my way over to the hidden button on the counter, I pause. "You're *sure* the plants aren't going to poison me?"

Another beep and spin.

"Did you see a man, a Rep man, in here yesterday?"

Bin-ro erupts into excited beeps and twirls.

"You like him?"

She beeps an affirmative.

"And he's been in here before?"

Another yes.

I turn this new information over in my mind. That Rep couldn't have built the garden on his own. He must have been helping someone. If someone wanted labor, and they also wanted to keep it quiet, a Rep would be the perfect choice, but how would a Rep—or anyone really— know the first thing about growing a garden? It's not like there are how-to guidebook holograms for that on the market—*How to Grow an Impossible Moongarden in Twelve Easy Steps!*

After lying on the floor to double-check the position of the triangular reflection on the countertop, I activate the button and wait as the counter retracts into itself, leaving a gaping hole in the floor. Gingerly, I lower myself onto the slide and let go. The whoosh of air as I whiz down is more exhilarating than terrifying now that I know no monsters are waiting for me at the bottom. I land more easily this time, too, managing to stay on my feet.

Wandering, with every turn something new catches my eye: Short, bushy plants that are clearly overgrown, but probably once bordered pathways. Plants that reach far over my head, their tendrils trickling down like a meteor shower frozen in time. Thin, stringy shoots that wind determinedly up a wall, covering it in a quilt of green. It's probably my imagination, but it's like the garden perks up to greet me. A scattering of teardrop-shaped leaves tickle my arms and face as I pass by, while tangles of branches covered in tiny, spikey balls snag on my shirt as if asking me to stay and visit for a while.

I'm supposed to be looking for my pendant, but I can't seem to tear my eyes away from my surroundings. There's a magic in here I've never experienced before. Not at home. Not at S.L.A.M. Not anywhere.

Leaves and stems and branches swish and whisper in my wake, filling the garden with a soft, rustling melody more tranquil than any lullaby I've ever heard. Tiny white bells hang from a patch of jagged leaves sprouting from the ground. I nudge them gently to see if they jingle or chime. They don't. Still, I can almost hear their notes added to the natural symphony humming around me. I must have walked in a circle, because I realize I've ended up back where I started at the bottom of the chute. After a few steps down another path, I pause. A strangely shaped object rests at my feet. Stooping down, I study what must have once been a flower. *I wonder if it was beautiful before.*

I gently prod it, and it flops over. With its petals dark and withered and its stem half-severed, it's clearly dead now. It looks like something crushed it. *I hope it's not my fault.* I might have fallen on it when I tumbled through the garden yesterday. I wish I could fix it, but I have no idea how, or if that's even possible. I rack my brain for the little I can recollect about plants, which truthfully isn't much. I know they need water and sunlight, neither of which seem available here.

Grief like I've never felt before grips my heart as I realize there's nothing I can do to help, and without thinking, I lay my hand over the flower. Heat streams from my chest into my fingertips, and my hand tingles like its fallen asleep. *What's happening?* My pulse is racing, but I resist the urge to pull back. I'm not sure I could if I wanted to. But instead of feeling afraid, a peculiar confidence floods through me, like I'm doing exactly what I'm meant to be doing.

After a few moments the strange sensation fades, and

when I pull my hand away, the now-bright yellow flower slowly floats upright, its stem intact, once again rising from the ground. I give the flower a gentle tug, but it stays put. It almost seems to be waving at me from its new home.

For some reason, my eyes burn, tears collecting on my lashes. My left arm burns, too, just above my wrist. I look down and my mouth falls open as tiny green lines weave themselves together on my skin. My eyes devour the emerald-green marking in the shape of a vine that's appeared like magic.

An Inscription.

Rustling off to the side makes me jump, and then Bin-ro rolls up, my pendant clasped in some sort of hook protruding from her hull. Without a word, I take the pendant, climb to my feet, and leave the garden.

For the rest of the weekend, I wander the school. In the Rec hall, I turn on a virtual game, then just stand there as aliens blast my ship to pieces. I go to the cafeteria and shuffle perfectly uniform and perfectly jiggly squares of food around my tray. I honestly don't know if any makes its way into my mouth. In the modulab, I type a zillion-and-a-half messages to my old friend Hannah, and don't send a single one.

Before I know it, I'm sitting in history on Monday morning while Mr. Ford drones on and on about some long-ago war on the Old World—something about the Third Water Conflict. I'm hardly listening, and I'm not the only one. Kids around me lounge in their seats, doodling on their desktop screens. No one likes these classes. No magic. No demonstrations. Just lectures and text glowing on page projections.

I shift from staring mindlessly at my hologram textbook to stealing glimpses beneath my sleeve at the green markings to replaying the flower coming back to life when I touched it.

It can't mean what you think it means.

But what else could it be?

Anything but what you're thinking.

There isn't anything else, is there? No other explanations that makes sense. Nothing except the M *word.* Magic.

I wave my fingers in front of my workstation's sensor pad aimlessly, accidentally highlighting random words on the page. A new hologram screen turns on, offering a catalog of potential synonyms.

You've never heard of a Creer related to plants.

Of course not, stupid. There hasn't been plant matter outside of labs for hundreds of years. Why would anyone learn plant theory when there's nothing to try the practical magic on?

I drum my fingers on the screen, causing more words

to populate and additional hologram pages to pop up. I'm sure there isn't a single textbook file in the whole modulab that explains plant magic. And why would there be? As far as anyone is concerned, plants are history.

I sit upright. If there *was* a book that might tell me more about plant magic, it would be the history textbook in front of me. I swipe away the thesaurus screens and flip through the hologram pages so fast the headings are almost a blur. I pause when I reach a section called *Toxic Plants* and roll slowly over each word. There's no new information—just the same stuff I've heard my whole life. Plants on the Old World started releasing poisonous fumes—scientists called it *carbon asinoxide.*

At that time, there was no test for this never-before-seen toxic gas, though later a protocol was developed verifying its existence. By then, the compromised growth had spread so widely, it had already veered out of Creer control and, despite mitigation efforts, could not be stopped. As a result, the noxious fumes from botanic emissions overwhelmed the atmosphere. Oxygen masks were required, both indoors and outdoors. Even this protocol could not stop those already exposed from perishing. Approximately three billion people died, roughly a third of the planet's population. This, combined with frequent droughts, floods, and wildfires, among other natural disasters, *ultimately led those who remained to flee to off-world Settlements.*

All this is old news. Even so, I read the entry over and over again, looking for a hint, a clue, a seed about the plant magic. I flip to the index just in case, my eyes darting to Mr. Ford to make sure he's not about to call on anyone. He's not; he's just scribbling notes on the holo-projector as usual.

"Jupiter Jackpot!" I whisper, and the boy in front of me turns around to glare. I shrug an apology—maybe I woke him up—and hunch over my projected page, lasering in on the solitary number listed after *Plant Magic.* Holding my breath, I flip to page 1,214 in the glossary and immediately zero in on the words:

> **Botan** *(extinct): Creer known for the practice of Botanic magic, more commonly known as "plant magic," related to the study of flora. Abilities: able to commune with plant life.*

Thoughts and questions and feelings bubble inside me like a thermal-heat kettle set on high. In seconds, they reach full boil. My hand shoots into the air before I even realize what I'm doing.

Mr. Ford stumbles back like I've thrown something at

him. I can't remember the last time someone raised a hand in his class. Maybe this is a first.

"Oh, yes. Miss—er, you. You have a question?"

"What happened to the Botans?"

"The, er, the *Botans*?" He glances at the notes behind him. "I was discussing the efforts to control the water rations and—"

"I know, but I was wondering."

"Well." Mr. Ford presses his fingers into his chin. "They all died out a long, long time ago when the human population left the Old World."

"What could the Botans do?" I ask. "Could they talk to the plants? Or make them grow?"

"Hard to say." Mr. Ford paces, deep in thought. "The records indicate both, but perhaps it was one or the other, or something else entirely. There isn't much written on them, to be quite honest. Botans have been gone for generations. And there were certain *prejudices*, I would say, that perhaps made the historians of the time less inclined to record much about them and their abilities."

"Who cares?" a boy calls out. "We don't need them anyway now that the Chemics can make our food and stuff in labs."

"Well, Mr. uh, um . . ." At least I'm not the only one in the class whose name Mr. Ford doesn't know.

"Kyle Melfin, sir." The kid beams proudly. "My dad is

the Chemic rep on the Creer Governing Council, and he says without his food cloning company, the Settlements would starve."

His dad. The man from Director Weathers's office flashes in my mind. I open my mouth to say that the Chemics seem to be having some trouble with all that, but then remember my bargain with Director Weathers and snap it shut again.

"He is very likely correct," Mr. Ford agrees. "Moons don't have gardens, after all."

Mr. Ford settles back into his lesson, drawling on about who-knows-what. I'm concentrating hard, but not on what he's saying—on what he *said*. If all that's standing between the population of the Settlements and starvation is the Chemics and their food cloning, then the future is not looking very bright (or well fed).

But what if the secret moongarden could help? What if *I* can help?

Hope bubbles in my chest. Maybe my future is tied to mathematical equations after all, because right now, it seems like a secret moongarden plus secret Botan powers might just equal saving the galaxy.

But first, I need to find out more about this food cloning business and what's gone wrong. And if I'm going to get the garden in order (and learn more about my magic), I'm going to need to learn a lot more about plants. For that I need a teacher. Where would I find one of those?

I almost bolt from my seat. There *is* one person at this school who could teach me about plants *and* keep quiet about it. I just have to find him.

CHAPTER TWELVE

I RUSH OUT OF MY LAST CLASS OF THE DAY AS soon as the bell rings, not even waiting to hear what homework Ms. Goble has assigned on cross-communicating fractions. The days I have my Number Whispering theory class last have always been my least favorite, and today in particular I don't have time to waste studying a Creer I'll never have. I've got more important things to do, and they all start with finding that Rep who knows about the moongarden.

I start at the bottom of the school and scour the building room by room, floor by floor. I see lots of Reps but not the one I'm looking for. It never occurred to me how many Reps actually work in the school before I started looking for a specific one.

I'm rounding the corner of the Chemic wing when a familiar voice freezes me in place midstep.

"Miss Hodger," Director Weathers calls from behind me, exiting a classroom. "Just who I was hoping to see."

That's the last thing on the Moon that I want to hear. "Hi, Director Weathers." I manage a weak smile as I turn around. "I was just looking for my Chemic professor to see if I could do any bonus work to make up for the class I missed last week."

"Good, good," he says, folding his hands in front of him. Even though his tone is cheerful, his expression is serious. "That's what I was hoping to hear. Sounds like our, er, *arrangement*, is still in place, then?"

I rock from my heels to my toes and back again. "What arrangement?" I reply, hoping it's the answer he's looking for.

He smiles approvingly. "Let's keep it that way, shall we?"

I nod, hoping that will be the end of our discussion.

Director Weathers takes a step forward, then pauses. "Seven months."

I raise my eyebrows. "Sir?"

"That's how long our year is now. Back on the Old World, it was twelve. Do you know why the original off-world Settlements chose that new time frame?"

"The Old World's orbital year was three hundred sixty-five days, but the Moon's is only twenty-seven," I answer automatically. "That's how we ended up with our one hundred ninety-six-day year. It's the average of the two."

"Seven months, each with a perfectly uniform four weeks, seven days apiece. Most students don't know the history of how our calendar came to be. It's interesting that you do."

I shrug. "That was one of the first formulas my parents taught me."

"My point is, Miss Hodger, that only five of those seven months are devoted to schooling. In your first year, the weeks spent here are even more critical, what with your Creer test in the fifth month."

I clench my hands into fists at my sides. I already have enough people badgering me about that test. I don't need another one.

"A single wasted class is a wasted opportunity," he continues. "I wanted to remind you of that."

He turns to go, but irritation churns inside me. Director Weathers isn't the only one with something to lose if our deal falls apart. And I can leave *reminders*, too. "My mother mentioned that the Lunar University is going to have the same menu as S.L.A.M. soon," I blurt out.

"Did she now?" The wrinkles around his eyes deepen as he looks over his shoulder. "I hadn't heard." He adjusts the Creer pin on his tie. "Tell her hello the next time you speak to her." He continues on his way, his stride faster than before. This time, he doesn't look back, and I return to my hunt for the Rep from the moongarden classroom. I finally find him on the fifth level wiping down some counters in a Chemic lab. He swipes a wrinkled hand across his forehead, pushing a wisp of gray hair out of his eyes. I hover in the doorway, waiting for him to look up.

He doesn't.

I clear my throat.

Nothing.

"Ahem!"

The Rep man just keeps scrubbing.

I stomp a few feet into the classroom. "Uh, excuse me?"

The man glances up at me. "Need me to call a Mender?"

"What?"

He looks back down at his work. "All that coughing and hemming and hawing you were doing. Sounds like you need to be in the Mending wing."

I cross my arms in front of my chest and move a few steps closer. "I was *trying* to get your attention."

He sprays some cleaner on the counter and rings out his buffer. "Most people use *hello*."

I shift my weight. "Hello," I finally say.

He nods but doesn't look up. "Hello."

This is going to be harder than I thought.

"I need your help."

He glances up at me again. "Got a project?"

"Sort of." I take a breath, trying to figure out the best way to word my request. I go for the direct route. "I need you to help me in the garden—the moongarden."

He stops and turns to face me. "Don't talk about that out in the open like it's some sort of traveling space circus." His voice is a harsh whisper. "You could get in real trouble for even mentioning it." He turns back to his work. "Could get both of us in trouble, as a matter of fact."

"Okay," I snap. "I need you to help me in *the place*."

"Nope."

My eyebrows shoot up. "What?"

"You heard me."

"But you have to!"

"All I have to do is finish these counters in here, then buff the floors in this wing, then clean up after the dinner rush. I don't have any other work orders on the docket today." He shoots me a stern look. "And you'd be smart to forget all about that place and any wild ideas you have for it."

My mouth hangs open as I process all he's said. He just ignores me.

"But you've worked in there before. I *know* you have."

"Doesn't have anything to do with right now."

"But . . . but I need your help!"

He glares at me out of the corner of his eye. "What do you want with that place?" He hesitates. "You need to steer clear of there."

"Why? The plants aren't poisonous. I know they're not."

"I know they're not, too, but that garden is still dangerous."

My stomach drops. "What happened to the person who created it?"

He shakes his head. "Nothing good."

I wait, but he doesn't elaborate. "But how—"

"You don't need to know," he says firmly. "You just need to stay away."

"I can't," I blurt out, fiddling with the sleeve concealing my main reason.

He glances up at me, but this time there's a different sort of look in his eyes. I can't quite decipher it, but it's gentler than a moment ago, like he just saw something familiar. "And why would that be?"

"I want to learn about the plants," I say softly. "I want to make them grow. I want to . . . to *fix* the garden. I don't know what it's supposed to look like, but it seems wrong right now. Like chaos. I want to make it right." I look up into the man's pale-blue eyes. He's stopped cleaning, his buffer forgotten on the counter. "And then I want to show it to the galaxy and prove that plants aren't all dangerous. They can be good—do good. They can help us. But to do that, I need *your* help."

The Rep focuses on a spot on the counter. "What do you need an old . . . old man like me for?"

"I know you know about the garden. I think you helped whoever created it, didn't you?" He doesn't respond, but I take that as confirmation. "I need someone to teach me how to make it right—teach me about the plants. They can help the Settlements. I know it.

The Rep's quiet for a while—a long while. So long, that I worry he may have drifted off. When he looks up and reaches out his hand toward me, I jump.

"I'm Bernie," he says.

I reach out and gingerly shake his hand. "I'm, uh, Myra."

"Hello, uh, Myra," he says, the ghost of a smile on his lips.

"So . . ."

"Yeah, I'll help you. I have some time after dinner tomorrow." He starts scrubbing the counter again, like he agreed to just come sweep the dormitories.

I can't help the grin spreading across my face. I should say thank you, but "Why?" comes out instead.

He nods to himself. "Because you remind me of someone I used to know."

I have both an idea and no idea of who that could be. But it doesn't matter. For now anyway.

CHAPTER THIRTEEN

THE NEXT AFTERNOON, I DON'T EVEN BOTHER going to dinner. The block between the end of mealtime and the start of curfew isn't long—barely two hours—and I don't want to waste a second of it with something as silly as *eating*. So with a few minutes left before the meal block ends, I weave through the deserted halls to the moongarden. There doesn't seem to be anything in this wing besides offices and classrooms, so thankfully I don't cross paths with anyone. Until I turn the last corner.

I skip into the corridor with the moongarden classroom and skid to a halt. There's a light on in the room next to it. I slow my pace and creep closer. I'm not breaking any rules being here, but the last person I want seeing me lurking is a teacher. *Maybe a Rep was cleaning and left the light on*, I think hopefully.

No such luck. As I inch closer to the window streaming its square of yellow light into the hallway, I see the back of someone's head at a desk. I recognize the dark bob instantly. It's Ms. Curie. *This must be her office.*

Calling up all my class-cutting rules, I hold my head high and walk swiftly by her door. She doesn't look up, and I blow out a nervous breath before hurrying into the moon-garden classroom. I make my way behind the teacher's workstation and activate the door, then slip inside.

"About time, missy!"

The voice knocks me over as easily as a sonic cannon, and I tumble back onto the floor. "Bernie! That was fast! How did you get in here?"

The old Rep peers down at me with one eyebrow raised. "Walked. How did you get in? Teleportation?"

"Ms. Curie's in her office down the hall. Did she see you?"

Bernie shrugs. "No one notices Reps coming and going."

"Must be nice being invisible. Like having a super-power."

"Not exactly," Bernie says, his gravelly voice sounding even more solemn than usual. "Let's get going. I've got a project to do in the Rec hall at curfew, so that doesn't give us much time."

Do Reps get tired? I narrow my eyes at the man. No, at

Bernie. I never thought about it before, but Reps must sleep. They're human, after all. I shrug and follow him down the chute and into the garden.

It's even more beautiful than I remembered. I stoop to brush a fringe of green near my foot, the long, thin leaves curling over the ground like fingers. To my left, a tree with leaves the size of dinner plates rises over me, its branches drooping as if it's straining to touch the ground. To my right, a prickly mound covered with dry, stringy growth looms like a big, hairy monster. A vine with heart-shaped leaves curls around another trunk, as though it's hugging a friend, and a fuzzy plant, so soft and light it's practically invisible, brushes my cheek as I pass by it.

I turn in circles, spinning faster and faster, until the emerald hues swirl around me and I'm twirling, an orbiting planet in a universe of green. Scents stream toward me on my makeshift breeze, some crisp and fresh, others sweet, the rest damp and slightly musty. I inhale deeply, soaking in the sights and smells. A chuckle sounds behind me and I stumble, blushing as I realize how silly I must look. "I've never seen anything like this before," I say sheepishly.

Bernie grins. "It suits you here."

All I can do is smile.

Without another word, Bernie disappears into the dense foliage. As soon as he's out of sight, I drop to the ground, searching for another dead plant. It only takes me a second to spot one. But the closer I look, the more I sense that the whole garden seems to be in trouble. Dying, even. Brittle branches cloak all the shrubs in this section, and the ground is littered with blackened leaves and flowers.

Crumbling petals tickle my palm as I close my eyes, willing the bloom back to life, just like last time. But when I open one eye to peek, the flower looks exactly the same.

I rack my brain, pulling together everything I know about plants. Focusing on the flower again, I imagine water pelting down, soaking it. Maybe the petals form some sort of cup for the flower to drink from. Or maybe the leaves move to catch the water. I have no idea how it all works.

I lay my hand over the flower again, picturing water and light cascading over it. I imagine the plant growing.

Still, nothing happens.

A commotion cuts through the dense brush, and I scramble to my feet. A few moments later, Bernie returns with an odd-looking tool, a long stick with metal teeth on one end. He also has a friend in tow.

Bin-ro whistles brightly at me.

"Hi, Bin-ro!" I bend over and pat her metal hull as she scoots by, a strange apparatus emerging from her side. "What's that?" I ask, pointing at the webbed plate Bin-ro's hovering over the ground.

"A scanning mechanism," Bernie explains. "This little

robot is mighty helpful. The scanner can tell which sprouts need a little extra care, even before you can see it written on their leaves."

"Plants can write what they need on their leaves?" *They really are magic!* I kneel down and begin searching for words.

Bernie guffaws. "No, not like that. I just mean plants give off signals when they need a little something extra to grow."

"Oh." My cheeks flush.

Bernie pulls the metal part of the stick across the ground, tearing up bits of brown and green along the way.

"WHAT ARE YOU DOING?" I rush over and snatch the stick out of his hands, throwing up my hands to protect the scraggly growth. A few sparks seem to drift through the air toward him, but it's probably just a trick my eyes are playing on me. "You're ripping them apart!"

Bernie starts chuckling, then full-on laughs. A moment later, he's doubled over howling. Has he glitched?

After a few seconds, he straightens, trying to catch his breath. "Your heart's in the right place, missy, but you don't know a thing about horticulture." He wipes a single tear from his eye. "That's the proper word for gardening."

He's not wrong. Still, it sure looked like he was tearing the garden to shreds. "What do you mean?"

"This rake here," he says, pointing at the tool, "helps

clear the ground so the flowers and trees we want to grow have space to do it. I'm only pulling up the weeds."

"They looked like plants," I say defensively.

"They are plants, but not good ones."

"Bad like the—you know?" I nod toward the ceiling where the Old World is hovering somewhere, my palms suddenly sweaty.

"No, no. *Weeds*. They won't hurt you. They just stop the good vegetation, the healthy ones, from growing." He gently pries the rake from my hands. "They're like a virus, bad cells attacking good, so we gotta pull them so they can't strangle the parts of the garden we want to help."

"Let's get rid of them then!" I start frantically pulling up all the green at my feet.

"Wait, wait now." Bernie chuckles. "Those aren't all weeds you're pulling."

I look at my fingers snarled with leaves and vines and stems and feel sick. "Did I just kill healthy growth?"

"It's all right, missy. You didn't know. They'll bounce back, you'll see. Plants are resilient. They're survivors. They have to be to live here."

"But how do you know the good from the bad?" The tangle of stems and leaves in my hands doesn't look any different from the ones Bernie was pulling with the rake.

"I can teach you," Bernie says, "but it's going to take a

while, especially with just the bit of time between dinner and curfew."

"You can't get away during the day?" I ask. "I could cut class sometimes and meet you here."

He shakes his head. "I'm booked with projects from before breakfast until after dinner most days." His eyes narrow. "And you shouldn't be missing class."

"What about after curfew?" I ask, ignoring his scolding.

"I'd have more free time then, but getting here won't be easy for you."

He's not wrong. "I'll try and think of something." I look around at the sprawling garden. "Getting this place in order is going to be a lot harder than I thought."

"There's an art to horticulture," Bernie says. "Not to mention a little bit of magic."

My stomach drops. "Ma-magic?"

"Of course. All life has a little bit of magic in it, if you know what to look for. Plants aren't any different. Sometimes you just need to coax them a bit to help it come out. But once it does . . ." He leans on his rake and scans the room. "This place used to be a real sight to see. Enchanted, I used to call it." He starts scraping at the ground again. "We'll get it back in order, then you'll see."

I study him for a minute. I've talked more to Bernie than I've ever talked to all the other Reps I've come across in my life combined. He's a lot smarter than I thought he'd be.

"How do you know so much about plants?" I ask. "Do all Reps know about them?"

"No." He frowns. "The others, the—I'm the only one."

"So how do *you* know?"

"I was a gardener once. A master gardener, actually. I had my degree and certification and everything. Well, my original did," he says quietly, resuming his scraping at the ground.

"Really?" I gasp. "But that had to be hundreds of years ago!"

"Yep, I suppose it was." Bernie's rake is the only sound for a moment. "I'm one of the first of my kind," he finally says.

"Wow." I don't know how else to respond, so I start pulling up weeds by hand. I wonder if Reps don't like being called Reps. But what else would I call them? That's what they are. With a shake of my head, I scoop up all the weeds we've gathered and place them in a pile.

The work is hard, but I don't mind it. Bernie shows me how to dig up plants in a way that doesn't ruin their roots (long, tangly things like hair or spaghetti) so we can replant them. He says they work like straws, pulling what they need out of the ground.

"How do they know what to take?" I ask, gently packing a small, fuzzy sprout into a freshly dug hole. The leaves are soft and delicate, like a handful of feathers.

CHAPTER FOURTEEN

A WEEK LATER, I SIT ON MY BED, WEDGED INTO the far corner, trying to move as far away from the other girls as physically possible in one tiny dorm room. They're swapping gossip about the boys at S.L.A.M.

Algebraic theory would be a vastly more interesting topic, and that's saying something.

"Canter Weathers asked me if I knew Ms. Curie's office hours today," Bethany says breathlessly. "He could have asked anyone in his class, his year even, and he asked *me*!"

Lila smirks. "No way! Have you picked out a planet for your wedding?"

The girls dissolve into giggles as Bethany's pillow arcs through the air. I mime throwing up onto my desk, though none of them notices.

"Oooh, what about Kyle Melfin," Sloane coos. "He's so

talented! I bet they accept him as a Chemic Novice before we even take our Creer test."

"He seems like a know-nothing know-it-all to me," I mutter.

Three heads swivel in unison toward me, and as one, they all turn back around without a word. Ever since I, er, *borrowed* Lila's pendant, even she's taken to ignoring me.

Normally, I wouldn't care. But today I do. I need a favor. I've been meeting Bernie in the moongarden every day for the past week, but it's never enough time. His daily tasks don't always end with dinner. Sometimes, he's only got a few free minutes before curfew. If I'm ever going to learn enough about plants to set the garden right and figure out how to work my magic, I need more time in the moongarden. That means breaking curfew. And Lila might just know a way to do it.

Maybe I could leverage her secret to my advantage. Threaten to tell what I learned about her dad in exchange for what I need. The second the thought materializes in my mind, it turns sour, like splashing vinegar into juice. If my plan with the garden doesn't work out the way I want it to, I may end up being the last person on the Moon who doesn't think I'm a total villain, but I'd like to at least keep it that way.

"We're going to go study in the modulab," Bethany says to Lila as she and Sloane bound off the bed. "Want to come?"

Lila shakes her head. "All the good screens are probably taken by now. I'll just stay here."

Bethany and Sloane leave, and Lila powers up her book-pod at her desk, squinting at diagrams and complicated-looking vocabulary words. She shoots me a sideways glance, and I take it as my one and only opening.

"I'm sorry for taking your pendant," I blurt out. "I should have asked. Mine was . . . dead, and you were all sleeping. If I missed my call with my parents, they would have gone cosmic."

She doesn't say anything, just raises her eyebrows.

"But I guess that doesn't matter," I add quickly. "I still should have asked."

She studies me for a second. Then another. And still she says nothing.

I pluck at my bright Number Whisperer-yellow socks (a Worship Day gift from my parents, obviously). *It's no use.*

"It's okay," she finally says. "My parents would freak, too, if I missed a call. Just, next time, ask or leave a note or something. I wouldn't have minded."

"Deal," I say, some tension easing from my shoulders.

"And about what you saw . . . ," Lila continues, her cheeks flushing.

"I didn't see anything."

She cocks her head, her whole face bright red. "But the picture."

I look her dead in the eye. "Lila, I didn't see *anything*. And even if I did, I wouldn't say anything about it."

She stares back at me, unconvinced. "Having a non-Creer parent, it's not a good look around here."

"I know."

"Kids can be awful, especially stuffy S.L.A.M. students."

"Believe me, I know." I fold my legs beneath me.

"How?" Lila asks.

"*How?*" I repeat, startled.

"I noticed you don't really have friends from home here, or none that you're friendly with now. Didn't anyone from your old school come to S.L.A.M.?"

"A few people," I say slowly. "But no one I was close with. Most of my old group of friends decided to go to other Lunar schools. One went to the Martian School of Magic, and another picked the Venusian Academy of Magical Arts." I shrug. "But we weren't really friends by then anyway."

"What happened?"

For some reason, I tell her. I go through the whole CHARM story. As I talk, pressure seems to leak from my chest, like air being let out of a balloon. When I'm finished, I actually feel a bit lighter.

"Crashing comets," Lila says, leaning back in her chair. "That must have been really tough."

I rest my chin on my hand. "Kids are awful, remember?"

"They really are. Sometimes." Lila pauses. "That happened at my school, too, but it wasn't all my friends, at least. Bethany and Sloane didn't care about what my Creer was, anyway. That's why I roomed with them."

She raises her eyebrows at me, like she wants to ask me who I was supposed to room with, since I obviously was dumped in here last-minute. But before she can, I blurt out a question: "If you're not too mad at me still, could I ask a favor?"

She glances up, startled. "You mean in exchange for—"

"No! No, not at all. I'm not going to tell anyone about your dad, Lila. I swear." I fidget, nervous she'll say no. "I was just going to ask if you knew what the JV hoverball boys use to get by the curfew trackers."

She considers my question for a moment, then pushes off her bed and goes over to her dresser. "I do, actually. Here." She tosses me a roll of something shiny. "It's reflector paper. Canter Weathers invented it. It reflects the transmissions from the trackers. The boys said they wrap it around their feet when they walk through the halls. They don't know where the trackers are, but they know they're low to the ground."

"And this stuff stops the trackers from detecting them?" I unroll it and pinch a piece between my fingers. It's crunchy and shiny, like paper-thin metal.

She shrugs. "They said it would. We didn't get to see it in action, though."

"Can I borrow a couple pieces?"

"Sure." Her brow furrows. "What do you need it for?"

What do *I need it for?* "I, uh, need it to go to the modulab."

"The modulab?"

"Yeah." Wheels spin quickly in my mind formulating a believable excuse. "It's kind of hard to study with all the Number Whisperer kids always trying to talk to me." I shrug. "They know my dad's on the Governing Council, and my mom's on the admission board for the Lunar University. I guess they think I have connections. But I have some big projects coming up, and it'd be a lot easier to study if I could go when it's empty."

Her eyes narrow. "But wouldn't the modulab be locked after curfew?"

"Er, they don't lock it. They don't need to since they have the trackers all around the school." I have no idea if that's true, but it sounds good.

"Oh," Lila says, but she doesn't seem convinced.

"I do have something to offer in exchange, though," I say quickly. "If you want to keep practicing your Mender scans on someone, you can use me." *Can't hurt to have her do it anyway if I'm going to keep going to the garden. Just in case.*

She grins. "Fine by me."

116

I break off two pieces of the metal paper and hand her back the roll.

She tucks it into her dresser. "Let me know how it works."

The warning note in her voice is clear. She really means, let me know *if* it works.

"I will," I reply, swallowing down a wad of dread. "I'm going to try it tonight."

CHAPTER FIFTEEN

THAT EVENING, ONCE ALL MY ROOMMATES ARE in bed, I carefully pull the sheets of metal from under my pillow. I listen for three sets of sleep-breathing, counting at least two. I peek over the covers and catch Lila's eye. She mouths *Good luck*, before rolling over.

As quietly as I can (which is hard since the paper is crinkly), I mold the metal around my socked-feet, then slip out of bed and then out the door, heading in the direction of the modulab. My lie to Lila about needing to sneak past the trackers actually wasn't a half-bad idea. A deserted modulab sounds a lot safer for the kind of research I need to do than one crowded with nosy kids, and if the reflector paper doesn't fool the curfew trackers, the last place I want to be is near the moongarden classroom.

I tiptoe past darkened doors, the decorations that usually

glow there muted for the night. The normally bright lights dotting the ceiling are set to low-power, casting strange shadows throughout the hall.

I skulk down the corridor and around the first corner. There are definitely trackers in this hallway—there have to be—and I have no idea what happens when one is set off. A blaring alarm seems unlikely. It'd wake half the school. I'd bet Bin-ro that when a student trips a sensor, it pings a teacher, or worse, the director.

Thankfully, when I get there, the modulab isn't locked. I hurry inside and pop one of the multisized, multishaped screens off the wall, then settle into a workspace in the very back, out of view from the door. The soft, moldable material of the putty-lounger auto-adjusts with my movements, stretching and extending until it's practically a sofa. I prop the long, rectangular screen on my knees and get to work.

I start by searching for anything about the food cloning issues that Director Weathers and Mr. Melfin mentioned happening last year. I sift through hundreds of articles posted to the school network from news sources all over the solar system, but none of them mention any problems with the food codes. It's like it never happened. And any headlines that look even slightly helpful are blocked. Director Weathers's handiwork?

Out of sources and out of ideas, I try a new angle.

Chemics must have to study food cloning as a part of their curriculum. Maybe there's something useful there. I log on to S.L.A.M.'s main site and scroll through the course listings for Chemics. I'm about to give up on that, too, when my gaze snags on the word *micropropagation*. I don't have a clue what that means, but tiny print next to it says *organic tissue cloning to stimulate food growth*.

I tap the bullet and the syllabus expands. It's a fifth-year lesson plan, so it mostly reads like Chemic gibberish to me. A few words catch my eye: *genetic variability, growth inhibiting*, and *contamination*. I don't know much about food cloning, but clearly, this translates to *problem, problem*, and *problem*. There doesn't seem to be any solutions listed, either. Not on this syllabus, anyway.

I stretch out my feet, pushing the putty-lounger to its limits, then sit cross-legged, the material folding around me like a nest. I'm not going to get far, limited to the school network . . . at least not *this* school's network.

Scooping my bag off the floor, I dig through it, pulling out my rarely used messenger, then quickly type a message to Mom, hoping against hope she's not buried in grading or recording a lecture for her class.

Almost instantly, a response pings back to me:

OF COURSE you may log into the university's archives of advanced numerical studies! I am so thrilled you asked! I'm not surprised Ms. Goble's lessons aren't challenging you enough. It's a Novice class, after all. And good for you, taking such initiative. I was a late-night studier, too, in my day. (But don't stay up too late! You need your rest for class.) Are your roommates sleeping? Do you need me to mail you a screen darkening cover? That way, your late-night studying won't bother them if they want to go to bed. I've made you a temporary university log-in. We use them for prospective students, so it will expire in a few days. If you need a more permanent one, just let me know and I'll speak to my director. I'm sure she'll approve!

I grimace at the length of the message. A simple *Yes, here's the log-in* would have been plenty.

I eagerly type the username and password she sent into the Lunar University's network. *Jupiter Jackpot!* Without the safeguards of S.L.A.M.'s network, I'm able to access way more, including the links that were blocked.

Turns out, they were blocked with good reason.

I scroll through article after article, all authored by Jake Melfin, and all about the many benefits of cloned foods grown in controlled environments, rather than "unstable and unpredictable" natural settings. After some more poking, I stumble across a post authored by a Chemic named Nathan Hackett that contradicts almost everything Mr. Melfin's coverage says. According to this report, the food cloning technology is an unavoidable dead end. Labs are not perfectly controlled environments at all times, free from contamination, and the plant tissue cells being used for cloning *could* eventually stop working. *Will* eventually stop working. The only way to prevent the inevitable problems connected with food cloning is to have a fresh source of genetic material, such as new plant tissue samples.

Why wasn't this bigger news?

Several clicks later, I get my answer. A few weeks after his article was published, Mr. Hackett was fired from his teaching position at the Martian School of Magic over some sort of scandal. The story about it includes an interview with Representative Jake Melfin, and quotes him as saying that Mr. Hackett was "discredited, disproved, and removed from the school before he could infect any more young minds with his nonsense." I can't find any trace of Mr. Hackett after that.

Ignoring more pings from my messenger—apparently sending Mom one message means I'd like her to send me fifty—I keep digging.

I uncover more information on Mr. Melfin and his company, Melfin Food Industries—MFI. It looks like they've been the main supplier of food for the Settlements for generations, dating all the way back to the evacuation of the Old World. They have two types of production: *micropropagation* or traditional plant cloning, and *imitation*, which is a fully artificial way of creating food without any natural elements.

I scrunch my nose. That's clearly what the cafeteria's been serving us. The MFI company blog has all sorts of articles about how great imitation is, how much easier and less expensive it is to produce. But I smell something fishy, and the Reps didn't serve fish-stick blobs in the cafeteria tonight.

Remembering Mom's lectures to her students about making sure sources are impartial before citing them in a paper, I start searching for data outside MFI's site on imitation food production, and immediately have a flood of hits, including interviews with Mender and Chemic experts on the nutritional content of the imitation products. A few say the new-form diet is great, and no different from goods produced by traditional cloning processes. But a quick cross-search reveals that those same "experts" actually work at MFI.

The responses from other experts are far less complimentary. Words like *malnutrition, health adverse,* and *toxic* stick out. One Chemic expert (not from MFI) worries that without new plant matter, the cloning process may break down completely, and all we'll be left with is the imitation method. Like the discredited Martian professor, he agrees that clean plant samples could restart the food cloning process, fixing the issue of overused plant cells. "But, unfortunately," his statement concludes, "moons don't have gardens."

I settle back in the seat, turning over all this new information in my head. *They do now.*

A thump at the front end of the modulab makes me jump. My putty-lounger snaps at my sudden movement, nearly dumping me on the floor. I reach out and grab the edge of the table, scanning the room as I steady myself.

No one's here, and the hallway outside the entrance is deserted, too. I notice a chair on its side near the front of the room. I don't remember it being knocked over when I came in. Sometimes kids leave them tilted against walls and tables. It probably just shifted and fell.

I take a breath, and as I push back into my chair, I catch a glimpse of a speck of green on my exposed wrist. Any lingering nerves dissolve into determination.

Maybe there's another solution to the food problem. I type *Botan* into the search field. I'm surprised that results appear. Not many, but enough to make my stomach fall faster than the modulab chair.

"Should Magical Negligence Be Prosecuted: A Legal Case Study of Botans."

"Op-Ed: Are Botans More Trouble Than Their Magic Is Worth? An Argument for Leaving Them Behind."

"Deadly Incompetence or Sinister Plot: Humanity Flees to Outer-Space Settlements after Botan Failures."

I squeeze my eyes shut, blocking out the headlines, and close the search window. These articles are centuries old. Whatever happened with the Botans back then shouldn't impact what happens today. The garden may be a mess now, but I'm betting it wasn't always that way. If I can get it back in order and prove that the plants aren't poisonous, it could change everything. And if I can use my Botan magic to do it, maybe my parents won't be devastated their daughter isn't following in their Number Whispering footsteps. For them, a galaxy-saving Creer has to be better than no Creer at all.

At least, it *should* be.

CHAPTER SIXTEEN

AFTER THE SUCCESS OF MY FIRST POST-CURFEW adventure, and with no detention greeting me the next day, I decide to push my luck and head to the moongarden the next night. Once the others are asleep, I slip out of the room. My metal-clad feet tiptoe down the corridors. Peeking around the corner, my heart lodges itself in my throat. There's a light on in the moongarden hallway. *Ms. Curie couldn't be working this late, could she?* Holding my breath, I dare a quick glimpse.

Apparently she can. There she is, hunched over her desk just like she was the first time I secretly met Bernie.

I shift from foot to foot, debating what to do: Go forward to the garden and risk Ms. Curie's wrath. Go back, giving up on the garden, and risk everything else.

I take a step forward and freeze.

The metal is only wrapped around my shoes. If I crawl past her door, and there are trackers on in this hall, I'm done. *Only one way past.* I squat and carefully shuffle down the corridor. I know I must look ridiculous, but strange contortions are far better than tripping the alarm. Or being seen.

I hold my breath as I cross under her office window and can't help glancing back over my shoulder once I'm past. No face appears in the window.

As I slip into the classroom, the door slides shut behind me, but my sigh of relief is drowned out by the sound of another door whooshing open.

"Blast it!" I whisper, scampering for cover as footsteps clomp nearer and nearer. I throw myself behind the teacher's workstation, curling up as small as I can.

The classroom door slides open. I can just see the top of Ms. Curie's dark hair as she wanders around the room, then leans against the workstation I'm hiding behind. All she has to do is turn her head and she'll see me.

Excuses and stories and lies scroll through my head like lines of computer code. I weigh the best, most-plausible reason why I would be hiding in an abandoned classroom after curfew with metal wrapped around my feet, but all I can seem to focus on is the back of Ms. Curie's head.

I don't know how long she stands there. It feels like a millennium.

Finally, she pushes off the desk with a sigh and drifts over to the wall I fell through my first time here. Now, there's absolutely nothing shielding me from her line of vision. I will myself to be a statue, trying not to even blink.

Thankfully, Ms. Curie doesn't turn around. She stares at the wall for a moment, reaching out to press her hand against it. My heartbeat thuds loudly in my ears. *Was that Ms. Curie's garden?*

Her hand slowly drops and she rubs at her eyes. "I'm sorry," she whispers.

My eyebrows shoot up, and I silently curse myself for the movement. Any flicker of motion could draw her attention, and then I'm space dust. Still, the words echo through my mind like a lunar boom. *I'm sorry?* Sorry for what? For closing up the garden? Abandoning it? Or sorry for something else?

Ms. Curie stands there for another few seconds, and then, with a small sigh, turns and leaves. I wait as her footsteps echo in the distance, then disappear. Finally, when I'm sure she's far, far away, I rise from my hiding spot.

As I do, a flash of movement from behind one of the remaining student desks across the room catches my eye.

Ms. Curie may be gone, but I'm not alone.

CHAPTER SEVENTEEN

I STARE, HORRIFIED, INTO CANTER WEATHERS'S face. He gapes back at me, his expression more confusion than anger.

"What are you doing in here?" he barks as I edge my way toward the door. "And where'd you get those?" He stabs a finger at my metal-coated feet. I can't help but notice his own pair flickering in the dim light as he positions himself between me and the door.

"None of your— What are *you* doing in here?" I stammer angrily. "You're not supposed to be out after curfew, either."

"I asked you first."

"I was hiding from Ms. Curie," I finally say, fixing him with my best glare.

"No, you weren't. I saw you. You came in here, and then

she came into the hall and you ducked behind the work-station."

I force a *who-cares-not-me* expression onto my face and shrug. "I was out seeing if these things would work." I hold up one foot.

"You must be friends with Bethany and her roommates," Canter replies, shaking his head. "I *told* them not to show anyone the reflector paper. If you got caught with it on, any teacher would know it was an Elector invention."

I plant my hands on my hips. "Sounds like it's not my problem then."

Canter glowers. "Who are you, anyway? What's your Creer?"

"My name is *none of your business* and my Creer is *get out of my way*." I push past him, heading for the door to the hall. I know I'm playing with fire—or electricity, really—but I don't have a choice.

My hand's already reaching for the door panel when a shuffling sound behind me makes me freeze.

"Hey, missy. What's the holdup? I thought we were meet-ing around—" Bernie climbs through the now-translucent wall, then stops.

"What in the Moon . . ." Canter's eyes flick between me and Bernie, like a holo-hockey puck. For a moment, no one says anything, then Canter stomps past Bernie and disappears through the wall and into the lab.

I shoot Bernie a hopeless look and climb after him.

I find Canter turning in a slow circle, taking in the whole room. He wanders over to the pile of magnifiers I'd dumped on the floor, picks up one of the slides, and examines it, just like I did my first time here, then drops it back into the pile. "What is this place?" he asks.

"A lab."

He shoots me a furious look. "I can *see* it's a lab."

I glare back. "Then be more specific."

"What's it *for*?"

"I don't know."

His eyes flash, and he opens his mouth, but I cut him off before he can say anything else.

"How would I know? I see the same things as you: dirty slides, a few magnifiers, and a lot of empty drawers. Figure it out yourself."

"You!" Canter says, pointing over my shoulder. "Tell me about this place, Rep."

I turn in horror to find that Bernie has followed us. I try to shoo him away, but it's too late. Canter would never have remembered him from the few seconds in the classroom. I'd bet Bin-ro on it. But now . . .

"He has a name!" I growl. "And Bernie doesn't take orders from you."

"I'm the director's son. Of course he takes orders from me." Canter's eyes widen. "Wait, did you say *Bernie*? You know his name?" He snorts. "I knew you were some sort of weirdo."

"Listen, you—"

"It's a research lab," Bernie says quietly.

"What sort of research?" Canter asks, stepping closer.

"Couldn't say," Bernie replies. "I'm just tasked with cleaning it."

Canter studies him for a minute, then turns his focus to me before his eyes dart around the room again. *He's buying it.* "So, where's the rest of it?" he finally asks, and my stomach drops.

I take a breath before trying for a casual, confused tone. "The rest of what? This is it."

Canter nods over to the counter where the tunnel is hidden. "Then where did all *that* come from?"

I have no idea what he's talking about. The counter looks perfectly normal, but then I see it. The traces of gravel on the floor. We must have been tracking it in all this time and never noticed.

"Now," Canter says, a smug smile on his face, "you're going to tell me what this place really is."

CHAPTER EIGHTEEN

I STAND IN FRONT OF THE STILL-HIDDEN passageway. "Please," I plead. "You can't tell *anyone*. Seriously. You just *can't*."

"Show me," he says, taking a menacing step forward.

I chew my lip for a moment, but I really don't have a choice. Reluctantly, I touch the secret spot on the counter and wait for it to retract and reveal the tunnel, then slide into the chute, flying down the smooth metal, my hair whipping away from my face. In the few seconds that pass, I hope Canter's had second thoughts about diving into the darkness, but a skid and whoosh of movement behind me confirms I'm not that lucky. I land easily on my feet, and he comes tumbling into the garden a moment later.

"How— What— Crashing comets," Canter stammers, his head swiveling side to side. With most of the dead plants cleared away, the garden looks much less threatening now than it did when I first stumbled upon it, but even a pretty moongarden must still seem deadly given what we've always been told about the fall of the Old World.

"It's not dangerous, I promise," I blurt out.

Bernie bobs his head as he emerges from the tunnel. "She's right. This garden isn't toxic."

"How would you know anything about that?" Canter scoffs.

"He knows plenty," I snap. "His original was a gardener."

Canter raises his eyebrows. "His original?"

I nod, and then a commotion makes us all jump. Bin-ro comes barreling out of the brush, beeping and whistling. She zips between Canter's legs, looping around and around each foot. Canter bursts out laughing, crouching down and patting Bin-ro as if she were a pet. "You're sure they're not toxic?"

I nod. "I had my Mender roommate check me out. Just in case."

"She knows about this place, too?"

"No," I say quickly. "I told her she could practice her scans on me for class."

Bernie bends down to pick up some tools, then heads off out of sight. He gives a little whistle and Bin-ro scoots after him.

"You're their roommate," Canter says, snapping his

fingers. "Lila, Bethany, Sloane, and some other girl. The Number Whisperer. Myra something."

I roll my eyes. "Yes, that's my name: Myra Something the Third."

Canter ignores me and wanders farther into the garden as if in a daze, brushing bits of plant off his clothes. Bernie and I finished clearing the garden's paths of debris, but they're still overgrown and hard to see. Somehow, Canter's feet still manage to find them, as if he knows exactly where he's going.

I hold my breath as he stops and runs his hands down the trunk of a large tree. "This place is amazing," he finally says.

I eye him, intrigued. Most people would've bolted out of here in a nanosecond, no matter how safe I insisted the moongarden was, but Canter doesn't seem to care. "We've been working on it," I say slowly, watching his reaction. "Trying to clean it up."

"Why bother? If anyone else finds out about this place, you'd be expelled for sure. Maybe worse. I've heard of people being sent to the prison on Mercury just for having seeds."

My stomach drops, but I pull myself together quickly. "I don't know. I just had to because . . ." I realize I'm twisting my hands together. There are so many reasons why the moongarden matters to me, none of which I want to share with Canter, and only one that I can. Even if it's not entirely accurate. "It's because of my parents."

"Your parents?"

"Yeah . . . They expect me to do all these great things. They're both super-accomplished Number Whisperers. *Beyond* accomplished. Like, math legends. So anything I do, they'll already have done it. But if I can turn this garden—this impossible but somehow possible garden—into something amazing, even if it's not exactly Number magic, they might . . . I don't know . . ."

"Be satisfied?"

I raise my eyebrows. "Yeah, exactly. Or at least stop badgering me a little." Crossing my arms, I take in the boy standing in front of me. "So that's my story. What's yours?"

"Same as you," Canter says. "You're not the only one with a famous parent."

I eye him suspiciously. "But you're an Elector. That's one of the most powerful Creers. And you're on the hoverball team. And you're, you know, *you*."

"Oh sure, I can excel as an Elector." Canter rolls his eyes. "I can score all kinds of points in hoverball, too. Big deal. A bunch of other kids can claim the exact same things. I've got to do something *extra* extra just to matter at all."

"To your dad or to everyone else?"

Canter shrugs. "Pretty much the same thing, isn't it?" After a moment he says, "So what's the plan for this place?"

I pause. What he's saying does make sense, but something tells me there's more to it than he's revealing. Maybe because there's more to why the garden is so important to me than what I'm revealing, too. Still, I don't press him. I can't afford to give him anything else to hold over me. "Bernie's helping me fix the garden up. Grow some food— some safe food. Then show it to the galaxy."

Canter scrunches up his face. "Anything grown here has got to be better than the space junk they're serving in the cafeteria now."

I weigh my words carefully, my deal with Canter's dad orbiting around my head. "I think there's something wrong with the food cloning process. That's why they changed S.L.A.M.'s food. They don't have anything else."

Canter raises his eyebrows. "What makes you think that?"

I shuffle my feet. "I was poking around my mom's school network—she teaches at the Lunar University." I tell Canter about the articles I found discussing the problems with the food cloning process and how MFI is trying to sell everyone on them. He listens, but doesn't seem surprised.

He kneels down next to a cluster of plants with heart-shaped leaves covering the ground like a teal-colored carpet, stretching out his hands. "It's funny. I can feel electricity buzzing in them."

"Plants give off a faint electric charge," Bernie says,

walking over to join us. I notice that he's looking oddly at Canter, as if seeing him for the first time. "Not enough to do anything with. But enough for an Elector to know it's there."

"I think Ms. Curie mentioned something about that in class once," I say.

Canter eyes Bernie warily. "How did you know that?"

"Picked up a lot of odds and ends of information in my time."

Canter's gaze slides up to the ceiling, taking in the panels and bulbs lining the panes of glass. "What's all that?"

"The perforated panels release water and the lights distribute nutrients," Bernie explains, "but they stopped working a long time ago."

"I could fix them," Canter says, patting his Elector-silver jumpsuit. "I'd like to help," he adds more quietly.

I study the second-year in front of me. *Why isn't he scared? He's got a lot more to lose than I do if this all goes supernova.*

"Okay," I say softly. "But you can't—"

He shakes his head. "I won't tell anyone." A smile tugs at his lips as his gaze travels over the tangled golds and emeralds and umbers surrounding us. "No one else can know about this place. Not yet."

CHAPTER NINETEEN

THE NEXT DAY, I SIT IN MS. GOBLE'S CLASS stifling a yawn and waiting for the bell to ring. Only one more day until the weekend. One more day until I can spend as long as I like in the moongarden without sacrificing hours of sleep. Granted, Canter will probably be there, but I think I can deal with that. He'll stick to his work, and I'll stick to mine. Hopefully, he'll be too distracted by repairing all the electrical damage to pay much attention to what I'm doing.

I peek into my sleeve at the green markings hidden there and smile, then glance around to make sure no one noticed. No one has. In fact, everyone seems immersed in hushed conversations. I listen, trying to catch bits of the exchanges as a strange tension fills the room, but I can't make sense of any of it. After a few moments, I tap my pendant, pulling up today's agenda to see if it holds any answers, but Goble arrives before the screen loads.

"Good morning," she says. "Now that we've finished the first unit on theory, I think those on the Number Whisperer track are ready to dive into magical application. The Creer test is three months away, which may seem like a long time, but I assure you, it goes faster than you can imagine." She clasps her hands and scans the classroom, eyeing us the same way she looks at fractions she's about to dissect.

My palms begin to sweat. *No, not now. Not today.* I've always known that at some point, we'd divide the class into Number Whisperers and other Creers to prep for the test at the end of the year, but I didn't think it would be *now.* And no magic equals big trouble for me. I don't need a Creer for that math.

"I'd like all those pursuing Number Whispering on that side of the room"—Ms. Goble gestures to her left—"and all other Creers over here on the right. Your assignment is on the holo-board. Let me know if there are any questions."

I haul my bag and body over to the left, choosing a spot in the back corner. A girl with two strawberry-blond braids and way too much energy springs into the workstation next to mine. She quickly arranges all her materials on her desk, bobbing, while Ms. Goble reviews her notes. I roll my eyes. *These seats had better not be permanent.*

"These will be your stations for the rest of the school year," Ms. Goble says, glancing up over her portable screen, "and your neighbor is your partner for the practical portion of class."

I fix my gaze to the front, doing everything I can to ignore Bouncy Braids, who's trying to catch my eye.

"Hi," she whispers, leaning over to my desk. "I'm Cammie. You're Myra, right? I've heard a lot about you! Well, about your parents, anyway, and how amazing they are. Your dad's the Number Whisperer on the Governing Council, right? And doesn't your mom teach at the university?" She doesn't pause for me to answer, and I wouldn't offer one, anyway. "I saw her name in our textbook. She's even published some Number studies. Wow! Everyone says you'll be at the top of our Creer. And now we're partners!" Cammie beams. "I mean, you probably already know how to do all this stuff, but it's still pretty cool, don't you think? What do you expect we'll start with first?"

I tap my pendant to bring up today's lesson plan. "The syllabus says cascading multiplication tables."

"Oh, that's right. I read that, too. It's right here." She nods at her computer screen. "They sound so fun! Have you done them before? I mean, you must have, right? Do you have any tips?"

I shake my head and turn my attention to Ms. Goble. She's put her notes down and walked to the front of the

Number Whisperer side of the classroom. Cammie zips around in her seat, resuming her bouncing.

Goble did this on purpose. I bet she told the Number Fanatic to sit next to me to get back at me for those classes I skipped weeks ago.

"I assume you've all read the assigned chapters pertaining to this topic, so I'll skip the scientific side and jump right into the magic," Ms. Goble says. All the Number Whisperer kids are on the edge of their seats. Even the other Creers watch closely. "Now, most of you have been practicing multiplication tables since kinder-school, but as you read in your text, the tables fall into each other, all interconnected, flowing as one. It's almost like a choreographed tumble. As you imagine the first set of tables"—she waves her hand and a simple set of multiplication tables emerges from her fingertips, hovering like mist before her—"let them fall into each other. Like so." She flicks the corner of the top number, as if it's a piece of lint, and the number cartwheels through the air. As it does, other numbers spin off, following the proper multiplication order. The cascading line of numbers rolls downward, hits the ground, and bounds back up, again and again, until the numbers form the outline of rolling hills. The kids around me all *ooh* and *ah*.

Ms. Goble's eyes sparkle as she waves her hands. The numbers crumble then disappear. "Work with your partners to try and duplicate the technique. Start with simple tables, and don't get frustrated if they don't fall very far at first. I'll be walking around if anyone needs assistance."

"Want to go first?" Cammie's face is inches from the edge of my desk, all smiles and eagerness.

"No, thanks."

"Okay, I'll go." She scrunches up her face, and I fight the urge to roll my eyes. "Just got to think of a starting equation. Okay, got it." She touches one finger to her temple and slowly draws it away. As she does, a number trails behind her fingertip as if she pulled it directly from her brain, which I suppose she did.

"Ms. Goble!" she howls, and everyone turns toward us. "I've got one! I've got one!" She points excitedly at the slowly drifting numbers.

"Very nice, Cammie."

"Okay, now the cascading." Cammie mashes up her nose again, as if making her face as small as possible will somehow increase her brain size. Face still crumpled, she flicks the edge of the number and it does a slow pinwheel. As it turns, a few other equations twist out of the first. "Ooh," she squeals, then punches the air. "Nailed it!"

You've got *to be kidding me.*

"Okay, your turn." Cammie's eyes are wide and expectant. "I bet yours will spin across the whole room!" The kids in front of us turn around and stare at me, waiting.

"Is she doing magic?" the girl whispers. Her partner leans in eagerly.

More and more eyes flick my way, and my palms start to sweat again.

"Are you sure you don't want to try again?" I ask Cammie. "You were on a roll." I give her a shaky smile and nod toward the fading stream of numbers lingering in the air.

"No way. I've been dying to watch you since the first day of class!"

I take in Cammie's wide eyes and the sea of others turned toward me, then lift my arm slowly, hoping for the bell to ring or a meteor to hit the school—anything to get me out of this. I hear gasps and murmurs as I raise my hand toward my head as slowly as possible. . . .

"Miss Hodger. The director would like to see you in his office."

My hand falls and my eyes jolt up to meet Ms. Goble's. She places her messenger on her desk and nods to the door. "Better hurry."

Without another word, I grab my things and all but run out of the classroom. I glance back, and Ms. Goble is still watching me. As I dart down the hall and around the corner, my stomach drops. *What could the director want? Does he know about my modulab searches? Or worse, did Canter snitch?*

I pass another few corridors before entering the administration wing, then hover outside the closed door with S.L.A.M. DIRECTOR ROBERT FRANKLIN WEATHERS stamped on the front. A reception screen glows beside it. I blink at the words, then read them again: OUT FOR THE DAY. RETURN EXPECTED, MONDAY, 9:00 A.M."

I recall Ms. Goble's expression as I left. I only met her eyes for a second, but suddenly it's entirely clear what she was thinking.

She knows.

CHAPTER TWENTY

Third Month, 2448

FIRST THING SATURDAY MORNING, I CREEP into my dormitory hall, careful not to wake my roommates. I don't know why I bother, though. It's not like I'll have to deal with them much longer, anyway.

I tap my pendant and call up the message Goble sent right after my non-visit to Director Weathers's office, hoping to find some clue about what's to come, but it's hard to find any hidden meaning in the words.

Hi, Myra. Would you please stop by my office Monday morning at nine to chat?

Great. Just great.

I have exactly two days to either develop Number

Whispering magic or come up with a non-expellable reason why I can't. The odds aren't looking good either way. With few ideas and even less sleep, I shuffle down the hall toward the moongarden. Maybe the plants will inspire me. And if they don't, at least I'll spend every last minute I can at S.L.A.M. in the garden.

When I arrive, the moongarden is bustling with activity. Despite my current situation, I can't help but feel a rush of excitement. Even though it's strange and new, somehow the garden feels like home. Like my whole life, it's been trying to reach me, but I couldn't hear its call. Until now. Deep in my bones, I know I belong here in a way I've never belonged anywhere.

I skip along the newly neat-and-tidy paths we created, trailing my fingers through the leaves, and ignoring my aching muscles. Caring for the garden is surprisingly difficult work. I can't remember the last time my shoulders and legs weren't sore, but I don't mind.

I pause to inspect a bush overflowing with ruffly, crinkled leaves the color of limes. Moving closer, I notice the plant is a riot of color. Violet stems form a web beneath the flourescent foliage. The edges of the lime-green leaves fade to a lemony yellow, the tips so pale they're almost white. Tiny red veins creep across their surface, forming an interconnecting grid. The pattern reminds me of

Mr. Ford's map showing the man-made River of Ingenuity on Mars. The Mars Settlement created the waterway, along with Perseverance Bay, decades ago.

I trace the tiny crimson lines with my fingertip, the smooth surface of the leaf punctuated by the grooves. Leaning in, I inhale deeply, and the sharp, fresh aroma makes my eyes water. Tiny buds form a network of polka dots, hints of bubblegum pink just visible beneath the minty-green shell. I imagine the shrub a few weeks from now, cloaked in fuchsia petals, and wonder what it will smell like when it blooms. Will it be tart like lemonade or sweet like strawberry taffy or some combination I can't even conjure yet? I gently brush my hand over the surface and the crisp buds flick across my palms, echoing the anticipation fluttering in my chest.

A grunt nearby snaps me out of my moment of joy, and I frown at Canter, who's standing in the heart of the garden, his hands outstretched as streaks of lightning dance from his fingertips, flashing up to the ceiling. The bulbs overhead crackle in response, the darkened ones blinking on one at a time. Bin-ro is hovering around his feet, watching him work.

"You got here early," I grumble, heading over to where Bernie is crouched, digging up some sort of fruit bush for relocating. Clusters of tiny green balls hidden among the leaves bounce and bob as he works.

"What'd you do, get lost?" Canter asks with a smirk.

"*No.* I had to get dressed in the dark so I didn't wake up my roommates."

"You definitely got lost."

"Listen, hotshot," I say, rounding on him, my hands planted on my hips. Bin-ro beeps, then takes off, disappearing into the brush. "I *found* this place. You could have hung out in the classroom outside for a year and never known it was here."

A wounded look flashes across Canter's face before it's replaced by irritation. "What'd you scare off Bin-ro for? He was helping me."

"She," I snap.

"No, it's *he*!"

"How do you know?"

"I asked him," Canter says, looking smug. "Didn't you?"

"I—"

"You do know you can use one-beep-yes, two-beeps-no with him, right?" Canter's voice drips with condescension. "It's really simple."

"I know *that*," I say through gritted teeth. "I invented it with her."

"*Him.*"

"All right!" I say, taking a deep breath. "How long have you been hanging around in that classroom, anyway? You never told me why you were there."

He shrugs, turning back to his work. "Same as you. Testing out the reflector paper."

For some reason, his reply rings false, and I notice he didn't answer my first question. "How long were you—?"

"I need to go check out the light bulbs on the other side," he says, turning and walking away.

I'm about to ask him why he's avoiding responding, but he's already too far away. "Hey, Bernie," I say, flopping down beside him. "Whatcha working on?"

"These plants need more room for their roots to spread out," he explains, swiping his sleeve across his face. "This one should be a lot taller, so I'm replanting it."

"What is it again?"

"It'll be a blueberry bush once it's back in good order," he says, lugging the tangle of branches to a hole a few yards away.

"Wow. How many do we have? And how much room will it take up?"

Bernie rattles off some dimensions, and I add them up in my head, then immediately stop, since the math only reminds me of my meeting with Goble on Monday and what could happen after.

"You're pretty cool," I whisper, turning back to the blueberry bush as Bernie heads off to tackle some other task. *Imagine eating something that we watched grow!*

I've only ever seen photos of the Chemic food labs—

they have to be kept clean and free of contamination, so hardly anyone gets to go inside. I always thought the labs looked pretty boring: rows and rows of solution bottles, carefully labeled jars of chemical compounds and powders, grayish blobs suspended under fogged glass or trapped in cloudy tubes. You can hardly see anything. In comparison, our garden seems like a science fiction movie. You drop a speck of something in the ground, pour water on it, and *poof*, food. I grin at the spindly, jade-colored plant with its small, round leaves narrowing to points, and right before my eyes it sprouts up half a foot.

Warmth washes over me, like I've just stepped under a sunlamp. The sensation retracts until one small spot on my left arm tingles with heat. I sneak a peek under my sleeve and can just make out a heart-shaped leaf next to the first line of green. *A new Inscription!*

"I think that blueberry bush already looks better," Bernie calls from behind me, making me jump. "It's spreading out, all right."

I peek over my shoulder. Bernie catches my eye and grins. My cheeks redden, and before he can say more, I turn away. *He couldn't have seen anything. He probably wouldn't even know what happened if he did. Reps don't have Creers.* I glance back at Bernie again. Thankfully, he's not looking at me anymore. But he is still smiling.

"Hey, Myra," Canter calls, and I welcome the interruption.

"What's up?" I ask as I trot over.

"I have a question for you."

"I know." I fix him with my best deadpan stare. "That's why I said, *What's up?*"

He shakes his head. "I've been thinking about this place pretty much nonstop. I swear, I didn't take one note in any of my classes yesterday."

I know the feeling. "It's distracting, right?"

"Sure is. Boy am I glad I caught you stealing my epic invention," he says, his eyes sparkling.

I cock an eyebrow at him. "It's shiny paper, Canter."

He swings around, looking highly offended. "For all we know, I may be the first S.L.A.M. student to *ever* find a way past the curfew trackers!"

I fight back a laugh. "You'd be a S.L.A.M. legend *if* we could tell anyone. Which we can't."

"Well, as my lone witness, you'll have to admire and celebrate me enough for everyone else," he says. "Canter Day has a nice ring to it."

This time, I can't help but chuckle. "That'd be a definite no."

"Then you at least have to thank your metal-socks whenever you wear them." He's laughing now, too.

"If they work long enough for us to get this garden together, I'll think about it," I reply, gaining control of my giggles, and an idea forms in my mind. "But only if you tell me what you were really doing in the classroom that night."

He opens his mouth to answer, but I cut him off.

"And don't say you were just testing out the reflector paper, because I know that's not the whole story."

He looks me straight in the eye like he's weighing out whether or not I can be trusted. I stare right back, not backing down.

Finally, he sighs, and it's like a mask falls away. For a moment, I can see the real Canter standing in front of me. No jokes, no snark, just a kid with sad eyes and fidgety feet. "My mom was a teacher here before she died."

I nod. That's why the auditorium is named after her.

"Sometimes, I like to wander around, trying to guess which classroom was hers." He rocks from his heels to his toes. "It's hard to do during the day. People start to ask questions if they catch you poking around random class-rooms."

"Never go to the same place twice," I murmur. "If you get caught somewhere more than once, it's a lot harder to say you were there by accident."

Canter's eyes brighten. "Exactly! That's what I say." His eyes narrow. "Why do you know that?"

Now it's my turn to fidget. "It's my Rule Number Two for skipping class."

"Why would *you* cut class?"

"It's just . . . everyone expects a lot from me. Not just my parents. The other kids, too, *because* of my parents. Sometimes I just want a break." It might not be the whole truth, but it's pretty close.

Canter studies me and I wonder if I've let my mask fall away, too. Or at least shift a little.

"So, why don't you just ask your dad?"

He blinks. "Ask him what?"

"About your mom. He must know which classroom was hers."

Canter's gaze hardens. "Probably, but it doesn't matter."

"Why not?"

"He doesn't like to talk about her. He almost never does. I stopped asking him questions a long time ago."

"That doesn't seem fair. She's your mom. You've got a right to ask."

He shrugs. "I'm used to it."

An awkward silence builds between us, and I don't know what else to say. "Uh, didn't you want to ask me something?"

"I did? Oh, right!" He runs his hands through his blond hair, his expression warming again. "Do you have a plan for how you're going to unveil this place once it's done?"

I cock my head to the side. I knew I'd have to show people the garden once it was ready, but I hadn't really thought about *how*. "Well, not exactly."

"You can't just take pictures or a recording," Canter says in a rush. "They'll say it's fake. And you can't invite people in and show them, either. They'd just freak out and burn the place down. If we show people, it has to be everyone. *Everyone* everyone."

I turn his words over in my mind. He's right. "So . . ."

"We could livestream it on the open network," he says softly.

My eyes go wide. "How?"

"I could build a broadcaster. And then hack us in," he adds quickly. "I picked up a few tricks from my Tekkie friends. I know I could do it. Then we could broadcast the moongarden to all the Settlements at the same time."

"It could work," I reply, chewing my lip. It's a good idea. Perfect, really. But I would never tell Canter that.

He nudges me. "Ah, c'mon. You can do better than that. It's a good idea. Admit it."

"It has an above-average likelihood of being successful," I answer in a clipped tone.

Canter barks a laugh and turns back to the generator. "You love it. I know you do."

"As long as you can build the broadcaster *and* hack into the network," I say, smirking as I walk away. "That's a tall order, hotshot."

"You just get all the green stuff looking good. I'll take care of the rest."

I wince. *Hopefully I'm here long enough to do that.* I push the thought away for now, since there's nothing I can do about it until Monday. "You sure came up with that idea fast," I call back. I swear Canter turns his head in my direction, but he doesn't reply, so maybe he didn't hear me.

"What do you think?" I ask Bernie, rejoining him.

"Could work." He shoots me a serious look. "It'll be risky though."

"I know." I twist the hem of my sleeve around my wrist. "You never told me what happened to the person who created this garden."

Bernie pauses, then heads away muttering something about pruning. Defeated for the moment, I walk over to a second newly planted blueberry bush placed beside the first, significantly taller one. *How did I do that?*

Focused on the blueberry bush, I imagine its roots reaching out through the soil, pulling in the water soaking there. In my mind's eye, I see glittering specks traveling up its thirsty roots, illuminating the stems, and then the leaves. I picture the whole plant bathed in a sparkling light. Then I reach out to brush my fingers against the bush.

Nothing happens.

I squeeze my eyes shut and imagine the plant growing taller and taller, its branches sprouting dozens of new jade-colored leaves. I open my eyes. The bush is exactly the same.

A rustling under a nearby tangle of hedges makes me tense, but I relax as Bin-ro emerges from under the leaves, rolling over to me. "Hi, again," I say, settling back on the dusty ground. I'm quiet for a moment, then shoot Bin-ro a sideways glance. "He, er, him. Is that right or—?"

"Beep!" Bin-ro spins in a circle, his lights flashing.

"Got it," I say, patting his hull. "Sorry, buddy."

Bin-ro whistles a tune and rolls off, disappearing under the blueberry bush.

Maybe it looks a teeny bit greener. I stick my tongue out at the uncooperative plant, then turn back to see what the others are up to. Canter's helping Bernie haul a small tree fern across the garden. All the lights in the section he was working on glow overhead like a constellation of stars.

No way am I letting Canter Weathers outdo me here. I'll get the *green stuff looking good.* I know I will, once I figure out my magic. But currently, it's: Botan Magic: 1, Myra Hodger: 0.

CHAPTER TWENTY-ONE

ON SUNDAY AFTERNOON, I TUCK MYSELF INTO a reading cove in the Rec hall. The inside of the egg-shaped structure is small, not much bigger than a closet, but cozy. I settle into the layers of adjustable foam and power on my bookpod.

Normally, the Rec hall is the last place I'd choose to study, but one, it was surprisingly less crowded than the modulab, and two, I've decided that I can't give Goble any other reasons to chuck me out of S.L.A.M. I'm determined to turn in the best homework my teachers have ever seen from me—seen from *anyone*. At the very least, maybe it'll buy me a little more time in the moongarden.

I imagine what it would be like to leave school. To have my parents come and pick me up and take me home. The embarrassment would be bad enough, but the thought of never seeing the moongarden again, never using my magic again . . . I shudder. It's unbearable.

I can't let it happen.

Determined, I snuggle deeper into the foam and bury myself in homework.

I'm only through the first set of instructions when a commotion in the Selfie-Station section catches my attention. Curious, I peek over the top of my hologram page to find the source of the noise. A herd of kids has crowded onto a makeshift sofa after pulling and stretching a putty-lounger until it's long enough to accommodate a half-dozen bodies. They all grin and a camera flashes. A few seconds later, their image projects on the wall opposite them. It'd be a cute picture if they didn't all have thick, curly mustaches plastered over their faces.

The kids guffaw as another friend pops up from behind the computer that controls the photo enhancements. He gives a small bow and holds out his hand, and the others dig into their pockets and drop small parcels in his outstretched palm.

Figures. I roll my eyes and settle back into the pillows. Today is Trickering, a silly holiday left over from Old World days. Everyone spends the day acting absolutely ridiculous, dressing up in silly costumes, and more important, tricking each other to earn candy. On Trickering morning, the school distributes a small stash of candy to each of us. We're supposed to keep the pieces in our pockets all day, and if someone successfully pranks us, they get rewarded with a piece of candy. I sigh, balance my bookpod on my lap, and fumble around in my bag. That's why the modulab was so busy today—kids studying are easy targets.

I turn up the music in my pod, drowning out the mayhem going on around me. I don't know how long I'm at it, but it must be a while, because I've submitted all my history, Elector, and Chemic assignments when a knock thuds on the side of my reading cove.

Startled, I jump and my bookpod goes tumbling off my lap. When I look out, an older boy in Chemic-purple is leaning toward me. "Rec hall's closing. Better pack up."

Behind him, the room is dark. *How long have I been in here?*

"Oh, sorry," I mutter, collecting my bookpod and shoving it into my bag. I scramble out of the cove and immediately need to shield my eyes from the bright lights shining overhead. "What the—"

The boy doubles over laughing. The dark, foggy cloud hovering outside my reading cove bursts, and the magic fades away. "Got you!"

I glower. *Light-absorbing mist.* Trickering. Of course.

"Good one," I say, rolling my eyes and hoisting my back-pack over my shoulder. *Apparently, I'm not going to get all my work done in here, either. Not on Trickering.*

"Pay up!" the boy exclaims, holding out his hand.

I dig in my pocket and drop something onto his palm as I stomp by.

"Tha— Hey! This is just a wrapper!"

I turn and smirk over my shoulder as I shrug. "Oops. Ate them all."

I head toward the cafeteria. *May as well get something to eat.* I have no idea what time it is, but my grumbling stomach is telling me it needs food.

I hurry along, dodging a stun pulse and tripping over a couple of out-of-place stairs some Tekkie student added to the corridor. *Crashing comets, do I hate Trickering.* As soon as the thought crosses my mind, I walk through a Chemic stink-cloud. *Great, just great.* I stomp faster and dart into the cafeteria.

Phew. Safe. One quick scan around the room tells me my relief was premature. For a second, I think I ran into the wrong room. The cafeteria is unrecognizable. Volts of purple- and blue-colored electricity spark back and forth across the ceiling in what must be an Elector-created loop. The effect is eerie, the colored lightning casting strange shadows and ominous flashes over the entire room. Fog shields one corner of the cafeteria, clearly powered by Chemic magic. Kids stumble in and out of that section, some clutching goodie bags, and others shrieking as they drop the "tricks" that must also be lurking inside—oversized fake bugs, snakes, and gooey blobs.

Director Weathers stands at one end of the cafeteria, pointing at an assortment of glowing, misty orbs hanging over the heads of the kids clustered there. The Chemic-powered mystery balls spin and rotate, switching places and scrambling around each other. A girl reaches up and pokes one, and the bubble bursts, showering her with candy. She squeals as she stoops to collect the pieces. The boy next to her isn't as lucky. He taps an orb, and thick green ooze trickles out onto his head. He laughs and smears it in his hair, making it stand on emerald end.

Director Weathers turns in my direction, locking eyes with me for a moment. Maybe it's my imagination, but his gaze seems to harden. I quickly look away.

I make my way to the tables set up at the far end of the cafeteria, ready to inhale whatever's there, before hiding in my room for the rest of the day. Joining the end of a long line, Moon monsters, space goblins, and more versions of Galactic Warrior Princess Zylstra than I can count form a mob in front of me. I wince as I see more than one student dressed up as a Mercurian prisoner, decked out in bright red from head to toe. Inching forward, I reach ahead, trying to grab a tray so I can hurry and make my escape.

But as soon as I touch the tray, it shocks me, then clatters to the floor, knocking over the rest of the stack in the process. "Crashing comets," I mutter, sucking on my wounded finger as I bend to collect them when a *zap* makes me freeze.

"Marco! You know the rules," Ms. Curie snaps, her lightning bolt fading into the air. She's dressed as a simple witch, black makeup highlighting her already dark features, along with a bushy black wig that bounces around the shoulders of her gray cloak as she marches toward us. "No injuries, messes, or chaos caused by a Trickering prank. And it looks like you've caused all three here."

"It's all right," I mutter as I pull the fallen trays into a pile. "It didn't hurt that bad."

"See, Ms. Curie," Marco chimes in. "She's fine."

"She'd be better if you helped her clean up that mess rather than just watching her," Ms. Curie replies, her dark eyes flashing.

Marco drops down beside me, slowly adding one tray to my almost-complete pile. "I got you," he whispers. "Pay up."

I shove the stack of trays into his outstretched hands. "Paid."

I scan the table, trying to decide between all the

nearly identical blobs of food. After a moment, I snag a red-and-yellowish square I can only assume is some sort of pasta or pizza concoction, then walk into the seating area, ready to plop down wherever there's an open seat. Spotting an empty space, I steer between the tables, and as I do, a name drifts from the buzz of conversation. My name.

"Who's Myra Hodger?" someone says. A girl. I don't recognize the voice.

I freeze midstep, a pizza-blob brandishing statue.

"I don't know, some first-year who thinks she's the galaxy's gift to Number Whispering," a boy replies. "My sister's in her class, and she told me Goble lets her leave lessons all the time. Doesn't even have to do the practical work."

"Who does she hang around with?" another girl asks.

"No one." The boy scoffs. "Who'd want to hang around with an obnoxious know-it-all?"

I've got to get out of here.

"Aren't her parents famous Number Whisperers or something, though?" the first girl asks.

"Yeah, exactly," says the boy. "Mommy and Daddy probably already have her acceptance to the Lunar University filed and framed."

"Wait a second," someone else says. A chair screeches. "Isn't that *her*?"

More chairs squeal against the floor and my cheeks burn

as I swivel, searching for a quick exit. But the paths between the tables seem to have been swallowed up by kids, like the tide coming in, removing all routes to safety.

"Oh, that's her," a familiar voice calls out. Bethany. I'm eighty percent sure. "I got stuck with her as a roommate, and she won't even help us with our homework."

"More like I got stuck with you," I shoot back, but it mostly comes out as a squeak, which is promptly swallowed by muttered names and words I do my best not to hear. I try and squeeze by a cluster of kids and chairs.

"Are you really already accepted into the university?" a girl wearing Number Whisperer yellow asks, blocking my path. "Because that is *completely* unfair! There are only so many spots, and you don't even do the work!"

"They don't accept first-years," I huff, stumbling a few steps toward an escape route between tables. Chairs slide in to block my opening as kids twist around to catch a glimpse of me. I try and slip through, but no one will move.

"She didn't say her parents won't get her in once she graduates," sneers a boy in a silver jumpsuit at the next table.

"I didn't mean—that's not what I—that's not true," I stammer as I turn in a circle. A blond head catches my attention. I look desperately at Canter hunched over his lunch tray at the table in front of me. *He knows I'm not a know-it-all. He knows how my parents are.*

Canter holds my gaze for a moment, then turns to his friend. "Slammers don't like show-offs," he finally says, but he won't meet my eye.

Everyone laughs, and soon people are repeating Canter's words until it forms a chant. Kids press in, trapping me in the center of their gossip storm, and I do the only thing I can: I drop my plate and climb up on one of the tables. The kids go quiet, caught off-guard. Two quick steps between plates and cups, then I hop down on the other side, and with a clear path before me, I race for the door.

Someone is coming through it, though.

"Myra, are you okay? What happened?" Lila, clad in a moon-fairy costume, backpedals out of my path, confusion and concern in her eyes.

My face on fire, I ignore her and race down the hall. I don't have a destination—just *away*—and before I know it, I'm throwing myself behind the workstation in the moongarden classroom and slapping my palm to the wall. I barrel through the lab and into the garden, only stopping when I'm surrounded by vibrant shades of green. Dropping to the ground, I curl into myself and put my head in my hands, squeezing my eyes shut against the storm of tears fighting to crash through.

All I wanted was to be left alone. I wasn't trying to be top of my class or hoverball champion. Shooting stars, I wasn't even hoping for an invite to Apolloton. Not really, anyway. Being ignored was fine. It was working for me. But, apparently, even that was too much to ask.

And just think what the kids will say once Goble expels me. That'll really give them all a laugh. At least I won't be here to see it.

A tear tracks a hot line down my face, slips off my chin, and splatters on the ground. It soaks into the gray gravel, leaving behind a solitary wet dot in the dust, a reminder of how very alone I am. And then the ground shudders beneath me. I jump to my feet as a stem springs up from the earth, from the exact spot my tear fell. Up and up it grows, leaves and then flowers popping out to cover it in a turquoise haze.

How did I do that? How am I going to explain this?

A smile somehow edges its way onto my face as I take in the flower. Even without leaning closer I can smell its sweetness, like sugar carried on a breeze. I lift a hand to brush its leaves, and as I do, a wispy trail of golden dust seems to follow in my hand's wake. Plants burst up from the ground beside me following the same path as my hand, a whole row of flowers like the blue one. Colors explode in a riot of hues—from cobalt blue to canary yellow to saffron and crimson and every shade in between.

Grinning now, I turn and wave my hand in the other direction. More plants streak up from the dusty gravel, blooms bursting to life and spilling over back toward the ground. Their delicate petals brush my ankles, my cheeks, my fingertips, as if saying *hello,* or *you're not alone. We're here with you.* Some grow tall enough to tangle over my head, and the air is filled with the scent of them, prettier than any perfume in the galaxy. In a few seconds, I'm surrounded, just like in the cafeteria, but this time with friends. Vibrant flowers form a rainbow around me. It might be the most beautiful thing I've ever seen. And, somehow, it came from me. I turn in a circle, marveling at what my magic can do, even if I don't know how I'm doing it.

The kids in the cafeteria suddenly seem much farther away now, so much less important. My cheeks burn again as more tears fall, but this time they're happy ones. My left arm burns, too, just above my wrist. When I look down, my mouth falls open. Thin yellow lines are weaving themselves together on my skin.

I hold my wrist up to my face, and my eyes devour the cluster of tiny goldenrod flowers that now bloom next to the leaf and stem.

I don't care about how I'll explain all these new plants to Bernie and Canter. Nothing matters now, except that they're here, and they're beautiful. And they came from me.

Still, creeping up the wall of my mind like a vine weaving its way over a trellis is the fact that Inscriptions don't fade. Sure, they can be written over if someone develops another magical affinity, but they'll never disappear—my Botan Inscriptions will always be there, announcing my Creer to the galaxy. And a girl expelled from S.L.A.M. covered in flowers and leaves won't be a good look. How bad, I have no idea.

CHAPTER TWENTY-TWO

ON MONDAY MORNING, I HANG BACK IN MY room rather than going to the breakfast block. I can't help checking the time on my pendant, counting down the minutes until my meeting with Ms. Goble.

Lila sits on her bed, a breakfast bar in one hand and a bookpod in the other, but she's not looking at either of them. She's been trying to catch my eye since the other girls stomped out to breakfast, throwing snarky grenades in their wake. It's bad enough dodging the gossip and sneers in the halls and classrooms, but I can't even escape it in my own room.

Lila clears her throat. I know that trick. My eyes remain glued to my pendant as I pretend to skim today's lessons plans, but really, I'm just reading Goble's message over and over, trying to find some way out.

"Myra," Lila says softly.

I instinctively glance in her direction then away. *Blast it, she got me.* I've given her the opening she needs.

"I'm sorry the other kids are being so awful to you," she says.

I shrug, still not looking at her. "It's fine."

"No, it's not. And I told Bethany and Sloane to lay off, but—"

"Lila, it's *fine*. Really." I give in and meet her gaze. "I deserve this. I'm a know-it-all. I skip class. I didn't help you with your homework, and I should have. And it's true— Goble did let me leave class without doing the practical magic lesson."

Lila frowns. "Why?"

I look down at my pendant. "She said Director Weathers wanted to see me."

"Well, that's a perfectly good explanation. Once you have another practical class, they'll leave you alone."

"I'm not going to do any practical magic in class," I blurt out. "Not ever."

Lila's eyebrows shoot up.

"Er, because then they'll just say I'm showing off."

"I don't think Goble will let you get away with that," Lila says slowly.

I shrug. It doesn't matter. I probably won't be here by the time class rolls around anyway. Lila must think I'm just being stubborn, though.

"Listen, I know what it's like when everyone gangs up on you and it feels like you'll never escape them."

I sit up straighter. *Friendly, popular Lila?* "You do?"

"Yeah." She flinches as if whatever she's thinking zapped her with a burst of electricity. "At my old school, we had a Parents Day to show off our end-of-the-year projects. I made a full-scale replica of the human body's nervous system. My teacher was an Elector and gave it a charge that made different portions light up. It was really cool."

"Sounds like it."

"My dad came to see it. He'd been to the school before, but he'd just come off a job on Mercury. It's really hot there, so he was wearing short sleeves. . . ."

"Oh." I see where this is going. "I'm sure the other kids weren't interstellar about it."

"Nope," she says with a little sigh. "My point is, they eventually moved on. I even had a few friends who stuck by me through the whole thing."

I wish I had that. Lila smiles at me encouragingly. *But . . . maybe I do?*

We're both quiet, and I'm about to change the subject when Lila says, "I've been meaning to ask you something." I cringe. "How did you end up in our room, anyway? Not that I mind," she adds quickly. "It just seemed so last minute."

"It was," I mutter, picking at my bedspread. I rack my brain for a way to deflect the conversation. Somehow, the truth comes tumbling out instead. "I was supposed to room with my best friend, Hannah, from home. We had a fight right before the school year started, and she ended up switching schools."

Lila nods, her eyes sympathetic. "Bad timing, huh?"

"Couldn't have been worse."

"What was the fight about?"

A warning siren is blaring in my brain telling me to be quiet, but now that I've started, I can't seem to stop.

"I . . . I told her I couldn't hear whatever secrets the numbers whisper to each other—I never have—and I wasn't even curious about what the secrets could be."

Lila's eyes widen. "Can you hear them now?" she asks gently.

I shake my head. I guess it won't matter who knows after my meeting with Ms. Goble.

"Is that why you don't participate in the practical lessons in Goble's class?" Lila asks, and I nod. She's quiet for a moment as she turns this new information over in her head. "What did Hannah say when you told her?"

"That it didn't matter," I reply, my voice barely more than a whisper. "I was still me, magic or not."

"She's right," Lila says.

I shrug. "I'd never really thought of it that way, though. It seemed . . . scary somehow to think there was another path for me other than math. Number Whispering is all my parents care about. They think if you don't have magic, you don't matter. Sorry, I—"

"It's okay," Lila says, blushing. "A lot of people think that."

"Well, I don't."

She flashes me a bright smile. "And then what happened?"

"Hannah tried to convince me that there was still time." My bedding is a twisted knot in my fist. "That people can even change Creers after a while."

"It's rare, but it does happen."

"I know. But I . . . I didn't want to hear that right then. I was getting upset. Not at her, really. Just at the whole situation. I snapped and said, *And some people don't have Creers at all, like your sister.*"

"Her sister's a non-Creer?" Lila asks, and I nod.

"It just got worse from there." I study my wrinkled bedspread.

"And you haven't spoken to each other since?"

"Nope."

"That's really rough, Myra. I'm sorry."

"It's my own fault," I say bitterly. "I'm a terrible friend."

Lila shakes her head. "You said some bad things, but that

doesn't make you a bad friend. Have you tried reaching out to her and apologizing?"

"I thought I'd get the chance to when we got to school, but she never showed up."

"Send her a message," Lila suggests.

"I've tried, but I can't get the wording right. Besides, it's too late. She's probably off at some other Lunar school with a whole new crew of friends."

"I bet she'd still like to hear from you."

"I'll think about it," I say, and I even mean it. Maybe.

"Good," Lila says. "And thanks for telling me about her . . . and everything else, too."

"Thanks for listening." I offer her a weak smile.

"So what are you going to do, you know, about the other thing? The Number Whispering?"

"Or lack of," I mutter. "Nothing. I have a meeting with Ms. Goble about it this morning."

Lila's eyebrows shoot up. "She knows?"

"Unfortunately. Looks like you might get your triple room back."

Lila actually seems upset. "Maybe you can convince her to let you stay. Try another Creer or something. What time is your meeting?"

I glance at the clock and stiffen. "Uh, now!" I bolt for the door, but pause in the entryway. "Hey, Lila?"

She looks up.

"Thanks. For everything."

She meets my gaze, her eyes warm. "Hang in there, Myra. It'll get better."

Without another word, I turn and rush through hall after hall, skidding to a stop outside my Number Whisperer classroom.

I've been over and over this conversation in my head, imagining what Goble might say and how I'd reply. I've tried every angle, every dodge and lie and bluff. But the conversation always ends the same way. With expulsion. With my parents' endless disappointment. With a life without magic once I'm sent away from S.L.A.M. and the moongarden.

I take a deep breath and walk into the classroom.

Ms. Goble's perched on the edge of her desk conducting wispy, jumbled numbers into neat rows. When I enter, she snaps her fingers and they burst into a million pieces, then fade away. "Shut the door please, Miss Hodger."

I turn and punch the keypad. The door whizzes closed.

She nods toward the desk in front of her. I don't sit behind it, though. I settle on the edge, like her. I can't meet her eyes, even though I feel them watching me. *Just breathe, Myra. Just breathe.*

"I think you know why I asked you here, Miss Hodger."

I glance up and nod, then drop my focus back to the floor.

"And why would that be?"

"You're expelling me." I manage to say the words so quietly I'm not sure they came out at all.

Ms. Goble studies me. "Why haven't you told anyone? Your parents obviously don't know."

I shrug. "I don't think they *want* to know."

"I'm surprised they wouldn't have picked up on the same signs I did."

"My parents are a bit self-involved."

She nods slowly. "You know, there's nothing wrong with not having a Creer."

"That's not what my parents think."

"They'll adjust. They just need—"

"How much time do I have?"

Ms. Goble peers down at me. "What do you mean?"

"Until I have to leave." *Maybe I can wheedle a week or two out of her. Tell her I need time to say goodbye to my friends or some nonsense, and then spend my last days in the garden.*

"I'm not expelling you, Miss Hodger."

My head pops up. "What?"

"I'm only required to record grades. Not suspicions."

"But I just told you—"

"Owning up to who you are is a personal decision. I can't force you to do it. I can only encourage you to accept yourself, exactly as you are. You don't need magic to matter."

"But my parents—" I begin.

"You should give them a chance to prove you wrong." Ms. Goble leans toward me. "They might surprise you."

That's the thing my parents always boast about math: it's reliable. One plus one always equals two. Two times two always equals four. The Hodgers are as predictable as a division table. They don't do surprises.

"And what if they don't?"

"The galaxy is bigger than your parents, Miss Hodger." She adjusts the Creer pin on her collar. "And I've known both your mother and father for a long time. I think they'll come around."

"So in the meantime, I can stay?" I try and keep hope from creeping into my voice, but I know Ms. Goble still hears it.

"Technically, a student has until their Creer test to display magic. Although, as you know, most show an affinity far before then. If you haven't by now . . ."

"I know I'm not going to be a Number Whisperer."

"Then why stay, Miss Hodger? Why not try to find other talents? The Lunar Settlement has many fine non-magical schools—"

I sit straight up on the edge of the desk, not quite believing my luck. "I can stay until the Creer test?"

"I'll have to grade you on assignments until then. And I'm afraid that without magic, your grades will suffer quite drastically."

My face falls. "Will you tell my parents?"

"They can see your grades on the academia network. Knowing your mother, I imagine it's only a matter of time until she inquires."

"And then you'll have to tell them."

"As I said, I don't have to report my suspicions. Only grades. But if you continue to refuse to participate in the practical magic in class, your grades are going to fall quickly."

That's fine. I might be able to explain that away to my parents. All they care about is the test.

"You may also have to deal with some backlash from your peers. I imagine they'll want to know why you're not participating."

"They already do." I shrug. "It doesn't matter."

"Well," she says, crossing her arms. Formulas and equations cover every inch of them. And something else, too. Something that doesn't look like any Number Whispering Inscription I've ever seen. . . . "Since you won't be completing your practical magic homework, I have another assignment for you."

I tear my eyes away from her arms. *What on the Moon could she want me to do?*

"You'll complete a research paper for me on the various non-Creer jobs, to be handed in during your end-of-the-year exam."

My mouth falls open as humiliation crawls up my throat. "It is non-negotiable."

I consider the assignment for a few moments. There's really no harm in a little extra work. It seems a more than fair trade.

Ms. Goble taps her finger on the desk as she waits for my response.

"I have a question."

"There are a variety of jobs you could look into. I could suggest—"

"No, not about that. Ms. Goble, are those Chemic Inscriptions on your arm?"

She looks down, startled, then the ghost of a smile plays across her lips. "Yes, actually. When I began at S.L.A.M. many years ago, I was on a Chemic track." She touches the markings on her arm, clearly the remnants of the periodic table, though they're almost completely covered by Number Whisperer Inscriptions. "But as I delved into my classes, I found I was more and more fascinated by the numerical side of calculating chemical compounds than on the compounds themselves. Eventually, I switched tracks and developed magic for Number Whispering." She gazes into my eyes. "That leads to a good point, Miss Hodger. Life takes strange turns sometimes. At first, they can seem wrong, but as you travel farther down the path, you see you're exactly where you were meant to be all along."

I'm suddenly grasped by the urge to tell her about the secret moongarden, but I fight back the bizarre notion and change the subject back to the assignment. "If I do this essay, I won't be expelled until the Creer test?"

She studies me for a moment, then nods. "Yes. But, Miss Hodger, you're only avoiding the inevitable."

That's fine. As long as the inevitable doesn't show up anytime soon.

CHAPTER TWENTY-THREE

THE NEXT NIGHT, I POSITIVELY SKIP TO THE moongarden, my metal-wrapped feet glinting in the dim hallway light like stardust. No longer weighed down by the worry of being caught magic-less, all I can think about now are the months ahead among the plants. The thought lifts me up like I'm on the low-grav hoverball court. By the time my Creer test rolls around, I should definitely have my Botan magic sorted out, and we'll easily have the garden ready to show to the galaxy.

Inside the glass-enclosed space, Canter huffs and puffs, rifling through some sort of toolbox not far from the slide. He tries one contraption, grunts, then tosses it behind him into a growing pile.

I roll my eyes, determined to ignore him. Even as I

feel his gaze following me across the garden, I pretend he doesn't exist.

"Hey," he says softly as I pass him.

I settle myself in the far corner, where I pull out a laser-line generator and punch the pointy end into the ground. I tap one of my precalculated measurements into the stick-shaped device, and a thin red line projects out, dividing a third of the garden. Sitting back against a tree trunk, I inspect my work area and brush a tangle of leaves off my shoulder before the branches can snarl in my hair. They belong to a nearby blueberry bush, the stalks weighed down by clusters of ripe fruit. I lean over and pluck a couple of the tiny indigo balls, popping them into my mouth one at a time. The delicate skin of the first berry bursts in my mouth, and an explosion of tartness makes me shiver. The next one is as sweet as candy. My eyes drift shut while I chew, savoring the sugary flavor. Forcing myself to focus on my work, I enter a few more calculations into the machine, and another line generates from the middle of the first, dividing the section in half. I lick my lips, the berry juice dancing across my tongue as I skim my calculations.

Bin-ro scoots over, rolling parallel to my lines, whistling softly. He gives a beep of approval. Out of the corner of my eye, I see Canter fiddling with the broadcaster he's building, grunting and sighing far more than is probably necessary.

Finally, he stands and walks toward me, dust kicking up in small clouds around his feet. "Done slicing up the place?" he asks, eyeing the red lines.

"Done fixing the nutrient system?" I grumble back, nodding toward the light bulbs in the ceiling. I stand, then stoop to tap another measurement into the laser-line generator. A new red line appears, curving to form a crescent-shaped section in the back. Bin-ro goes to check it out.

"Sort of." His cheeks flush slightly. "That's why I'm working on the broadcaster for now. I need some new parts for the rest of the light bulbs. The connections in the last section are fried beyond repair."

"Beyond *your* repair," I add under my breath.

"What, did you need help cutting this place up like pie?"

Bin-ro spins around and blows a loud raspberry at Canter, who ignores him.

"For your information," I say, patting Bin-ro appreciatively on his metal hull, "this plan will ensure everything has room to grow once I start filling the sections with the new plantings." Bernie found a stockpile of seeds hidden away, most of which were plants used to grow food. "Without those, you won't have anything to broadcast. And we've gotten along just fine without all the light bulbs working so far. Seems like it's a little too big a project for you, anyway."

"I don't see you using your magical skills to help out,"

Canter says. "Aren't you a Number Whisperer? Can't you, like, multiply some of these plants or something?"

"Number magic doesn't work like that, genius."

"Anyway," Canter says, shifting from foot to foot. "About the broadcaster. I've been thinking . . ."

"Hope you didn't blow a fuse." Bin-ro beeps loudly, then turns and rolls painfully over my toe. "Ouch, Bin-ro! Don't you have anything better to do?" He turns and rolls away, whistling a shrill robot lecture at us.

"Can you let me finish?" Canter snaps. "We're going to need a lot more parts for the broadcaster. It was hard enough getting these." He nods at the collection of metal bits and pieces making up the machine he's working on. "Curie guards Elector supplies like they're her kids. I practically had to pry some of these parts out of her hand. I'll need to sneak them out bit by bit so she doesn't notice."

I frown. "What if she tells your dad some of her parts have gone missing?"

"She won't. I'd have to steal her whole closet, including the door, before she'd say anything to him."

"Why?"

He shrugs. "They don't get along."

I wonder why. I file the thought away for later. "It's still risky, but I'm okay with you taking that chance."

"It's not going to matter what you're growing if we don't have a way to broadcast it," he says, ignoring my last dig.

"So get going, then."

"I need to get a bolt off so I can swap out some fuses, but I can't reach it," he says, nodding toward an open panel on the half-built machine. "And if I take this whole thing apart to get at it, it'll take days." He eyes me. "Your arms are smaller than mine. Can you give it a try?"

I look up and lock him in my best glare. "Why should I do you any favors?"

He winces. "What was I supposed to do, Myra? If I defended you in the lunchroom, everyone would have wanted to know why we were friends all of a sudden. It's not like we hang outside of here."

"That's true," I reply coldly. "Except that time I saved your table for you and your buddies, right?"

Recognition dawns in his eyes, and his cheeks burn redder than a supernova. "We were just kidding around," he says weakly.

I don't flinch as I stare into his blue eyes. "Glad you guys got a good laugh."

His blush deepens. "Look, Myra. I'm sorry, okay? I shouldn't have said that at lunch. I should have, I don't know, just shut up I guess."

I roll my eyes and turn back to my garden plan. "Yeah. That would have made a big difference."

"I don't know what you want me to say."

"Nothing!" I snap, looking back up at him. "That's the best way to fix something, right?"

Canter musses his hair. "Can you just help me with the bolt? It's not like it's for *me*. It's for the garden."

I sigh. "Do I have to do everything around here? I'm even picking up your Elector slack."

"Not my fault you can't Number Whisper the ground clear," he replies, flashing me a small smirk.

No, but I can do something better. I walk over to Canter and he hands me a small tool to twist off the bolt. I tuck it against my palm and reach my left arm inside the panel. The metal innards pinch and pull at me as I stretch. "Where is it?"

"There's a J-curve on the right. You should be able to feel a bolt at the very end."

The angle is wrong, so I pull my left arm out and try my right. I twist my hand around and find the opening to the J-curve, but something snags my sleeve, holding my wrist in place. "Hang on," I mutter. I pull my arm back out, push up my sleeve, and reach my right hand back inside. Finally, my fingertips brush the bolt. "Got it." I maneuver the tool to twist it off. When it's loose enough, I twirl it the last few rotations by hand and carefully pinch it between my fingers.

"Don't drop it."

"Don't jinx me." I retract my arm, holding the screw out on my palm toward Canter. He doesn't take it. "What? Is it the wrong one?"

"No, that's it. It's just . . ." His eyes travel from my palm to my wrist and up my bare arm. "You, er, you don't have any Inscriptions."

My fist closes around the bolt as I rip down my sleeve. *Too late. Far too late, Myra.* "Of course I do," I snap. *Just none I can show you.*

"Um, where?" Canter asks, his voice surprisingly soft. He studies me with concern, not the judgment I expected. "Your other arm?"

"What do you want me to say, Canter?" I demand, whirling around. "That I don't have any magic? That I don't have any Inscriptions? Fine. I don't, okay?" I toss the bolt at him and stalk away. "Go ahead and be pleased with yourself for figuring it out."

"Magic isn't everything." He looks uncomfortable and awkward and, worst of all, sad, like he feels bad for me. Which he clearly does. It's all over his face. *Poor little Myra. No Inscriptions and no magic.*

I fling the tool onto the ground, stomping it into the dust. The only thing worse than being pitied is being pitied for something that isn't true. Before I let something stupid slip, I cross to the mouth of the chute, but as I'm about to rush into it, a form blocks my way.

"Hey, now," Bernie murmurs, stepping out in front of me. "Where's the fire, Missy? What happened?"

"Just move."

"Hold on there." Now I'm caught between Bernie and Canter like a Ping-Pong ball of humiliation. Bin-ro, curious about the commotion, emerges from under a bush.

Just as I'm about to shove him out of my way, Bernie points over my shoulder at Canter, his eyes flashing with something I've never seen. "You do something to her? Say something?"

"No! I just saw—" Canter stops and looks at me again with those pitying eyes.

"Don't you look at me like that!" I shriek. *"Don't you dare!"*

"I'm sorry." He genuinely looks like he means it.

I want to scream that I've got magic, way better magic than stupid number powers, but I can't. Not to the school director's son. Telling Lila was one thing. She's never given me a reason not to trust her. Canter, on the other hand . . .

"I didn't mean to upset you. Myra, I'm sorry."

My frustration boils over. "Stop saying that!" I shout, lunging at him, but something stops me. Bernie's got me around the waist and is pulling me back.

"What in the name of Pluto is going on here? What'd he see?"

"This!" I shriek as I rip up my right sleeve, showing him the clear and unmarked skin. "He saw *nothing*."

"Is that all?" Bernie asks, gently releasing me.

"What do you mean, *is that all*? Magic is *everything*! Canter knows that better than anyone." I pull my sleeve back down. If Canter knows I'm not a Number Whisperer, it won't matter if Goble doesn't tell anyone. The whole school will be calling me a magical hack by tomorrow. And what if he tells his dad? Ms. Goble said she wouldn't expel me, but would Director Weathers? Would he call my parents? I wilt as the fight drains out of me. "Without magic, I'm going to get kicked out of here. Expelled. And then I'll just be . . . nothing." I sink to my knees and Bin-ro rolls over, hovering silently by my side. I stare at the ground, concentrating on a small sprout trying to poke its way through, fighting the tears pooling behind my eyes.

With a jolt, a bud catapults out of the gray dirt. *Get a hold of yourself, Myra! Before your real secret comes out.*

"Look around at this place, now," Bernie says, sweeping his arm out. Neat paths wind through the garden. The plants still look wild, but in a welcoming way. They stretch across the ground, curling over the newly cleared trails like they want to tousle your hair, brush your shoulders, or provide a perfect nook for a game of hide-and-seek. Bursts of color blossom in every corner. Oranges, purples, reds, and yellows mix in with the green like a mosaic come to life. "How can you see all this and believe any of that nonsense?"

"All that matters is my Creer test and the fact that I'm going to fail it."

"Not true." Bernie shakes his head. "This place matters. Look at you two. You've transformed it. That's a once-in-a-lifetime kind of accomplishment. And this garden has changed you both, too."

"The only accomplishments my parents care about are magical ones."

"Just because your parents are Number Whisperers and you're good at math doesn't mean that's your Creer," Canter says gently. "Try a different type of magic."

"I have tried. I've tried them all." I sigh, suddenly exhausted as I push to my feet. "Can we talk about something else, please?"

Bernie gives my shoulder an encouraging pat. Bin-ro beeps softly and nudges my foot, then the pair head off into the garden.

Canter turns back to his machine. "My mother was a non-Creer," he says quietly. "She mattered. Not just to me. To the whole school."

I raise my eyebrows. "What did she teach here?"

"History." His eyes cloud over as a sad smile crosses his lips. "I heard back when she was teaching, people even liked it."

"Do you remember her?" I ask softly.

He nods. "A little. She was funny. I remember laughing with her a lot. . . . Not much else, though. I was little when her shuttle crashed."

We're quiet, lost in our own thoughts.

"I'm not going to tell anyone, Myra," Canter says, looking over at me, "if that's what you're worried about."

"I'm worried about a lot of things."

"Well, that's one less, at least."

I nod, unsure what to say. Only a few minutes ago, I was celebrating being in the clear. For a while, anyway. Now I'm back to wondering if the plan for the garden (and me) will all fall apart. It's like being tethered to a streaking meteor, with no idea if I'll soar like a shooting star or crash into a planet.

I sigh and walk back toward the exit. Even though I should be using every minute I have to sort out how to control my magic, my heart's no longer in working here tonight.

Canter seemed pretty sincere about keeping my secret.

But can I trust him?

CHAPTER TWENTY-FOUR

A COUPLE WEEKS GO BY, AND NO ONE mentions my lack of Number Whispering magic. Not Ms. Goble, even though her *all-knowing* looks say volumes. Not Lila, though she shoots me encouraging glances whenever we see each other. And not Canter, even though the first few days after he discovered my (supposed) lack of Inscriptions were galactically awkward. And most important, no one else. Canter might just be true to his word. My classmates haven't missed my nonexistent magical participation in Goble's lessons, but their snarky comments are nothing compared to my relief at not being expelled.

I make my way back to my room after classes finish for the week. On any other Friday, I'd be excited for a weekend working late in the garden, sleeping in the next morning, but not today. It's Family Weekend, and the school is bursting with extra people. Bernie, Canter, and I decided it'd be too risky to go to the moongarden post-curfew. Who knows if we'll run into some parents wandering the school after-hours, reminiscing about their glory days at S.L.A.M. a millennium ago.

I snort and head toward my room, dodging the slowmoving parents and zippy younger siblings. There's a welcome reception scheduled for tonight, then a big fair tomorrow for the older students to show off class projects. I've never been so glad my parents are total number maniacs. They probably don't know there's such a thing as Family Weekend, let alone when it is. At least my roommates are sure to be occupied.

I flash my pendant in front of the sensor, scoot through the door, and start to throw my bag toward my bed, when a tall figure standing in front of it startles me. The bag goes flying, scattering its contents in all directions.

"Aargh! Blast it—*Mom*? What are you doing here?" I shriek. *This is bad. This is bad bad bad.*

"Can't I visit my daughter on Family Weekend without being bombarded by flying schoolwork?" Mom tries to smile, but it comes out more like a grimace.

I know that look; it means disappointment, displeasure, disapproval. And for me, *distress distress distress.* My mind blinks a warning like a crashing space shuttle. "Come on, Mom. We both know it takes a math-related natural disaster to get you out of your office. Some stupid Family Weekend isn't going to cut it. How'd you even find out about it, anyway? I know you aren't reading the S.L.A.M. newsletter."

"Myra, that's not fair. Please don't start with the whole *deserted daughter* routine. You never once wanted to come with me to the university, and I offered hundreds and hundreds of times."

"Are you sure you added up those hundreds correctly?"

"*Myra.*" She narrows her eyes and drops her chin. I recognize that look, too. The trouble that brought her here is about to be revealed. "Speaking of adding, why don't you tell me what's going on with your math classes lately?" The volume of her voice rises with each word, so the last is almost a screech.

Uh-oh.

I don't have any way out of this, so I do what anyone in my position would. I pick a fight. "Oh, classic, Mom," I fire back as I gather the contents of my bag, spiking my messenger, bookpod, and a bottle of eyeglass-cleaning mist at my bed, though they bounce off and fall back to the floor. "For *months* you hardly check in at all—you don't even know my roommates' names—but then you hear one little thing about my precious *math class* and you lightspeed it to my room to interrogate me." I chuck a portable computer screen at my headboard.

"One little thing?" My mother has her hands on her hips and doesn't even glance at my now probably-cracked computer. "I've been watching your grades do a steady freefall for months! This week, you're on the threshold of failing. I called Ms. Goble and we had a very *interesting* conversation."

I spin to face her. "Oh, so *that's* how you found out about Family Weekend. Ms. Goble told you!"

"Don't change the subject," Mom snaps. "She had quite a lot to say about you—skipped classes, lack of participation, and some other nonsense." She waves her hand dismissively, but I have a fairly good idea what the nonsense might be.

"You're the smart one," I say, throwing my hands in the air. "Why don't you explain it to me? That's all that matters to you. Math! Numbers! That's all that's *ever* mattered to you. I'm not just some equation for you to figure out! And guess what. Math is *boring*. That's why I don't participate. If you'd just called and talked to me like a normal human being, I would have told you that, but nooo. You had to sneak around my back and talk to my teachers, then swoop in here like an evil math monster."

"Myra—" It's her warning tone. I know I have to move fast. Up the ante.

"No! All you care about are my math classes, what my teachers say, what equations they're teaching. Why don't you ask one of my math teachers to be your daughter instead? You'd probably be happier!"

"That's not—that's not true, Myra." Mom's hands fall to her sides. It's a good sign. We've gone from a Stage Five threat to a Stage Three. "You know I care about you— *everything* about you. Not just your skills as a Whisp."

"Oh please, Mom." I throw my head back and roll my eyes. "Please don't call it that. You know I hate that name. Number Whisperer is bad enough. You don't need to make it sound even more ridiculous."

"Now you're just being dramatic." She gives me a shaky smile.

Bingo! Hit a nerve. I mentally downgrade the threat level to a One-point-five and press on. "Math is all you and Dad ever talk about. You can't even take ten minutes out of your day to have a video call with me without doing equations on the side."

"That's not—"

I raise my hand. "Mom. I'm twelve years old, and I've known when you and Dad are hiding your work since I was about three. You both think you're so slick—that I don't notice your eyeballs ping-ponging on our calls. Dad is *always* working on something during our video chats. Admit it!"

"Well, um, honey, he's had a lot of deadlines and—"

"See! That's exactly what I mean! He's been on deadline every single call we've had this year? Wow, he should really get a raise."

"Myra, just listen, please," Mom says as she wrings her hands again. "Math is what we're passionate about. It's who we are. And it's who you are, too."

If she only knew.

"I know it seems boring now, honey. I do. I—I was even bored in my math classes when I was your age."

I gasp and stumble back onto my bed, clutching at my chest. "Mom, *no*."

She gives a small laugh and settles beside me. "It's true," she says as she pats my knee. "To be honest, your father and I knew you were going to be bored this year."

My eyes go wide with real surprise this time. "You did?"

"Well, of course, honey. This is a *placement* class. Introductory. Way below your level."

Oh, right. That's why.

"We actually even considered having you put in a higher class, you know, with the actual Novices. I'm sure we could have—we've known the director since we were at S.L.A.M. Regardless. We decided you'd be better off with kids your own age. Kids in your Creer. We know you had a little trouble in the friend department at your preliminary school. . . ."

I wince, and Mom quickly shakes her head.

"Only because those kids were so far below your level, sweetie. Most of them won't even have a Creer at all. You shouldn't take it personally. But here"—a smile inches across her face—"here, we knew you'd be fine. Bored at first, maybe, but at least you'd be with kids somewhere near your league."

I flop back onto my bed, hoping she takes the hint. No luck.

"And with your Creer test right around the corner—"

"Mom, *please*. Can we not talk about that test *again?* I bet my first word ever was *test*! Shooting stars, you probably had a baby mobile of numbers above my crib."

Her cheeks go pink.

"Crashing *comets*. You had a number mobile above my *crib*."

"It was a gift from my colleagues at the time."

"That is not normal! Menders don't make baby mobiles with tiny hanging *organs,* do they?"

She chuckles as I cover my face with my hands.

"Freaks," I mutter through my hands. "My parents are total math freaks."

"All right, honey. I know you're sick of hearing about it, but we really should discuss the test. Ms. Goble thought—"

"All you care about is this stupid test." I blink furiously and turn away while I pretend to clean my glasses. I'm nowhere near crying, but she doesn't need to know that. "I swear, if I didn't pass the thing, you and Dad would probably put me up for adoption."

"Don't be silly, sweetie. There's no way you're going to fail your Creer test."

I close my eyes and count to ten. "Can we please just not talk about it anymore? Seriously. I'm a *Slammer*, just like you wanted me to be, surrounded by the little math prodigies you wanted me to be around. Can't that be enough?"

I swear I can hear her gulping down her horror: *Not talk about math? What else is there to talk about?*

"If that's what you really want, honey, I guess we can try that. We'll take a break. For a little while."

Threat level back to zero. For now.

CHAPTER TWENTY-FIVE

"ARE YOU SURE YOU DON'T WANT TO STAY FOR the welcome reception, Myra? I bet some of the exhibits are really impressive. Val, I mean, Ms. Goble, mentioned some of the Whisp presentations to me when we spoke. I think you might—"

"I'm sure," I say quickly as I stare out the Crawler window. Mom suggested heading into Apolloton when I flat-out refused to go to the welcome reception, and it wasn't a half-bad idea. It'll be nice to get out of S.L.A.M. for a few hours, and with everyone at the welcome reception, there's less chance of her running into any of my teachers.

The Crawler transport is packed. I glance around the circular space, glad that I don't recognize any faces.

"Oh, for comet's sake," Mom exclaims suddenly, "I didn't even think of inviting your roommates to join us."

"I'm sure they have plans," I reply, then turn back to the window, thanking every lucky star in the galaxy she *did* forget.

A fog of moondust hovers over the barren gray landscape as the Crawler churns up the rocky ground beneath it. I've never liked the Crawlers much. They look like giant metal spiders, and they're not nearly as fast as the bullet trains. Unfortunately, they're the only option for travel to Apolloton.

Lights glow in the distance, bouncing off the clear enclosures encircling the town, and before long I can make out the buildings. Most of the Lunar structures are rounded, with the exception of S.L.A.M. The school's tall, spiral design is one of the draws in the recruitment catalog. Something about *innovative and cutting-edge environment.* I roll my eyes. Mom called it a marvel when she first took me to visit. I called it a stretched-out Slinky.

The Crawler presses into the glistening enclosure surrounding Apolloton. The shiny, nearly translucent material stretches and pulls like a bubble while we push through, then snaps back into place. The doors open, and the passengers exit into the street. Mom and I are the last to leave. Without Apolloton's enclosures, we'd have to walk around with oxygen masks—not exactly convenient. Artificial atmosphere technology was developed a century or so ago, with fabricated gravity enhancements added not long after. Everyone calls them the great inventions of the age. Truthfully, I wouldn't mind an oxygen mask right now if it meant Mom couldn't pepper me with questions.

"Where to, honey?" she asks, gesturing down the busy street. Computerized cars whiz past all the shops lining the sidewalk: Mixture Madness—Your Source for Household Concoctions; Home Mendables; Volts & Bolts; Classic Venusian Cuisine; Old-Fashioned Burger Discs—Voted Best Spud Sticks on the Moon!

"How about there?" I point to a small restaurant called the Lunar Diner. My guess is most people will visit the fancy Venusian place or the burger joint. Hopefully, the diner will mean no awkward encounters.

"Sure, sweetie. Whatever you want."

As we step into the road, all the cars in our vicinity immediately slow to a stop and we stroll around them. Once our feet touch the sidewalk again, they speed away like someone hit the Pause button again. A couple of boys clad in Elector-silver pass us on the sidewalk as a man talking on a messenger trails behind them.

Oh great. So much for not running into anyone I know. I fix my gaze on the restaurant ahead, fully prepared to be ignored.

"Hey, Myra," Canter calls.

My head jerks around just in time to catch Canter's friend's eyes dart between him and me, his brow furrowing in confusion. Mom's gaze burns a hole in the side of my head.

"Hey," I say.

Canter waves behind his back as the pair continue on. I just stare after him in bewilderment.

Director Weathers spots my mom and gives a small nod before sticking up his index finger. "I just ran into an old friend. I'll call you back," he says into his messenger, then clicks it off as he walks up to us. My stomach lurches, remembering my last meeting with him. "Good to see you, Claire," he says, extending his free hand.

"Robert," Mom says warmly as she clasps it. "It's so good to see you. S.L.A.M. has been a hot topic in the capital lately. Jake Melfin's been talking up the new menu he just rolled out. We're due to have it released in the university any day, and he's hoping to expand the new formulas to the other Settlements soon, too."

I send silent condolences to all the kids around the galaxy about to have their school menus destroyed by jiggly slime. *That must mean the food cloning still isn't fixed and the Settlement stockpiles are depleted. Or gone.*

The director's gaze locks on mine for a moment, as if checking to see if our deal is still in place. I have less to lose now that Mom has talked to Goble, but his icy gaze still freezes my voice in my throat. "I'm not sure the kids will be as enthusiastic as Jake is," he answers, grimacing as he straightens his tie. A purplish-black Chemic Creer pin in the shape of an atom glints under the streetlights. "Between us." His eyes flicker to me again.

"Jake always was . . . ambitious." Mom puts her hand on my shoulder. "Still, I'm sure the food's fine. And we won't say anything, will we, Myra?"

"I don't even know what you're talking about," I lie, my eyes shifting between them.

"That's the spirit, dear," Mom says, winking at Director Weathers, but his smile's become fixed.

"Right," he says, studying me. "Well, I appreciate it all the same." He glances back down at his messenger. "I've got to get back to the school for the reception, but it was great to see you, Claire. Give Joe my best."

"I certainly will." She nudges me with her elbow. "Myra, that was rude," she hisses when he's out of earshot.

"What? I wasn't even listening," I lie again, picking up the pace.

The diner is pretty much empty. Unfortunately, that also makes us easy to spot. Lila, her parents, and what must be her younger brother, sit at the table closest to the door. I give a weak wave, which she returns with a shy smile, glancing back and forth between her parents. They spin around to see who she's looking at.

"Hello," Mom says, walking over.

No, no, no.

"I'm Claire Hodger, Myra's mother. You must be one of my daughter's friends."

"Mom, this is my roommate Lila," I mutter, edging toward the vacant table in the back corner.

"Roommate!" Lila's mother exclaims as she stands up, blocking my escape route. "So this is the mystery roommate, then? We've seen Bethany and Sloane a couple of times, but Myra's always off in the modulab studying when we've visited. It's so nice to meet you, dear." She pulls me into a hug, which I awkwardly return, then she steps back, beaming. Lila's mom is a pretty woman. Lila looks a lot like her, with the same golden-brown skin; curly, black hair; and warm brown eyes. Her mom has a wide smile and crinkles around her eyes that reveal she uses it a lot. "You must join us, Myra, Mrs. Hodger," Lila's mom insists, settling back down in their booth.

"Claire," my mother corrects as she sits.

"Henry Crumpler," Lila's father says, leaning over to shake Mom's hand. "This is my wife, Nora, and our son, Landon."

"It's nice to meet you," Mom says, all smiles and sunshine. "And you, Lila. I've heard so much about you from Myra."

Great. She's doing her Mom-of-the-Year routine.

"Planning on joining us, sweetie?" Mrs. Crumpler asks, a twinkle in her eye. I'm still standing where she released me from the hug. My cheeks burn as I slide into the seat next to Mom. The only one who looks more miserable than I do is Lila. She hasn't glanced up from her sandwich since we came over.

"So, what have you girls been up to lately?" Mom asks as she taps her order into the screen embedded in the tabletop.

I press my fingertip onto the screen, waiting for it to do its reading. The computer scans your body for nutrient deficiencies, then offers food that can compensate for them. A list of menu items populates the screen, but half of them read "Out of Stock." *Is Mr. Melfin the supplier for Apolloton's food supply, too?* I swipe the list of suggestions away and stab the pizza icon, which, thankfully, is available. I'm suddenly not very hungry, though.

"Studying mostly," Lila says as she chews. She glances quickly up at us, then back to her plate.

"Such a dedicated student," Mom says as a stew is placed in front of her by a Rep server. She doesn't even glance at him. "What's your Creer, dear?"

"I'm a Mender," Lila says proudly.

"Very admirable."

Lila wouldn't notice, but Mom's tone rings clear to me. Admirable, but not as valuable as a Number Whisperer. *The core of all Creers*, as Dad says.

"Are you both Menders, too?" Mom asks.

Lila's whole face turns red, and I realize it's not a coincidence that she picked this diner.

"I am," Mrs. Crumpler says. "And Henry is the head of the new Settlement development team preparing Neptune for habitation."

"Oh, how remarkable," Mom says. Her eyes shift quickly between Lila's parents. They hover for a millisecond on Lila's mother's Inscriptions, visible on her hand and wrist beneath her long-sleeved shirt, then up to the pearly-white cross-shaped Creer pin clasped to her blouse. Lila's dad's sleeves are rolled halfway up, revealing pale, blank skin. Mom's eyes linger there for a moment more, then return to her plate. Lila's sneakers cross and uncross under the table.

"That must be quite a feat," Mom continues. "Given the conditions there."

"You have no idea," Mr. Crumpler says, leaning back in his chair. "The temperatures alone are a challenge, not to mention Neptune's landscape. Took a whole team of the best Tekkies in the capital five years to develop a plan. We're going to build right into the ice, using it to form the buildings. Nothing like it in the whole galaxy. It'll be a real stunner when it's done."

"I'm sure," Mom says, her tone like a bit of Neptune ice is lodged in her throat. Hopefully, I'm the only one who notices. Lila's sneakers continue to scuff the ground in front of me. "What Tekkies do you know in the capital?"

The conversation dissolves into a blur of who's who, and I tune out. Lila doesn't say anything. Her eyes are glued to her little brother's game. Something tells me she's not paying attention to that, either.

After a while, Lila's mother's voice jolts me back to Moon. "So, what do you girls do for fun when you're not studying?"

Mom's eyes bore into me, and my brain scrambles to come up with something. *Think, Myra. What do kids your age talk about? Look normal for once!*

"Oh, Myra," Lila says suddenly, nibbling on her crust. "Remember that band I mentioned? S.L.A.M. is streaming a virtual concert of them in the Rec hall in a few weeks. We should go."

I have absolutely no idea what she's talking about. I'm positive we've never discussed any sort of band or music. Then it dawns on me that she's helping me out.

"Oh right. What are they called again?"

"The Solar Flares. It's going to be awesome."

"What an interesting name." Mom beams. "It sounds like it'll be a lot of fun."

Lila chatters on for a few more minutes about the band and other virtual concerts she's been to. Apparently, the broadcasts from Venus are the best ones. The parents chime in here and there while I mostly nod and smile. Finally, everyone is finished eating, and Lila and her family leave to catch the next Crawler back to school.

When they've gone, Mom settles back in her seat. "Lila seems like a very nice girl. You should spend more time with her."

I fold my hands on the table. "We're going to a concert, remember?"

"Oh, right." She gives me her most infuriating know-it-all smile. "I didn't realize you liked that kind of music."

"What kind of music?"

"Whatever kind they play." She looks at me expectantly. When I don't say anything, she presses on. "Look, Myra. It's obvious you and Lila aren't super close, but I think you should try and spend more time with her. I know it takes work"—she puts her hand up when I open my mouth to protest—"but trust me, your time here will be more fulfilling if you make some friends."

I adjust my glasses, as if they can somehow hide the rising heat in my cheeks.

"Just think about it, okay? She seems like a bright girl."

For a Mender. I know she's thinking it. The fact that Mom is even suggesting I befriend someone who's not a Number Whisperer says a lot.

"So you don't mind me hanging out with her, even though her dad's a, well . . ."

Mom shrugs. "Not everyone can have our talents.

If they did, how would everything get done? We couldn't trust Reps to do all the jobs non-Creers do." She laughs, though it sounds more like a cackle. "What a disaster that would be!"

I want to tell her how wrong she is. How if she actually got to know Reps, she'd realize they're just as smart and capable as the rest of us. How couldn't they be—they're clones of us, after all. But if I pick that fight, there's no telling what other topics could surge back up.

"Who were your friends in school?" I ask, changing the subject. "Ms. Goble?"

"No. . . . I had a lot of classes with her, but we weren't exactly friends."

"Why not? I thought you grew up together."

"We did, and we were friendly at one point, but things change." A glazed look shadows Mom's face. "She and Sandra Curie were inseparable. Ms. Curie still teaches at S.L.A.M., doesn't she?"

I nod. "Her classes are . . . interesting."

Mom gives me a knowing look. "Sandra was always a bit odd. . . . I really shouldn't say that. Val and Sandra stuck close together—them and another girl, Fiona Anderson. She didn't end up having any magic, poor dear, so Fiona left at the end of the year. But she visited often." Mom pauses, her thoughts somewhere else. "That's when she and Rob—I mean, Director Weathers—became close."

"Fiona, as in *Fiona Weathers*, the director's wife?"

"Yes." Mom's eyes narrow slightly. "Have you heard of her?"

"The school auditorium is named after her."

"Oh, that's right," Mom says, relaxing. "I'd heard they did that a while back, after the accident. Anyway, the three girls met in a Chemic theory class our first year. Did you know Ms. Goble was on a Chemic track initially?"

I nod, and Mom sighs. "Of course, I've always believed that secondary Creers are weaker, but that's not proven theory. Ms. Goble took to the Number Whispering quickly, though," she adds.

"Wouldn't being on the same Creer track have made you closer with Ms. Goble, though?"

Mom looks away. "It made things worse, to be honest. When we were younger, our schoolwork didn't overlap, but once it did, things got a little competitive between us." She shrugs. "Friendships are complicated."

Don't I know it. I wrestle with a question for a few moments, before finally blurting out, "Have you seen Hannah around at all?"

Mom blinks once. Twice. "No. Her family moved away."

Now it's my turn to flinch. "She *moved*? Where? Why?"

"I thought you two had, er, grown apart," Mom says,

glancing sideways at me. "After that argument you had, when she made that *ridiculous* claim—"

"We had a fight, that's all," I snap. "Do you know where she went?"

"I believe her father accepted a new position on the Venus Settlement," Mom replies stiffly. "Obviously, he accepted to escape the embarrassment of—"

"You should have told me she moved." I clench my fists. I don't know why I'm so angry.

"I'm sorry, dear. I didn't know you'd be so upset!"

"*I'm not upset!*" I positively yell.

"Yes, I see that." Mom pats me awkwardly on the shoulder. "I know you girls were friends for a long time, but friends grow apart. Look at me and Val, I mean, Ms. Goble. People change, and that's perfectly *fine*, Myra. Really."

I take a deep breath, forcing myself to calm down. "I know," I say, just wanting to change the subject. "I know that."

"And I know you don't want to hear this, but I really think Hannah moving is for the best."

"Mom, I don't want—"

"That whole family was a bit odd, if you ask me. Her sister, Merida—"

"Meredith, Mom. And I really don't want to talk—"

"Clearly a non-Creer. Such a shame. Her parents were

fairly talented in their fields. It happens though, even in the best families. But making those wild claims—"

"Mom!"

"And her sister, believing them! She was old enough to know better, if you ask me. But telling you, all the same—"

"MOM, I DON'T WANT TO TALK ABOUT THIS ANYMORE!"

"Imagine telling people her sister had *seeds*—real plant seeds, of all things!"

CHAPTER TWENTY-SIX

"I DON'T HEAR THE NUMBERS WHISPERING," I SAY softly, staring at Hannah's bedroom floor. "I never have."

"There's still plenty of time," Hannah replies, combing her sleek black hair with her fingers as she lounges on her bed. "Most kids don't get their magic until after they start their Creer lessons."

"No, Hannah," I say, harsher than I mean to be. "It's not just that I can't hear them. I don't care if I hear them or not. I don't even want to try. I'm not . . . I'm not interested in math, or numbers or the numbers' secrets. Not any of it."

Hannah straightens up, sitting cross-legged on the bed. "Myra," she says slowly, looking at me intently. "I'm pretty sure you've got magic somewhere in you. You're the smartest girl I know. But even if you don't, that's okay. You're still you. You're still my best friend. And you're still Myra."

Up until that moment, it never occurred to me that there could be any path for me other than math. It seems . . . scary somehow to think of a future where I'm not a Number Whisperer. "If you don't have magic, you don't matter," I snap, then instantly regret it. She's only trying to help.

"Maybe you're just focusing on the wrong Creer," Hannah suggests, though I can see the hurt in her eyes.

"My aptitude test only showed math," I remind her, clenching my fists.

"Creers can change," Hannah says with a shrug. "Some people even have Inscriptions from more than one Creer."

"And some don't have any at all," I retort. "Like your sister."

Hannah's expression shifts so quickly it looks like she's wearing a hologram mask. The concerned kindness in her eyes is immediately replaced by betrayal, and then fury.

"Just because your parents are stuck up and think that magic is the only thing that matters doesn't make it true, Myra," she says through gritted teeth. "Plenty of people do important things for the galaxy that have nothing to do with magic."

"Like what?" I ask, rolling my eyes.

"Like this," she snaps, pushing off her bed and digging through her dresser. She pulls out an ornate emerald box small enough to fit in my palm. The clasp on it looks like it had once been sealed with a key. With DNA scanning technology, locks with keys are almost unheard of nowadays. You really only see them on toys. But this is clearly no toy.

I stand to get a closer look. "What's in there?"

She opens it, revealing an empty interior. "Nothing now," Hannah says in a hushed whisper, her eyes glowing with wonder. "But when Meredith found it, she said it had seeds inside."

"Seeds?" I say with a gasp. "Only Chemics are supposed to have those. Where did your sister get them? A food lab?"

"They weren't Chemic seeds," she says with a huff, like I'm the dumbest person on the Moon. "They were seeds from the Old World."

My mouth falls open, then I snap it shut. "That's ridiculous, Hannah. You're just making things up. Or your sister is, and you fell for it."

Hannah's dark eyes blaze. "You don't know what you're talking about. You don't always have to be such a know-it-all. Meredith is going to do something important with the seeds—something that matters, unlike you with your lack of Number Whispering magic."

It's like she's slapped me. Without another word, I storm past her and out her bedroom door. I leave her apartment, without even a goodbye to her parents, and stomp down the three hallways between my apartment and hers. I burst inside, startled to find Mom at the table, grading exams.

"You're home early," I snap.

"I could say the same to you." She looks up, studying my face, sweating and hot with anger. "What happened?"

I tell her the whole story, except for the part about my not *caring about Number Whisperer magic. Her expression shifts from surprise to irritation to concern. She doesn't say much when I'm finished, except to tell me that I shouldn't worry about it. Hannah's just embarrassed that her sister doesn't have any magic, and I shouldn't pay any attention to her nonsense.*

I know my mom, though, and I can tell when she's working out an equation. Her eyes have that distant look to them, and I don't think it's a math problem she's trying to puzzle out. She doesn't say anything more. Just turns back to her work.

The fight doesn't come up again. I don't speak to Hannah, either. Before I know it, it's time to move into S.L.A.M. and Hannah isn't there.

I've tried for months to block out the night of my argument with Hannah. I've told myself over and over that things got out of hand. That we were both angry and saying things that we didn't mean. That didn't make sense. That weren't true. Even when I literally stumbled into the moongarden, I refused to let my mind wander to our argument. Because the only thing worse than what she'd told me being a lie was it turning out to be the truth.

There's no way Meredith could have had seeds in that box. Where would she even have gotten them? And if she did have them, what did that have to do with her moving? Hannah and Meredith's dad had just gotten a new job. Case closed. Friendship over.

It's a lot harder to convince myself of that now, though, than it was before.

The next week, I emerge into the garden for the first time since Mom's visit. Red lines crisscross the space, the greenery beginning to conform to my newly created sections thanks to a lot of replanting work. The plants seem to be really taking to their new homes. The garden looks vibrant and lush, the vines and branches stretching taller and farther than ever. Twigs and burrs and vines catch on my clothes as I pass. I crouch down next to a patch of thin, tubular blades of grass, inhaling their sharp fragrance: *chives*. I pluck one the way Bernie showed me, hesitate, and then nibble the end of it. Heat blossoms across my tongue, making my eyes water. I pop the rest of the stalk in my mouth, closing my eyes as the fiery flavor erupts and recedes like a volcano.

I stroll deeper into the tangle, then freeze when I spot something foreign—something that was definitely *not* here a few days ago.

I rush back toward the bottom of the chute and hop up on a large, angled branch. After a while, muffled voices drift down the tunnel, followed by blurred forms streaking their way out into the garden.

"You guys!" I shriek as Bernie and Canter climb to their feet. "Come quick!" Before they can react, I'm rushing down a path and under an arched shrub.

Bernie bursts into the small clearing behind me. Canter's on his heels. A barrage of beeps announces Bin-ro as he comes skidding down the path. "What's wrong?" Bernie asks, looking left and right.

Canter gasps for air. "What happened?"

"Look." I step aside and gesture proudly at a cluster of huge gold and amber blooms.

"A flower?" Bernie gapes at me. "I thought you were being murdered! This whole place is filled with flowers now."

"But this is a *new one* from the seeds you found!" I grab Bernie's arms and start jumping up and down. "Aren't you excited?"

"Not enough to carry on like I've got a few bolts loose," Bernie grumbles, but I catch the corners of his mouth turning up.

Canter brushes his fingers over one of the flowers, which is bigger than his whole hand. "What are they called?"

"That's a sunflower," Bernie says.

I take in the cheery color. "Do we have moonflowers planted yet?"

Bernie doesn't answer. Instead, he takes one of the sunflower stems and points the bloom at his mouth, then taps his foot, bouncing in time to a silent beat.

I put my hands on my hips. "Bernie."

"'When vesper bells are ringing,'" he sings in a gravelly

voice. "'I hear sweet voices singing.'" Bernie spins around, still holding the flower like a voice amplifier.

"Not *again*," Canter moans, but he's grinning as wide as I am.

"'Moonlight and roses,'" Bernie bellows. "'Loves golden dreams sparkling anew,'" he croons as he throws his arm around another sunflower stalk. Bin-ro spins and turns along with the music. "'Tis then my heart grows fonder. As through the flowers I wander. With thoughts so true.'" Bernie bows down over his flower-o-phone. "'Moonlight and roses.'" He does a complicated series of steps to the side, then lifts the sunflower so it rests against his cheek. "'Bring wonderful memories of you.'"

Still laughing, Canter and I break into applause and Bernie bows dramatically. "Thank you, thank you."

"Hey, look at these!" I drop to my knees and peer at another plant growing up mesh strung between two posts, leaves sprouting along the vines. I prod a tiny flower the color of sunshine peeking through the green. "What are these? I thought this was a tomato plant."

"Tomatoes start as yellow flowers," Bernie explains, brushing one with his fingertip. "They'll turn into little green balls, then red, and then"—he throws a wink at us—"we can eat them. I bet they'll be the best thing I've tasted in, oh, a few hundred years."

"Do you remember your old life?" I ask. "Or, um, your first one? Your original . . ."

Bernie chuckles.

"I don't know what you call it," I say, my cheeks going pink. "Sorry."

"Don't be," Bernie says. He kneels down and starts trimming away a few of the leaves. "I remember some. They say it fades with each Repetition, but I seem to remember quite a bit. I was a gardener then, too."

"A Master Gardener," I add, remembering.

"That's right." Bernie stands, brushing dust from his clothes. "Took a lot of work and a lot of money to get my gardening degree. Had to beg, borrow, and work my tail off to finish. Didn't end up amounting to much, though, in the end."

"Why not?" I ask.

"Right after I finished school, the problems with the plants started hitting the news. Tough to find work as a gardener when plants might be deadly." He shakes his head. "I don't remember much after that."

"What's it like?" Canter asks. I'm a little surprised at the question. I've never heard Canter ask Bernie about anything other than gardening.

"What's what like?" Bernie replies.

"Remembering." Canter pauses. "Is it like seeing snippets

of your own life or recalling someone else's? Do you remember all the other Reps that came before you?"

"I don't know anything about the—about the others," Bernie says. "We're not a hive-mind. I've got my memories and what I guess you'd call my original's. They all seem like mine though." He leans back against a tree, rubbing his forehead. "Just feels like I started over again when he—or I, I guess—joined the program."

"Why'd he do it?" Canter asks.

"The usual reasons. Lack of money, lack of family, lack of options." Bernie spreads his hands out in front of him. "Maybe a little bit of fear of being lost to history—of having his story end. But the ending is part of life. I didn't get that then. These plants here, back on the Old World, when they'd die, they'd go back into the soil, just how they started, and then they'd help the next plants to grow, and the next, and the next, until forever. Now that's what you call immortality. Not this cloning business."

"Do you wish you hadn't done it?" I can't help but ask.

Bernie is quiet, and I wish I could take the question back. Finally, he looks at me and says, "I wish I understood then what I know now. But I had to live this whole extra life to get here, so I guess there's no good answer."

Canter looks up from the spot he's been studying. "What happened to him, er, you? Your original?"

"We're asking you too many questions." Suddenly, it feels like we're intruding. "You don't have to keep telling us all this personal stuff."

"I don't mind," Bernie says. "I'd rather be asked questions like a real human than passed on by like some kind of walking mop." He looks up at the glass enclosing the garden. The Old World glows in the distance, half obscured by shadow. "I don't know exactly what happened to my original. Must have died a long time ago since he lived on the Old World."

"Do you—what do you feel like?" I ask. I know I probably shouldn't—that I'm being rude—but I can't stop myself. "Do you feel like a Repetition? Or like us?"

Bernie scratches his head. "I feel like me. I don't feel different than I remember feeling before I entered the program. I still think and dream and breathe and eat. Just like I did. Just like you. It's just the world that's changed around me. People don't think I'm human anymore, and that wears on you after a while. So, I suppose in that sense I do feel different." He looks from Canter to me. "That make sense?"

I nod. It must be so strange having your life begin so long ago—*hundreds* of years ago—and then blink, and you've fast-forwarded straight into a new time, a new world. . . .

"What would you like us to call you?" Canter asks suddenly, breaking my train of thought. "You don't seem to like *Rep* or *Repetition*."

"It's not the word that bothers me so much," Bernie says, quietly hammering a stake into the ground. He secures one of the tomato vines to it with a loop of twine. "It's what's behind it. A Repetition is what I am. I can't deny that. But it's not *who* I am."

"So what should we call you then?" I ask, watching Bernie delicately wind twine around another vine.

"Just call me what you've been calling me. Just call me Bernie."

CHAPTER TWENTY-SEVEN

Fourth Month, 2448

A FEW DAYS LATER, I SIT IN MY CHEMIC THEORY class, waiting for the bell to ring and pretending not to hear the other kids whispering about me and my lack of magical participation in any classes. I lean over to pick up my bag and plop it on my desk to shield my face from view, but I immediately wish I hadn't.

Kids crane their necks at my movement, staring at my exposed wrist as my sleeve inches up my arm while I reach. I sigh and reflexively tug it back down, even though it's my right arm and there's no incriminating Botan Inscriptions for them to see. *Yet.*

I've noticed the whispers that usually trail me from class to class have intensified recently, and Lila filled me in on the latest school obsession: Inscription Hunting.

"Did you see anything?" a girl to my right whispers to her neighbor.

"I thought I saw a smudge of something on her arm, but I couldn't tell what it was."

"It's a freckle," I mutter, but they aren't listening. They're too busy arguing over if that counts as a *sighting*.

Apparently anyone who spots one of my Inscriptions gets bragging rights and a piece of leftover Trickering candy from the other players.

When the bell finally rings, I'm first out of the class, counting down the minutes until I can retreat to the safety of the moongarden. More and more of the new plantings are blooming now, including lots more of the plants that grow food. A tall, wispy one unlike anything else in the garden popped up yesterday. Bernie said it's used for bread, but the soft, feathery stalks don't look like anything I'd want to make a sandwich with. Another new plant apparently grows its food underground. We have to dig it out when it's ready, though I don't really understand how we'll know when that is without peeking.

I finally filled Canter in on my deal with Director Weathers. He didn't seem surprised his dad would be involved in a cover-up. Since then, Canter's been helping out a lot more with the actual gardening in between working on the broadcaster. I'd never admit it to him, but with all the new plants, I'm happy to have his help.

Dodging kids and Inscription Hunters in the hall, I stick my hand in my pocket and feel something crumbly. Drawing out a fist, I fold back my fingers to reveal a palmful of seeds. *Whoops.* I forgot to leave them in the moongarden.

Quickly, before anyone sees, I shake the seeds back into my pocket, then press my hand over it. *I'll give you a home later, I promise.* I give my pocket an affectionate tap. . . .

And then something taps back. The seeds shudder and roll like marbles in motion. Before I can sneak a few back out to investigate, *POP!*, there's a silent explosion, and a flower falls to the ground. I gasp and scoop it up, tucking it under the front of my sweater, scanning the hallway around me. Thankfully, no one's gaping or pointing.

I clamp my hand over the pocket opening in case one of the other seeds gets any funny ideas, and it's a good thing I do, because by the time I've rounded the next corner, I feel more pops under my sweaty palm. Before I know it, heaps of flowers poke out from my sweater and are cascading to the ground.

"Argh!" I whisper. "I told you *later*."

There's no way to get my bag open to shove the flowers inside without people noticing, so instead, I do the only thing I can think of—flop to the ground on top of them and start hastily stuffing them away. I know I look ridiculous, but all that matters is that no one sees the flowers.

I've almost got them all hidden when I hear the first snickers and comments.

"Whoa, did you see that dive? This isn't the hoverball court."

A pair of sneakers passes over my head as someone steps over—and almost on—me.

"What's that first-year doing? Some kind of new dance move?" More laughter.

Sneakers squeak on one side of me before thumping down on the other. Apparently, someone thought it'd be funny to use me as a human hurdle.

"Look, Canter. These newbie Slammers are really dropping like flies!"

I look up and see Canter and what looks like half the JV hoverball team huddled around me. My face flames. Canter's buddies are all doubled over laughing, but he's just standing there, mouth gaping, eyes wide.

"Hey, it's *her*," someone calls. "Quick, can anyone see any Inscriptions? A handful of Trickering candy to anyone that does!"

Oh no. Here we go again.

My face gets even hotter before a clenching feeling suddenly grips at my throat. I've spent years honing my ability to not care what the other kids think and say, but all that practice melts away when I see Canter's expression. *You're not friends,* I tell myself. *Don't expect this to go any differently.*

I ease up to my knees and glance around, trying to spot an escape route, but Canter steps in front of me before I can move.

"Shut it, Marco!" Canter shoots him a withering glare. "Give her a break."

I climb to my feet using Canter as a shield to hide the bulge over my stomach. Slinging my backpack off, I pull it in front of me and peek around Canter's shoulder.

"Whatever, dude," Marco mutters, his posture drooping slightly. "It was funny."

"Yeah, it's real funny to laugh at someone when they're down," Canter barks. "You ever think about maybe helping her up instead?"

"When did you get to be so noble? You've been acting real weird lately, dude. Usually, you'd be the first one laughing."

"Yeah, well . . . ," Canter says, glancing back at me. He raises his eyebrows slightly, as if to say, *What just happened?* I give a slight shrug and shake my head. "I decided to grow up. You should try it."

"Sure, have fun with that." Marco starts down the hall, stopping only to glance over his shoulder to see if his friends are following him. They aren't. They're frozen, looking between Canter and him. Marco groans and stomps away.

"You all right?" one of Canter's friends asks, and it takes me a second to realize he's talking to me.

I manage a small nod. "Thanks," I mumble. Canter flashes me a quick smile, then turns back to his friends.

I pivot to go the other way and find myself nose to nose with Lila.

"Hi there!" she says in a perky voice, but her eyes are narrowed to slits. "That was a nasty fall you took. I was right behind you and saw the whole thing. We'd better go check to make sure you didn't hurt anything. You could have a fracture."

I flash Canter a desperate look over my shoulder as Lila grabs my elbow and marches me away, but he's already disappeared into the busy hallway with his friends.

I trudge to our room like a hostage, Lila close on my heels, preventing any escape attempt. Excuses and explanations streak through my brain like a comet hurtling through space, but the only thing that could save me now is a meteor hitting the school.

"Myra," Lila says slowly, enunciating every letter of my name as she closes the door behind us, then taps at the controls a few times, flooding the room in sharply bright lights. "Do you have what I think you have under there?"

"Under where?" I fiddle with my backpack, scrambling to come up with a way out of this.

Lila puts her hands on her hips and looks down her nose

at me. "Really, Myra? *I saw you*. I saw everything. At least I think I did, since it's, you know, *impossible*."

"If I show you, you won't be able to unsee it." I stare into her eyes, willing her to understand. "You'll be *in*. I don't want to do that to you."

"Myra, I already saw them." She flops down on the bed. "And I'm already in, because you're my friend."

Any argument I might have had drifts away like smoke. She sets her jaw. "Okay, now spill it. Literally."

"Lila—"

"Listen, you've kept my secret, and I've been keeping your secrets for a while now, even if I don't know what all of them are. I know you've been up to something. Going to the *modulab* after curfew all the time?" she says, making air quotes. "And you were more excited about getting Mender scans than I was doing them. I could tell from the scans that something was up, too."

"You could?" My mouth falls open. "What do you mean?"

"You've been gaining muscle mass like you were lifting weights and running miles. Not things that usually happen in a modulab." She raises her eyebrows knowingly. "But I haven't said a word. Now, just tell me what secret I've been keeping. That's what friends do."

"I don't know much about friendship," I mumble.

"I know. That's why I'm teaching you." Lila raises her eyebrows, waiting.

Don't show her. Don't tell. She'll spoil everything.

Ignoring the voice in my head, I drop my backpack and lift up the hem of my shirt. A pile of flowers, enough to fill a vase, flutters to the ground.

Lila's eyes are as big as carnations. "Crashing comets," she whispers. "I mean, I saw a couple of them before you planked out in the middle of the hall, but I never—I can't—I mean . . . I don't know what to say!"

"It's a lot," I reply with a small smile. "And they're not poisonous, I swear. You can't—"

"I know they aren't. I've been doing your scans, remember? And I solemnly swear on my reputation as an awesome roommate and friend I won't tell anyone," she adds, raising her hand. She studies the flowers lying at our feet. "They're really . . . I don't know, *beautiful,* aren't they?"

I nod slowly. "So, what do we do now?"

"I don't know. I mean, where did these come from?"

I purse my lips, but there's no point lying about the moongarden. Still, friend or not, I can't mention my Botan magic. To anyone. After a deep breath, I say, "There's kind of this garden I found. . . ."

"Excuse me, what?

I grin. I can't help it. "It's a *moongarden.*"

"Okay, wait. Start at the beginning."

CHAPTER TWENTY-EIGHT

"I STILL CAN'T BELIEVE YOU DIDN'T TELL ME—didn't tell anyone!" Lila flops back on her bed. "Weren't you afraid the plants were toxic?"

"Not after you gave me a couple clean scans." I gather up the flowers from the floor and stuff them into my backpack.

"You trust my Mending that much?"

"Of course." I grin at her, but it fades, replaced with new worry. "Why?"

"Oh, don't get worked up," she says with a laugh. "I get top marks in all my Mending classes. You're totally fine."

"Who's fine?" someone asks as the door slides open. Bethany and Sloane dart inside before the door swishes shut behind them.

Lila and I exchange a quick glance. "Myra. She didn't

feel well. That's why we're here. I had a free period, so I told her I'd give her a quick scan."

Sloane's eyes bulge. "I thought you weren't supposed to practice on people until next year."

Lila crosses her arms. "Technically, yeah."

"And you'd risk all that for *her*?" Bethany asks with a sneer.

"Obviously," Lila replies, an edge creeping into her voice. "Plus it helps me, too. Most people wouldn't let me practice on them."

I shoot Lila a grateful look. "I don't mind."

"I would," Bethany says. "Who knows what sorts of awful things a bad Mending could do." She shudders. "No thanks."

"Good thing Lila's a great Mender, then."

Lila beams at me.

Bethany scowls, eyes roaming over my sweater. "What happened to your shirt?"

I shrug and glance down, pretending not to notice it's stretched out and drooping. "Too big, I guess."

"If you roll up the sleeves, it wouldn't look half as ridiculous," Bethany suggests eagerly.

Lila rolls her eyes. "Leave her alone. That whole Inscription Hunting game the other kids are playing is really immature."

"Well, why do you always change in the bathroom?"

Bethany asks me, tossing her hair over her shoulder. "It's so *weird*."

"Well, why do you always ask annoying questions," I mimic, flipping my ponytail dramatically. "It's so *rude*."

Lila laughs, and even Sloane lets a giggle escape. Bethany glares at them both, then swivels her gaze back to me. "All you have to do is show them a few Inscriptions and they'll lay off." Her eyes narrow. "Don't you have any?"

"'Course she does," Lila replies. "I've seen them."

Both shift their focus to her. I try my best not to look as surprised as they do. "Really?" Sloane squeaks, looking back and forth between us. "Why'd you show her?"

"Uh," I mumble, glancing sideways at Lila.

"She didn't *show* me," Lila says, casually tying her hair into a high bun as she talks. "I just happened to see them. We do live together, you know."

"So do we," Bethany snaps. "And I've never seen them."

"Maybe if you put half as much effort into being a nice roommate as you do being an Inscription Hunter, you'd have noticed, too," I say.

Sloane looks guilty, but Bethany just sneers and flops onto her bed.

Lila glances at her pendant. "What are you guys doing here, anyway? Don't you have class?"

"Skipping," Sloane says, then shoots me a worried look. "Don't tell on us."

"I wouldn't," I reply, getting up. "I'm supposed to be in class, too. I should probably go. I've got a Mender test this week I need to prep for."

"I can help you study," Lila says eagerly. "Throw me your bookpod, and I'll see what unit you're on."

"My bookpod?" My eyes dart down to my backpack, still bulging with forbidden flowers. My bookpod is squished somewhere at the bottom.

"Yeah— *Oh*." Lila looks anxiously at Bethany and Sloane, who are watching our exchange with vague interest, then at my backpack. *Sorry*, she mouths.

"I, uh, think it's in my desk," I say quickly, throwing myself behind my workstation before sliding open a drawer. I dig around, pretending to search for it. The drawer is chock-full, and a few things spill out the back. Kneeling down, I scoop up the items that dropped and move to stuff them back into the drawer.

"Why do you have two pendants?" Bethany asks, looking from the pendant dangling from my hand to the one hanging around my neck.

"It's not mine. It's—" *Shooting stars!* I forgot all about the pendant I accidently took the first time I was in the garden.

"What's wrong, Myra?" Lila asks.

"NOTHING! Nothing, I've just—I've got to go. To class."

"I thought you were getting Lila your bookpod," Sloane calls as I hurtle toward the door.

"I must have left it in class. I'll get it," I reply as the door swishes shut behind me. Safe in the deserted hallway, I press the power button on the old pendant, but of course, it's still dead. "Blast it," I mutter.

As I turn a corner, a glimmer of silver disappearing down the next hallway catches my eye. *An Elector student. Perfect!* I race after them, skidding into the connecting corridor, hastily tucking my pendant into my shirt. A tall girl in an Elector-silver jumpsuit glances back at me curiously.

Panting, I call out, "Excuse me. Can you help me?"

"With what?" she asks reluctantly, then her eyes narrow. "Aren't you that girl—"

"Nope," I say quickly. "I forgot to charge my pendant, and now it's dead," I say, holding it out to her. "I need it for my next class. Do you think you could give it a quick charge?"

"Oh, sure!" She looks around, all suspicion gone replaced by a clear desire to show off.

She taps the pendant and there's an audible zap as the energy surge makes the device jump.

"Thanks," I say with a small wave as she walks away.

The pendant doesn't stay on for long—the girl isn't nearly as good as she thinks she is—but it's enough to see the name of its owner flash across the screen: PROPERTY OF FIONA A. WEATHERS.

CHAPTER TWENTY-NINE

THAT EVENING, I LIE IN BED PRETENDING TO sleep, one lanyard hanging around my neck as usual (mine), and one wound tightly around my hand (Fiona's). *Fiona Weathers was in the garden. How else would her pendant have gotten there?*

But that's not what's worrying me. It's the fact that she'd been there, and now she's dead.

Once I hear a chorus of even breathing, I slide out of bed, wrap my feet in reflector paper, and tiptoe out the door.

Canter's not coming to the garden tonight—some JV hoverball team sleepover or something. Honestly, it couldn't be better timing. I have a feeling Bernie will say more without Canter there.

As usual, I slow when I reach the last hallway and peek

my head around the corner. Nothing but darkness greets me, and I hurry into the corridor, glancing into Ms. Curie's office as I pass, then jerk to a stop. The room's a total mess, but that's not the strange part. My parents' offices are usually littered with computers and bookpods and calculation instruments. Still, their devices are piled on their *desks*. Ms. Curie's is completely empty while a jumble of tools and equipment is heaped on the floor. Right above where the garden is hidden.

A chill runs through me. *Canter will know what that means.* I know what I think it means, but I'm no Elector.

Maybe it's just a coincidence. Maybe I'm overreacting, thinking Curie's monitoring electrical activity in the garden. I hope I am. I hope I'm wrong.

I tear myself away from the window and dash down the hall, my mind still lost somewhere in Curie's pile of parts. When I wave my hand in front of the panel for the moongarden classroom, nothing happens. I wave my hand again. Nothing. I press my whole palm to the panel. All it does is blink red.

This is a coincidence. It has to be. But a slippery, slimy feeling curls through my insides and my palms begin to sweat.

I tuck Fiona's pendant into my pocket. For half a second, I consider hunting down Bernie, then quickly reject that idea. He must know the door's locked, and if he's smart (which he is), he lightsped it away.

Just like I should.

With more worries and fewer options, I turn on my heel and hurry back to my room.

Early the next morning, gray overalls keep catching my eye as I whip from hallway to hallway. None are Bernie's. I laid awake all night trying to assemble all the puzzle pieces I've collected into a picture that makes sense. Too many are still missing, though, and I'm pretty sure Bernie has them.

After searching every level of S.L.A.M., which takes longer than it should since I have to keep dodging Inscription Hunters, I end up in the cafeteria. On a whim, I follow a woman in gray overalls through the STAFF ONLY door into what turns out to be the kitchen. A few Reps look up, surprised. I have absolutely no reason to be here, and it's definitely not allowed, but none of them question me.

I watch as they go about their business, cooking and washing and prepping breakfast. I'm about to turn to leave when I notice a nondescript door behind one of the counters. Pulling up my mental map of the school, I can't place what would be located behind the kitchen. An older Rep man opens the door and disappears behind it. I wait a few seconds before slipping through, too.

The empty corridor is lined with doors. I open the first few to reveal small apartments. These must be the living quarters for the Reps, though the ones I see appear to be unoccupied. The rooms each have a simple chair and table, a small food storage unit, and a flat, boxy bed, nothing like the ergonomically developed, curved beds the students use. The next door leads to a supply closet. I close it quickly before continuing farther down the hall. One more door, and then I'll have to just go back the way I came.

I press the enter button and the door slides open.

Laughter and chatter drift toward me but stop abruptly like someone hit a mute button. A half-dozen Reps sprawl across two couches or lean against the table between them. A few glance at me curiously before busying themselves with straightening cushions. Others ignore me altogether, studying the far wall. Only one man keeps his eyes fixed on me, though he doesn't say a word.

"Bernie! I've been looking for you everywhere!"

"What do you need?" he mumbles, looking around nervously.

"I have, er, some instructions for you. From the director. The kitchen staff needs help with breakfast."

Bernie pushes off the stiff-looking couch and nods toward the door. I follow him into the hall.

"What were you all doing in there?" I can't help but ask.

I've never heard Reps laugh or even talk to one another other than to discuss work.

Bernie shrugs. "Socializing. It's our off-shift, same as you and your friends when you don't have class."

Clearly, he doesn't know me very well.

"Is this about last night?" Bernie presses. "I got a late-night assignment, so I couldn't make it—"

"No, it's something else," I interrupt, pulling the pendant out of my pocket. "Or, um, someone else."

He raises his eyebrows. "Who?"

I take a deep breath. "Fiona Weathers."

Bernie jumps as though an Elector dropped a pulse in the hallway. "What'd you say?" he chokes out.

"She didn't die in an accident, did she?" I whisper.

"How do you know that?" Bernie demands. "Did some-one say—" He grabs my elbow, steering me farther away from the door. "Where is all this coming from?" His icy blue eyes are flooded with worry.

"I found this in the garden the first time I was there," I explain as I open my palm, revealing the pendant. "It belonged to the director's wife."

Bernie stares at the device for a few moments, then reaches out and gently closes my hand around it. "You need to get rid of that. Or I can do it for you. No one can know—"

"That someone got rid of her?" I ask, stepping closer. "Bernie, I know you know the truth. What really happened to Fiona Weathers's shuttle?"

"I told you from the start the garden is dangerous, Myra." He runs his hand through his wispy gray hair. "I should never have let you get mixed up in this."

"I was already mixed up in it before you knew about me," I say, planting my hands on my hips. "It was Fiona's garden, wasn't it?"

He nods toward my hand and the pendant still clutched within it. "You've got your answer right there."

"What really happened to her?"

"She had an accident."

I turn everything over and over in my mind. It's like reading the chapters of a novel out of order, trying to assemble them into a sequence that makes sense. I've got the gist of the plot, but I still can't quite figure out how the story ends. My thoughts drift to the locked garden door and the pile of equipment in Curie's office. "Did Ms. Curie have something to do with Fiona's accident?"

Bernie leans against a door and rubs his nose. "It's more complicated than that. Anything with the plants is complicated."

There's a loud bang from the room behind us, and we both jump.

"We can't be talking about this here!" he rasps, pushing off the door and shuffling down the hall.

"Wait! I have to tell you something!"

"Later, missy. Tonight, in the . . . in the place. You know where."

"But—"

The door clicks shut behind him.

CHAPTER THIRTY

I STAND ALONE IN THE HALLWAY FOR A LONG time. Minutes. Hours. Who knows? A bell rings, but I hardly hear it. I'm not going to class today, but where I will go, I have no idea.

The locked garden door is sending off all kinds of alarm bells in my head, a leftover defense mechanism from my class-cutting days, but the danger makes me want to go there more. It's as if the garden is calling out to me for help. *Why is it locked?*

After drifting down a few hallways, I find myself in the Elector wing. Classroom doors are locked with a code, and unless I find a way to hack into Director Weathers's network, I'll never figure out what it is.

Canter might already have access to his dad's passwords, though.

I peer through the windows until a familiar form catches my eye. Canter is hunched over his workstation, studying some sort of circuit breaker. He doesn't look up.

I start pacing in front of the door, hoping the movement will catch his attention. It doesn't, but a few of his classmates look up. I point from Canter to myself, until the boy in the next seat nudges him in the ribs. He just shoves the boy back, but doesn't even glance at me. The Elector boy meets my eyes and shrugs.

Blast it, Canter! I take a breath, then open the door. Ms. Curie whips around, her eyes narrowing.

"Can we help you, Miss Hodger?"

"The director wants to see Canter Weathers," I say, hoping the waver in my voice isn't as audible to her as it is to me.

Ms. Curie slides down from the workstation where she's perched and crosses to the messenger dock on her desk. "I didn't receive an alert."

"I was just in his office, ma'am, so the director sent me to find Canter," I explain slowly, choosing each word carefully. "I think he was having trouble with his messenger system."

"Oh?" Her eyes are slits. "I'll stop by after class and see what I can do."

"That's okay, Ms. Curie," Canter says as he pushes out from behind his workstation. "I'll take a look while I'm there. I'm sure I can fix it."

She sears him with her electric glare. "Based on your attention span during my class lately, I wouldn't be so sure, Mr. Weathers." She glances at me, then back at him. "Buzz me from your pendant if you have any trouble, and I'll come down."

"Yes, ma'am," Canter says quickly, before ducking out the door. "What's up?" he asks when we're safely down the hall. "Did something happen?"

"No, I just felt like getting grilled by Ms. Curie to get you out of class," I snap. "Of course something happened. The moongarden door is locked!"

"Is that all?" Canter asks, but his eyes have gone dark. "That's an easy fix. I can short-circuit the lock mechanism with a mini-surge."

"Well, the door's never been locked before, so I . . . er . . . kind of freaked out." I nudge him with my elbow. "Are you seriously complaining about skipping?"

"Good point. Let's go."

A few minutes later, Canter taps the panel outside the moongarden classroom and the sensor immediately glows green. "Nothing to it," he gloats.

"Why do you think it was locked?"

He shrugs. "The room's not in use. I'm honestly surprised it's always been open."

I nod, then follow him to the back wall. A moment later, we're in the moongarden.

Canter starts poking at a flowerbed. The gray ground has almost completely been overtaken by an array of colors, mostly arranged into neat little sections, and red laser-lines cut through the parts that haven't yet been sorted and organized. Bin-ro rolls around, scanning plants, beeping to signal a small oak tree needs some help. Canter heads over to take a look.

"Shouldn't you be working on the broadcaster?" I nod toward the heap of machinery and parts in the corner.

"Not much to do until I get a few more pieces," he says, pruning some of the tree's leaves.

"Everyone's in class. Wouldn't this be a good time to snag what you need?"

"Except I just left my Elector Industrial Applications class, genius." He picks up a shovel and begins digging in the moondust, stopping after a few moments to swipe a hand across his forehead. "What am I going to do? Go back and say my dad needs some parts to—"

"To fix his messenger?" I raise my eyebrows.

Canter pauses. "That actually could work. Some of the components I need work in messengers, too. Same sound amplification properties."

"What if Curie mentions it to your dad, though?"

Canter shakes his head. "She won't. I told you, my dad doesn't like her. And I'm pretty sure the feeling's mutual."

"Why?"

"Curie was friends with my mom, you know, before . . . Anyway. I think my dad and Curie had a falling-out or something after Mom died. Dad doesn't really talk about it, except to mutter under his breath about her being a troublemaker whenever her name comes up."

Canter drops the shovel and brushes off his pants, then grabs his bag and heads for the door while I turn over this new information in my mind. Fidgeting, I grip the pendant still buried deep in my pocket. *Just tell him, Myra! He has a right to know.*

"Canter, wait," I say, the words rushing out of me. I run through a dozen different ways to start as he stands there, curious, but none of them sound right. Finally, I opt for the simplest version. "I know who the garden belongs to. Or who it used to belong to, anyway."

Canter's eyes go wide, but not with surprise or curiosity. With dread. I know the look well. I'm sure it's been plastered across my face plenty of times the past few months. "You do?" he finally says hoarsely.

"Yes," I reply, still studying him. "Do you?"

He fidgets, but doesn't answer.

I pull the pendant out of my pocket and toss it to him. "I found this the first time I came to the garden. I'd forgotten all about it. . . . It'll probably need a charge."

Wordlessly, Canter taps the small white rectangle, and

a blue spark flares and fades, the light of the electric discharge and the subsequent glowing screen reflecting in his eyes. Still silent, he slowly looks up at me, his expression guilty.

"You knew." Memories click into place. "You told me you were wandering around, imagining which classroom *might* have been your mom's."

He nods, then turns and rummages in his backpack before pulling out a small tablet, much smaller than his usual one, and holding it out to me.

I take it gingerly, as if it might come alive and bite my fingers. After I press the power key, *Property of Fiona A. Weathers* flashes across the screen, then dissolves into a dashboard. I tap icon after icon, each more fascinating than the last. A catalogue of seeds and plant uses, plans for the garden, formulas for the nutrients delivered through the grate system. It's practically a gardening textbook.

"I used to roam around the school, wondering which room might have been hers, but then at the end of last year, I found that computer in a hidden drawer in the teacher workstation," Canter says softly. "I knew the classroom had to be hers. I used to go there to study . . . or just to sit. Sometimes, I'd try to imagine what it was like when she was teaching. What she said, what she did . . ." His voice trails off as he glances at the computer screen. "I didn't know what it was all for—what it meant—until I saw the garden."

Canter's first trip to the moongarden flashes through my mind. "I'd wondered why you weren't more freaked out. It was almost like you weren't surprised." My eyes widen. "Like you'd been here before."

"I think I was," he says softly. "I think my mom brought me here. It's hard to explain, but when I first slid into the garden, it looked so familiar, like a dream. And when I noticed the plants had electricity . . . It was like remembering something I'd forgotten. I *knew* the plants had their own electric charge, but I didn't know how I knew. It's not like I'd stumbled across any before."

"Did you remember Bernie, too?"

He shakes his head. "I was really young when she died, though."

"Bernie would remember. We could ask him," I say gently, and Canter nods. "I can't believe you knew all this time that your mom had been studying plants. And you didn't tell anyone? Not your dad or any of your friends?"

He scoffs. "Definitely not my dad. He doesn't like to talk about her, remember? And I didn't tell anyone else. I didn't want people to think she was weird or dangerous. I told you, people liked her, and I didn't want to damage her legacy. I was . . . I don't know. Maybe I was a little embarrassed." His cheeks flush, and he looks away.

Words finally make the journey from my brain to my mouth. "We've been taught our whole lives that plants are useless and long gone. Anyone would want to keep that kind of discovery quiet."

"I shouldn't have cared what people thought, though. She was my mom." He sets his jaw. "Well, I don't care anymore."

"I wish you'd told me," I say softly, still opening files. "This would have been helpful, and it's not like I would have judged you."

"Trusting people isn't really my thing."

I shoot him a small smile. "Me, neither."

Canter takes a deep breath. "There's more."

My head whips up. He's looking at me with a mixture of fear and determination.

"What?" I ask, although I'm almost afraid to know.

"I think—" He stops, then shakes his head and balls his hands into fists. "I think she was a Botan."

My mouth must drop open, because Canter quickly adds, "You've heard of them?"

I nod. "History class. Plant magic." Apparently, I can only form words two at a time now.

He rubs the back of his neck. "Once we started working in here, it all made sense—all her notes. She doesn't talk about magic, exactly, but she writes about channeling her emotions and *communing* with the plants, whatever that means."

"'The ability to commune with plant life,'" I say without thinking.

Canter gapes at me. "What'd you say?"

"I, uh, read it. In my history textbook."

"I've never covered Botans in history class."

I force a shrug. "It came up in class one day." *Because I asked.*

New facts streak and spin through my mind as I turn back to the computer. I open a file that appears to be plans for a broadcaster, the same design as the one Canter's been working on. I click another file and a blueprint of the nutrient delivery system opens, along with assembly instructions. When I tap the design, lines of text scroll across the screen. I skim through them, and my eyes go wide as saucers. I don't understand most of it, but the volts and currents are clearly Elector data.

"What do these mean?" I ask, shoving the tablet at Canter.

"How'd you get to this?" he asks, his mouth falling open. "I didn't know the nutrient system had pulse capabilities. I was wondering what all those extra circuits and capacitors were for. . . ." He looks up at me. "This is saying that the light bulbs can deliver an electric charge that kills any harmful plant growths. If this works, it would be an electrical breakthrough!"

I bite my lip. "There's no chance your mom was also secretly an Elector?"

"I think having clandestine plant magic was enough." He frowns, looking up at the rows of overhead light bulbs. "I've been wondering who built all this. I figured she could've had Bernie do it. The nutrient delivery system isn't that complicated. But this"—he shakes his head—"this would have taken an experienced Elector."

"Maybe it was Curie," I say, my voice almost a whisper. "They were friends."

Canter nods slowly. "That's true. She might have known about the garden and been helping my mom in here."

"She might still know about the garden." I tell him about the equipment piled on the floor in Curie's office.

"Could be a coincidence."

"We're starting to collect coincidences," I say grimly, my throat suddenly dry. "What happened to your mom's shuttle?" I ask slowly. "You hardly ever hear of space accidents nowadays, autopilot technology being what it is."

A shadow falls like a veil over Canter's eyes. "It had an electrical malfunction."

I don't say anything. I don't need to.

"We'll ask Bernie," Canter says.

I shift uneasily. "I already tried. He wouldn't say much."

"I'll ask him, then. I have a right to know."

"Maybe we're getting carried away," I say, twisting my hands together. "If Curie and your mom were friends and they were working together in here, why would Ms. Curie hurt her?"

"I don't know," Canter says, his eyes like ice. "But if she did, I'm going to find out."

CHAPTER THIRTY-ONE

CANTER RETURNS A WHILE LATER WITH A FEW more parts for the broadcaster. He tinkers with it while I tend the garden, but neither of us are all that productive. Even Bin-ro seems to have given up on work today. He just hovers between us, rolling aimlessly back and forth. Eventually, Canter forfeits and helps me prune some unruly shrubs. We just keep glancing at the door, waiting for Bernie. Close to curfew, we give up and head back to our rooms to wait until the school is asleep, and then sneak back to the garden. Bernie never shows up.

The next morning, I make my way to class bleary-eyed and with an uneasiness clenching my stomach. I hardly even notice the crew of Inscription Hunters loitering outside my room, hoping to catch me sleepy and off-guard. I hurry past them, ignoring the fact that they're still following me, resisting the urge to run and hide in the moongarden. I already skipped a day's worth of lessons, and there's no way I can miss more so soon—not unless I want another meeting with Director Weathers. Canter and I agreed to keep a lookout for Bernie, though. We'll meet in the moongarden tonight after curfew.

The day crawls by like we're on Mercury time. Finally, the dinner block rolls around. My stomach is too twisted to eat, so I head to my room. Apparently, I'm not the only one.

"Hi," I say as I trudge inside.

Lila's bent over a half-dozen projected books arranged in neat rows on her desk. "Hey," she says, glancing up at me. "Not hungry?"

I shake my head. "You either?"

She nods at a nutrient-bar wrapper on her bed. "Already ate. Oh, hey." She sits up. "I've been waiting to catch you while Bethany and Sloane aren't around. I figured out a way I think I can help you."

I must look confused, because she laughs. "With that whole Inscription Hunting thing?"

"Oh. That's okay. They'll get tired of it eventually."

"I know, but Bethany was right about one thing. The kids will get sick of it faster if they see your Inscriptions."

"But—"

"I know, I know. You haven't got any. But *they* don't need to know that!"

I raise my eyebrows. "How?"

"Come here." She gestures to her bed, scooting over to make room.

I sit gingerly on the edge as she leans over and rustles around in her dresser, before thrusting a short, thin, black tube triumphantly into the air. "Give me your arm."

Trying not to panic, I extend my right arm out to her, discreetly sitting on my other one. "What is that thing?"

"The most smudge-proof eyeliner in all of Apolloton." Lila grins as she rolls up my sleeve to expose my blank, unmarked skin. "I was studying Ms. Goble's Inscriptions in class today, and I think I can draw a few pretty well. Can I give it a try?"

I nod, and she sets to work. She's actually a pretty good artist. Before I know it, I've got a complicated algebraic theory and a basic multiplication table circling my forearm. "Wow, this actually looks real, Lila. Thank you!"

"Want me to do the other arm?"

"No, thanks," I say quickly, twisting it even farther behind my back. "I think if kids get a glimpse of this it'll be enough."

"Let me know if you need me to reapply," she says cheerfully, before tucking the eyeliner away.

"Thanks again, Lila. Seriously. That was really nice of you."

"Don't thank me," she says. "Just make sure I'm there when Bethany sees my handiwork."

I burst out laughing. "Deal. Her face will be priceless."

"I wouldn't trade it for a storm of Neptune diamonds," Lila agrees, giggling.

I nudge the remnants of her energy bar beside me. "So how come you didn't go to dinner?"

"I've got three tests this week and an essay for my Ethics and Compassion class."

I raise an eyebrow. "I've never heard of that class."

"It's only for Mender-tracks," she says, rubbing at her eyes. "We use so much emotion in our magic. We need to train ourselves so we don't burn out our compassion."

Didn't Canter say that Fiona's notes mentioned Botan magic and emotions? "What does that mean?" I ask as innocently as possible.

"Caring about our patients and making them better helps fuel our magic," Lila says. She tosses me her computer. "That's my essay on connecting with my desire to help and how to transform that feeling into magic."

I pore through the paragraphs, soaking up every bit of information.

"Boring, huh?" she asks after a few minutes.

"No!" I say, a little too enthusiastically. Lila gives me an odd look. "I mean, it's really cool. I've never heard about emotions playing into magic. Only data and theory."

"Mender is the only Creer that uses emotions," she explains. "I think I remember reading that because we use our magic on living things, it makes our tactics a little different."

Plants are alive, too! I reach the end of the essay and reread it from the top.

"Of course, we also use data and theory," Lila adds quickly, leaning over to click on another tab. A row of files scrolls across the screen. "Those are all my memorization charts for the week. Plus, I've got to learn how the body builds immunity against infection, bone development and structure, and the healing pattern of wounds."

I shoot her an awed smile. "Lila, this is like a *million* times harder than any of the other Creers."

She grins and motions toward the crumpled packaging on her bed. "That's why I have dinner in a wrapper."

I glance back down at her computer, noticing the open tabs on the side of the screen. Looks like they're textbooks borrowed from the modulab. I tap one—*Transitioning a Desire to Heal into Magic: What to Remember*—expanding it to full view. "Can I read this?"

Lila leans over to look. "Sure," she says, holding out her hand. I drop my pendant onto her palm, and she taps it to the screen, transferring the text to my school account. "The essay I used that for is done, so I don't need the book anymore."

I grab my own computer and sit cross-legged, burying my nose in the text.

"You really think it's that interesting?" Lila asks after a while.

I glance up, my mind already spinning with how the information could apply to plant magic. "Uh, yeah. Like you said, Mender is the only Creer that uses living things. I've never heard anything about magic using emotions in any of my other theory classes before."

Which is probably why I've had so much trouble controlling my own magic.

Lila settles back to studying. I do, too. At the very least, it'll keep my mind off Fiona Weathers. For a few hours, anyway.

Late that night, I creep by Ms. Curie's dark office window toward the moongarden classroom. Footsteps suddenly echo behind me. I freeze and peek over my shoulder, spotting Canter tiptoeing into the hall. He sees me and jumps.

"You scared me," we both hiss at the same time.

Canter quickly closes the distance between us, then peers through the office window. "At least Curie's not working tonight."

"But she's still been busy. Look." I point across the room, where tools are heaped in a pile.

"What is all that?"

"I thought you'd know." I adjust my glasses. "The tools look different from last time."

"Different, how?"

I squeeze my eyes shut, trying to remember. "There was a thin tube with long tentacle things on the end." I open my eyes, scanning the mess again. "I don't see it now."

"That could have been a reader," he says with a frown. "We use them to monitor electricity levels, usually to keep circuits from overloading." He squints and presses his face so close to the window, his breath fogs the glass. "I'm going in to take a closer look."

"Should we do that?"

"Should we be doing any of this?"

"Good point."

The door isn't locked and we creep inside. This almost feels scarier than sneaking into the moongarden full of illegal plants.

"Canter, you don't think Ms. Curie can sense the garden through the electricity the plants give off, right?"

He furrows his brow, concentrating. "No," he finally says. "I can't hear them from here. Their charge is way too dim."

"But she's a much more advanced Elector," I say, twisting my hands.

"I don't think that matters. She'd still have to be a lot closer to pick up on the garden's electricity."

"Okay," I mutter, but I don't really feel reassured.

I stand watch while Canter squats down, studying the various contraptions. "I don't recognize all of them," he says, "but some of these are enhancers."

"Enhancers?"

His eyes meet mine in the darkness. "They amplify faint traces of electricity to make it easier to detect."

My heart drops to my shoes. "What do we do now?"

Canter shrugs. "Not much we *can* do unless we want to give up on the garden or our plans."

I meet Canter's eyes. "We can't turn back now."

"I know."

Silently, we continue on to the moongarden. Inside, Canter tinkers with the broadcaster, but I can tell his heart's not in it. Mine's not, either. Shielded behind a particularly dense grove of trees, I settle in to practice channeling my emotions into magic, but it doesn't work. I must be too nervous. Every time I so much as reach toward a flower, it seems to lean away from me, like it's scared. I sigh and head back to join Canter.

"Where's Bernie?" I ask, flopping to the ground.

"Maybe he had a late-night project."

I chew my lip. "Maybe."

Canter focuses on the door as if he can will Bernie to come through it. "I bet he'll be here tomorrow."

But he isn't.

CHAPTER THIRTY-TWO

A WEEK LATER, AND THERE'S STILL NO SIGN OF Bernie. "Please just ask him," I plead with Canter the second he sets down his dinner tray. I know we're getting stares from all around the cafeteria, but I don't care. Canter doesn't seem to, either, even though his friends keep shooting bewildered glances in our direction. Let them gossip about what Big Loser Myra Hodger is doing sitting with School Hotshot Canter Weathers. I have more important things to worry about.

"How in the name of Pluto am I going to do that?" Canter spits back. "Hey, Dad. You know that old Rep, Bernie? Where'd he go? Oh, you have no idea what I'm talking about? Okay. Thanks. Good talk."

At that moment, Ms. Curie cuts a path across the cafeteria, passing too close to our table for my liking. I drop my voice. "I'm sure you could figure out a reason. And obviously your dad wouldn't know himself, but I'm sure he could tell you who would."

Maybe it's just my imagination, but Curie seems to slow, her eyes flicking to us more than once.

"Do you really want to go there?" Canter replies. His gaze follows Ms. Curie as she pauses to talk to a teacher. "I start asking questions about Bernie, my dad takes an interest in him, and that could lead him *you know where*."

"Couldn't you make something up?"

"Myra, just having a full-blown conversation with my father will be enough to make him suspicious."

"What do you mean? You guys must talk to each other." I've never really thought to ask how Director Weathers and Canter get along. I assumed well enough. Canter is pretty much the dream son, after all: An Inscription-covered Elector. Smart. Popular. How could Director Weathers not be proud of him?

Canter shrugs. "To be honest, we don't really spend much time together. He's always busy with school stuff." Canter stabs at his plate. "That's just an excuse, though. He was never really interested in any father-son bonding when he was the S.L.A.M. Chemic professor, either." Canter slides his food around some more. "It's not really his thing."

I focus on the cafeteria door as three men in suits walk

in, Director Weathers framed between two others. They've got their backs to us, but the sparkle of expensive cosmic cuff links catches my eye, and my breath catches in my chest as I turn away. "Maybe you just remind him of your mom," I say quietly, "and it makes it hard for him to be normal around you."

Canter shrugs. "That, or he just doesn't like me much."

"'Course he likes you. Shooting stars—even I don't totally dislike you."

Canter laughs. "Oh, you like me. I can tell."

"I said I don't *dislike* you."

"Sure." The corners of Canter's mouth turn up. "Don't worry. You're fairly tolerable yourself. I mean, you're not the absolute worst person on the Moon. I can think of one or two others I like less."

"Thanks a lot," I say, giving his shoulder a light shove. "I'm honored to be so far up your list."

"You should be."

We're quiet for a few moments before deep voices to my right snag my attention. Director Weathers is walking the perimeter of the cafeteria with a gray-suited, gray-haired man on one side and Jake Melfin on the other. I nod toward the trio. "What are they doing here?"

Canter peers past me and scowls. "Donors."

"For what?" Mr. Melfin glances toward our table, and I sink down in my seat.

"S.L.A.M., obviously. He takes them on tours of the school a few times a year, pinging them for contributions."

As Director Weathers passes our table, he nods at Canter, then locks eyes with me. Recognition flashes across his face. His lips press into a thin line before he hurries the others past our table. I wait until they're well out of earshot before turning back to Canter.

"You know what I'm going to say." When he doesn't respond, I press on. "Look, we tried. We've both looked *everywhere*, right? Bernie's not here. The only way we're going to find out where he is, is to ask."

Canter's eyes are dark. "Myra, where do you think he could be if he's not here?"

"I don't know. Maybe they transferred him? Or sent him to wherever Reps go when they retire. What happens when they get too old to do their jobs, anyway?"

"I don't know." Canter shovels a bite of food into his mouth.

"But I'm sure your dad does."

"Yeah, yeah, I get it." Canter sighs. "I'll see what I can do."

I study him another moment, then force a wide grin onto my face. "Great! So you talk to your dad, and by this time tomorrow, we'll be coming up with a plan to deal with Curie."

"You think I'm going to ask him *tonight*?"

I shrug. "Why not? The sooner we figure out how to find Bernie, the sooner things can go back to normal."

The last conversation Bernie and I shared flashes through my mind. Could someone have overheard us mentioning the plants? What would happen to Bernie if they did?

"All right," Canter says. "Let's meet in the garden tonight after curfew."

I throw him a mock salute before he rises with his tray and heads off.

But I can't just sit and wait. Resting my chin on my hand, I try to think of anywhere else Bernie could be. A moment later, I bolt upright and snatch my bag off the floor.

I hurry to the tray collector, then place my tray on the smooth metal surface. It sinks through the counter and disappears, off to be washed and sterilized below, then reappear sparkling at the other end of the counter.

As it slides out of view, I back toward the wall and slip into the kitchen. Like last time, all the Reps working look up at me. I open my mouth to apologize or explain, but before I can, they turn away, resuming their work like I'm not even there. I snap my mouth shut, hurry across the room and out the other side, then count the doors, trying to remember which one led to Bernie's common room.

One, two, three. Then that's a closet. Not this one or the next two . . .

I stop in front of a plain metal door, taking a deep breath before I punch in the entry key. The door slides open and a loud, boisterous voice greets me, along with a wave of chuckling.

A man stands in front of the two couches, frozen mid-gesture, his mouth hanging open. He must have been telling the others a story. A few others are seated, the smiles quickly fading from their faces. A quick scan tells me all I need to know: Bernie's not here.

But maybe someone here can still help me. It's worth a shot.

"Hi." I grin broadly, trying to sound as friendly as possible. The storyteller backs away like I've got some sort of plague. "I was hoping you could help me," I continue, taking another step into the room. "I'm looking for my friend. He was here before. His name's Bernie."

No one answers. A few eye me curiously before looking away. The rest pretend I don't exist.

"Please." I take another step toward the storyteller. "I need to find him. I've looked all over the school."

The man eyes me warily, but there's a glint in his gaze that reminds me of Bernie, so I press on. "My name's Myra," I say. "What's yours?"

"Paul.

"Please tell me where Bernie is, Paul. I need to find him."

"You won't find him here," he says quietly.

"Then where?"

Paul shrugs. "Not sure. He hasn't been back in days."

The others on the couch slowly edge away from us, as if our conversation is toxic.

"Can anyone tell me where he is?" I plead.

"Mr. McNamara," Paul says after a moment. "The janitorial manager. He'll know."

I want to touch Paul's hand, hug him, show him how grateful I am, but I know the only thing he wants is for me to leave.

"Thank you," I say as I slip out the door.

Back in the cafeteria, I pull out my messenger and text Canter about McNamara, asking him to meet me at the janitorial office after he talks to his dad. Then I poke around the school, trying to figure out where exactly the janitorial office is. Finally, I find it tucked in the school's farthest wing on the topmost level. I'm pulling out my messenger to text Canter again when the door swishes open so abruptly, I drop it and it goes clattering to the floor.

Canter storms by me, barely even glancing my way.

"Canter!" I call, scooping up my messenger and hurrying after him. "Canter, where are you going? What happ—"

"Forget it, Myra," he snaps, without looking back. "Just forget the whole thing."

Before I can catch up and demand an explanation, he throws himself into the Anti-Grav Chamber and disappears.

CHAPTER THIRTY-THREE

HOURS LATER, THERE'S STILL NO SIGN OF Canter, and he won't answer my messages. I even went back to McNamara's office and banged on the door until my knuckles ached. No one answered.

I send Canter one last text, then count the minutes to curfew.

The moongarden is empty when I arrive, but at least I have Bin-ro for company. Even he's not his usual chipper, chirping self. He stays at my feet, rolling slowly back and forth.

After what feels like forever, Canter stomps into view.

"It's about time!" I stand and brush the gravel off my pants. "What happened—"

I see his face and freeze. We stand there staring at each other, one of us wide-eyed, the other on the verge of tears.

"Canter—what—are you okay?" I don't want him to confirm what my gut already knows. Tears creep down my cheeks before he can find his voice.

"He's gone." The words sound like curses, the way he spits each one out.

"What do you mean, *gone?*"

"He's been *retired.*"

Bin-ro beeps softly, his light a somber blue.

"What do you mean, *retired?*" My voice trembles as my breath hitches in my chest. "Why can't they just bring him back? Or we can go find him!" I gesture toward the slide as if we should start our search now.

"What do you think they do to retired Reps, Myra?" Canter takes a step closer, and I don't know if he's going to hug me or hit me. "Reps don't just get to go off and lie around at some resort. Retiring a Rep means ending their cycle."

"But Reps are *people*! He's a person. He's Bernie! They can't just take him away." I'm sobbing now, loud, gasping, ugly. But I don't care. "What—what are we going to do?"

"Nothing." It comes out as more of a snarl. Canter grabs a small shovel and hacks away at the ground. He rips out a weed and part of the rosebush nearby, tossing both to the side. "Bernie's gone, Myra. Dead. Star vapor."

"They can't get away with this!" I swipe at my face with my sleeve, but it's no use. The tears keep falling like a meteor shower.

"Who can't, Myra? The rest of the Moon? They. Don't. Care. Get that through your head." Canter moves to another spot, ripping out another handful of green, clearly not caring what he's uprooting.

I follow behind him, bending down and whispering to the plants. Telling them I'm sorry. That Canter's sorry. That he doesn't mean it. He's just hurting. Or angry. Or both. I guess you can be both. One second, all I feel is rage. The next, I can't stop the tears. It's like a fire triggering a sprinkler system, one emotion just rolling into the next.

"Canter, stop." My hand prickles like it's fallen asleep. I look down and gasp as a golden bubble seeps from my palm and drifts toward the plants in Canter's path of destruction. Shock quickly dissolves into understanding and then to panic.

My magic's trying to protect them.

I dart forward and jab my finger at the shimmering orb before he notices, exhaling deeply as it pops and disappears. Guilt floods through me as I shove my hands in my pockets.

Thankfully, Canter doesn't seem to notice anything out of the ordinary. His movements slow like a battery running down. He sinks to the ground, the shovel still gripped tightly in his hand, and rests his forehead on the handle. I kneel beside him and put my hand on his shoulder, but he jerks away so ferociously, I fall backward.

"We *can* do something," I say quietly. "We can find out who did this, and we can *make* them care."

"And then what? It won't bring him back." Canter shakes his head, staring straight ahead. "No one even missed him."

I hurtle to my feet, wiping my face on my sleeve. "Except for us! And if we can show that Bernie meant something to us, that *we* miss him—"

"Don't you get it?" Canter flings the shovel aside and clambers to his feet. "It doesn't matter if you miss someone. *It doesn't matter how unfair it is.* IT DOESN'T MATTER! Missing someone doesn't bring them back. People stay dead."

My feet are rooted to the spot as tears stream down Canter's cheeks. He rubs them away angrily, but they don't stop.

"Canter—" I whisper.

"No one's going to care about all this, either! We're just two stupid kids trying to make something impossible happen. This garden is never going to do anything but cause trouble." He stalks away from me, kicking the shovel as he goes. "I'm done with this place! It's a tomb, and I'm never coming back."

"Canter, wait!" I choke out, but he's already disappeared up the tunnel.

A brittle silence consumes the moongarden.

I sit among the plants for a long time. So long, that I

don't need the reflective metal paper when I finally leave. A few students roam the hall as I shuffle along, hardly seeing where I'm going, not really caring, until—

"Miss Hodger!" yelps Ms. Curie, stumbling out of my path. A chill runs through me as she scans me like I'm a human circuit breaker. "I would ask what you're doing up and alert so early, but I'm afraid the latter isn't at all true."

"Sorry," I mumble, hoping the apology can substitute as an explanation.

Of course it doesn't.

"What are you doing in this hall at this hour?" she asks, her dark hair still swishing back and forth from our near-crash.

"I, er, went for a walk."

"I see." Curie studies me some more. "Remind me again what track you're on."

"Number Whisperer." Saying it aloud almost seems silly now. Nothing could be further from the truth. Not anymore.

"That's right. Hodger. I knew your parents." Her dark eyes drift to my arm.

I've gotten used to leaving my right arm uncovered, thanks to Lila's skill as an Inscription forger. Fortunately, it's helped take the fun out of the Inscription Hunting game for most kids. Unfortunately, my night in the moongarden must have been too much for the most smudge-proof eyeliner in all of Apolloton, because the formulas and tables are now nothing more than a smear across my arm. I hastily shove it behind my back, hoping Ms. Curie didn't notice. "I was uh, on my way to breakfast."

"You were. After your walk."

I don't know if it's a question or a confirmation. Or neither. She seems to be processing something I can't see.

"Go on, then," she finally says, and I try not to show my relief. "The cafeteria will be opening any minute. But, Miss Hodger." My stomach sinks. "There's nothing in this hall except my office. And I prefer to work in *silence*. Am I clear?"

I nod. "I won't come back."

Not right away, anyway. And not without Canter.

CHAPTER THIRTY-FOUR

Fifth Month, 2448

DESPITE MY DETERMINED EFFORTS, IT'S BEEN weeks since Canter abandoned the garden, and he's hardly said a word to me since. When we do speak, it's so he can tell me to go away or leave him alone or to forget the whole thing.

But I can't.

I also can't go back to the moongarden. I've crept out of my room half a dozen times after curfew, only to sneak right back in. It just doesn't feel right going there without the others.

Today will be different. Today I have a plan. I've been watching Canter all week, waiting for the perfect moment. Finally, as he's leaving the cafeteria after lunch, I spot my opportunity. He's the last of his friends to get up from the table, and when he makes his way to the tray collector, I follow.

Walking quietly up behind him, I wait until he's passing the door to the kitchen, then hip-check him so hard he stumbles through.

"What the— Myra! What are you doing?"

I grab his elbow and steer him through the kitchen and out the door into the deserted hall. "You've got to go back to the garden."

"I told you. I'm not going back." He starts to turn away.

"This was your mother's work," I say, grabbing his arm. "It's not finished yet. *She's* not finished yet."

"It *is* finished, Myra," Canter growls, easily pulling away and stepping past me. "She's dead. Bernie's dead. That place is cursed. It's over."

"Not for us!" I insist.

"How can you be sure our plan would even work? You know people will say it's a hoax or a fluke." He shakes his head. "I don't know what happened to my mom, but the garden definitely didn't help her. It might even be the reason she's gone," he finishes, his voice a whisper.

"Then it's even more important that we finish what she started!" I ball my hands into fists. "Whatever happened to her, we can't let it be for nothing, can we?"

He doesn't say anything, so I take it as a signal to press on. "Besides, there's more to show them than just the garden."

"What are you talking about?"

I take a breath and rip up my sleeve. "There's magic, too."

Canter's eyes bulge. "Wh-what are those?"

"Inscriptions," I say, tilting my head to look him in the eye. "Botan Inscriptions." Green vines speckled with curvy, swirling leaves crisscross my arm. Tiny yellow and blue flowers dot them here and there. And beneath my elbow, what I think is the outline of a tree has started to form.

Canter's eyes flick from my face to my arms and back again.

"I'm sorry," I say. "I should have told you. I wanted to. I almost did, when you told me about your mom, but . . ."

"You were scared."

I nod and give him a small smile. "Trusting people isn't really my thing."

The edges of his mouth turn up. "Me, neither. Until now."

I pull my sleeve back down and grin. "It can't just be me and your mom."

"It's not."

Canter's fingers grasp the fabric at his wrist. He hesitates, then slowly pulls up the sleeve of his silver jumpsuit. I'm not at all surprised to see that his right arm is covered in gray Elector Inscriptions—voltage formulas and circuit diagrams and an equation describing Ohm's law of conduction. But there's something else there, too, mixed in with the dark markings. Something green . . .

Canter straightens, his eyes shining in the dim light of the hall. "I'm a Botan, too."

CHAPTER THIRTY-FIVE

LATER THAT NIGHT, WHILE THE REST OF THE school sleeps, Canter and I meet in an empty hallway, halfway to the moongarden.

I elbow him in the ribs. "I still can't believe you didn't tell me."

"You didn't tell me, either!"

"That's different," I hiss. "I don't have another Creer to cover with. Plus, I thought I was the only one. You, at least, knew your mother was a Botan."

Canter shakes his head. "It still doesn't feel real."

I glance sideways at him. "How long have you known?"

"A month or so. I started fiddling with the plants when I was frustrated by the work on the nutrition and lights system, and I started feeling these weird . . . tremors, I guess you could call them. Pulses of energy, but different from when I use my Elector powers. Those are, I don't know, sharp. Intense. These were gentler, like comparing a rake to a feather. It was different, but I recognized the magic." He rubs at the spot where I know a sage-green vine winds around a diagram of a circuit breaker, as if the old Elector Inscription is simply a trellis for it to climb. "I got the Inscription a few days before Bernie—" He blinks and walks faster.

I scramble to catch up. "So what does that mean? Are you an Elector or a Botan?"

Canter shrugs, still walking at lightning speed. "Guess I'll have to figure it out. See which one I'm more drawn to."

I'm practically running to keep pace. "This isn't a hover-ball game," I whisper-yell as I race around another corner. "No one's trying to steal the ball from you."

"No one ever steals the ball from me," Canter says, glancing back over his shoulder with a smirk.

"Well, then, slow down! It's not like the garden's going to disappear. And if I fall trying to keep up with you, it's not going to matter that I've got reflectors on my feet."

"Oh, you're right," Canter says, his voice coated in thick, syrupy sarcasm. "I don't know why I'm in a hurry. It's not like we're breaking any rules being out here. Hey, do you want to go catch a vid-stream in the Rec center? Maybe head to the cafeteria for a snack?"

I clip his shoulder as I trot past. "There's a speed between turbocharged and moonwalk, hotshot. And other personalities besides jerk and super-jerk."

He huffs, shaking his head, but doesn't say another word.

In what feels like no time, we reach the last hallway. "All clear," I whisper, peeking around the corner. "Curie's office is dark."

Still, we tiptoe past her door.

I steal a glance inside, then grab Canter's arm. "It's not there anymore. All the equipment."

He squints through the window and shrugs. "Maybe it was nothing. She could have been working on a project or some demonstration for her class."

"Possible," I reply, sneaking a glance at Canter as we pad down the last corridor.

But all the air seems to leave my lungs as I skid to a halt in front of the moongarden classroom.

Or where the moongarden classroom used to be.

CHAPTER THIRTY-SIX

"IT'S—IT'S GONE." WHERE THE CLASSROOM door should be, there's only wall. Thick, solid, blank wall.

"When was the last time you came?" Canter asks, his voice like gravel.

"Not since we were here together. It didn't feel right going without you. Without Bernie."

Canter glances around, then grabs my elbow. "We've got to get out of here. This hallway could be watched."

We turn back the way we came. "Why would someone do this?"

Canter tugs at his hair. "First, the door's locked. Then Bernie is . . . gone. Now, the garden's sealed. It's too big of a coincidence."

I chew my lip.

He stops and turns to look at me. "What, Myra?"

"Someone might have heard me talking to Bernie in the Rep wing. About the garden."

Canter's eyes bulge. "You didn't tell me."

"You haven't been talking to me for the past month!"

"You could have sent me a message or *something*."

"I sent you a *hundred* messages."

"Not about that!"

I groan and rub my forehead. "The point is, someone could have heard Bernie and me talking."

Canter shakes his head. "Who would even understand what you were talking about?"

"Wouldn't your dad have had to approve—"

"WHAT ON THE MOON IS GOING ON HERE?" A new voice cuts through the silence of the darkened hallway like a sonic boom. Canter and I both jump, stumbling into each other as Ms. Goble marches down the hallway, her eyes blazing like twin suns. "I asked what is going on here, and someone had better answer me. *Now*."

"We were just—"

"I was just going—"

"We didn't—"

"I didn't realize—"

Our half-powered excuses pile up and up, but eventually, we both fall silent, our eyes glued to our metal-coated sneakers.

Ms. Goble's foot taps impatiently. "No excuse, then?"

We shake our heads.

"That's right, because there *is* absolutely no excuse for being out past curfew. And what are *those*?"

I have to look up to see where she's pointing, but of course it's at our feet. I drop my head again.

"Reflector paper," Canter mumbles.

"Excuse me?"

"We—uh—I invented it," he says, eyes still downcast. "I used a lasersaw to slice down ion metal into sheets, then charged it to reflect sensor beams."

"Really, Mr. Weathers," Ms. Goble replies, her foot still clicking. "I expected so much better from you. And you, Miss Hodger. Especially after our . . . discussions." I glance up and see her shaking her head in disappointment. "Though I suppose I do understand your . . . reasoning better now." Her eyes flick from my face to Canter's.

Reasoning? What does she— Oh. I glance sideways at Canter. She thinks I wanted to stay at S.L.A.M. because . . . I feel my face blush hotter than the sun.

"N-no, Ms. Goble," I say quickly, stepping away from Canter. "It's not like that at all. It's uh . . ." I look desperately at Canter for help.

He shoots me a confused look, and I groan.

"S.L.A.M. policy does not prohibit students from dating," Ms. Goble continues, "but the curfew is in place for good reason."

"D-dating?" Canter stammers, his eyes widening with realization. "We're not— She's not— We're just *friends,* Ms. Goble!"

"I don't have a particle interest in your personal business, Mr. Weathers, so long as your personal business occurs during regular school hours under appropriate supervision. I'm very disappointed in you both. I will be discussing this with your parents. And you will each, of course, have a week of detention."

"A week!" Canter yelps.

"Our parents!" I squeak.

"Yes. And I'll be confiscating *those*"—Ms. Goble juts her chin toward our feet again—"and any more you have hidden in your rooms. Let's go."

She marches us back to the dorms. My roommates are less than pleased to be awoken by me and Goble, and even less so when she takes Lila's roll of reflector paper. Thankfully, I think fast enough to pretend Lila's dresser is mine. At least she won't get in trouble, too. Canter shoots me a miserable look from the hall as Ms. Goble barks a good-night and firmly shuts the door. Ignoring my roommates' questions and protests, I climb into bed and pull the covers up over my head.

As the other girls drift back to sleep, I stare at the underside of my blanket.

What do we do now?

CHAPTER THIRTY-SEVEN

A FEW DAYS LATER, I'M HOLDING MY HAND over a doorway keypad, my fingertips brushing the buzzer. *This is weird. This is so weird.* If any of the other kids at school saw me about to buzz Canter Weathers's compartment, they'd probably think I was there to blow it up, not visit.

I shake my head, clearing any lingering doubts. With our reflector paper confiscated and our whereabouts limited strictly to class, the cafeteria, our dorm rooms, and detention hall, this was our only option.

I stab the button like I'm squishing a bug.

There's a hum from inside, then footsteps. The door slides open, revealing a tousle-haired Canter in sweats and a hoverball jersey. It's weird to see him in something other than his silver jumpsuit.

"Nice outfit. What were you doing? Napping?"

"Maybe I was." Canter smirks and leans against the door-frame.

"You are seriously elderly." I brush by him into the apartment. The inside is as beige as the Moon is gray. Beige walls, beige furniture, beige pictures hanging on the wall.

"Hey, hang on!" The door slides shut behind us, and Canter steps in front of me. "I haven't finished analyzing whether you're worthy to enter my living quarters."

I snort. "If *you're* worthy, I definitely am. I do feel like I should have worn something khaki, though. To fit in."

Canter laughs and glances around. "Dad thinks boring is prestigious. And nothing is more boring than beige."

A voice drifts from another room, and we both jerk our heads around.

"Oh, and also, my dad is home."

"You could have warned me," I snap, edging back to the door, my stomach dropping to my toes. "Should I leave?"

Canter and I have been meeting in the cafeteria during the lunch block (the only time we can these days) and decided that Priority One is to get inside the moongarden to make sure it's okay. We think there might be another access point—maybe through the vents in the ceiling. We need to get the school blueprints to know for sure. Priority Two is finding out where the work order to seal the class-room originated from, along with who issued the order to have Bernie's cycle ended. To do all that, we need to get into Director Weathers's office, which means he *definitely* can't be home.

Canter grabs my arm, before I can flee. "My dad's still leaving. Just not until dinnertime, which is good because it means he'll be out later."

"But won't he wonder—"

Canter shakes his head. "I told him I'm tutoring a first-year for her Elector class as part of my detention. It was the only way I could get around the fact that I'm grounded."

"And he'll buy that?"

"Oh yeah. I talked it up real good. Said the student was way behind and could definitely use my help. I wasn't even lying about—"

I punch him in the arm as hard as I can.

He just grins back at me. "C'mon, we can wait for him to leave in my room." I follow Canter down a narrow hallway. "Did your parents hear from Goble, too?" he asks over his shoulder.

"Yeah, but I just told them I was sneaking into the modulab to study."

"And they believed you?"

I shoot him a serious look. "Of *course*. What else would their math prodigy daughter be doing wandering the school in the middle of the night? Then my dad told me an epically long story about how he once got left in Apolloton because he was so distracted by a formula he was trying to decipher, he missed the S.L.A.M. Crawler." I shake my head. "And not by minutes, either. *Hours*."

Canter snorts. "At least you're not grounded."

"No, but now my parents have been checking up on me about twelve times a day, asking how my studying is going, what I got for homework, what I ate for lunch. . . . I swear Goble put them up to it."

I follow Canter through a doorway at the end of the hall, and almost have to shield my eyes. Bright shades of magenta, lime green, neon blue, and pretty much every other color blare back at me.

"Crashing comets, Canter. Did you electrocute a box of crayons or something?"

He chuckles. "Guess I'm just not very *prestigious*." He flops on his bed and I take the seat by his desk. There's a projection frame resting there: a pretty woman with auburn hair beams back at me.

"My mom," Canter whispers when he sees me looking.

"She was really pretty."

"Yeah, she was." Canter looks away, tilting his head back to stare at the ceiling.

Director Weathers's voice bleeds through the wall. It sounds like he's yelling. "Is everything okay in there?" I ask.

Canter glances at me. "It's fine. He's always yelling at someone about something."

"School stuff?"

"Mostly."

A chair scrapes, and suddenly there are footsteps in the hall. Canter tosses a bookpod at me and I jam the power key, silently willing it to turn on. The page glows to life the same instant the door slides open. I duck my face behind the screen, turning away so Director Weathers won't recognize me.

"Canter, I'm leaving— Oh. Who's this? A friend? You know you're groun—"

"I told you I was tutoring a first-year."

"That's right. Well, let's wrap it up by eight. It's a school night. I'll have one of the kitchen Reps send something up."

"Later."

As soon as the front door shuts, I blow out a breath, tossing the bookpod aside. "Let's get started."

Director Weathers's office is locked, but Canter scans his pendant and the door swings open.

"Why does he bother locking it if your pendant gives you access anyway?"

"It doesn't." Canter's face goes pink. "I may have swapped my pendant with his when he took the call."

I raise my eyebrows. "Won't you get in a ton of trouble?"

He shrugs, leading me into the room. "Nah. He probably won't even notice, and if he does, I'll just say it was an accident."

I'm uneasy, half expecting Director Weathers to come bursting back in at any moment. The room's nothing special—more beige, obviously. A square table sits in the center of the space with four chairs arranged around it; a small couch is against one wall; a big desk is in front of another. Canter slides behind his dad's desk, powering on the computer. I pull up a chair next to him as he starts tapping on files.

"Do you know what you're looking for?"

Canter shakes his head. "Not exactly. There were renovations on the school earlier this year, so he must have sent the Tekkies who did the work blueprints. Maybe if I can find their contracts, it'll be there."

"Maybe it'll show what triggered the newest *renovation*."

Canter nods. "There have to be notes, even if it was Reps doing the work." He taps a folder labeled *Contracts*, but the contents isn't about renovations—it's about the Reps. There are tons of files. Hundreds.

We sift through transfer contracts, work contracts, even what looks like the contracts Reps sign when they first enter the program, before they become Reps. Those are all pretty much the same. They list the date the "original individual" signed onto the program, what field or industry they wanted their clones to be used in, how many repetition cycles they'd agree to, and how much the original was paid based on the number of cycles. There's also a lot of legal language about what happens if the Repetition leaves the program early. I can't understand most of it, but the terms "fine" and "fee" jump out at me, paired with very large numbers.

Unfortunately, nothing we find has anything to do with Bernie or the reason his cycle was ended. Or who decided to end it.

Canter closes the folder, and we keep searching. Finally, we find another labeled *Labor*, and within that, *Work Orders*.

I gasp. "That's it!"

"No kidding," Canter snaps, tapping the folder. A small box demanding a password flashes across the screen.

"Blast it!" I clench my hands into fists on the desktop. "Why would those be password protected?"

"Hang on," Canter murmurs, rapidly typing and retyping in the password box.

As he works, I study the room. A projected slideshow of photos glows from the corner of the desk. Canter when he was young, probably no more than five or six years old. A wedding picture. Director Weathers looks so different—handsome, happy. A picture of a redheaded girl, who must be Fiona, surrounded by kids, some of whom look familiar. What must be a young Ms. Goble leans next to Fiona.

A grinning boy in a Chemic-purple sweatshirt jumps out, too: Director Weathers as a young teen. He looks almost identical to Canter. The kid-version of Ms. Curie stands on the other side of Fiona, an arm around her shoulders.

"Got it!" Canter calls out, throwing his hands up in the air.

The folder is almost everything we'd hoped for: The blueprints for the school. Even the work order to seal the classroom leading to the moongarden, though it doesn't say why the room was blocked off. But it does say who originated the request.

"Ms. Curie?"

Canter crinkles his forehead. "Why would she do that?"

"I don't know." I tap the screen, blowing up the work order.

Canter leans in. "That's my dad's handwriting."

"Maybe she went to his office to request it, and he wrote out the order."

"Maybe." But Canter doesn't sound convinced.

"I guess it doesn't really matter," I say after a moment. "We have the blueprints and a lead on who wanted the classroom sealed, even if we don't know for certain why."

Canter presses a few buttons on the screen, then holds up his lanyard, and a copy of the blueprints projects from his pendant onto the wall. "I'll study this tonight to see if I can find a way in."

I tap my pendant to his, then project my own copy to the wall. "I'll look, too. You've got another job to worry about."

"What's that?"

"Finding out why Curie wanted the moongarden closed."

CHAPTER THIRTY-EIGHT

BY THE NEXT AFTERNOON, I'VE GOT THE school's layout memorized, but I'm no closer to getting back inside the moongarden. There are plenty of vents near where the garden is hidden, but there is also a big problem. Neither the lab nor the moongarden are on the plans, and even though I know they're in the center of the school, it's impossible to tell which ducts might lead inside. I've got it narrowed to about a dozen, after tracing all the possible angles and paths of the ones nearby, but unfortunately none of their access points are easy to get to.

A good hour before curfew, I set out to patrol the school again, scoping out the various options, when a voice behind me calls, "What are you doing? Taking an evening stroll?"

I round on Canter and cross my arms. "Aren't you

supposed to be figuring out why Curie requested the classroom sealed?"

"Er, that didn't go so well," he says, his grin melting away. "I started asking about the renovation projects, trying to see if she'd mention the work order, but she ended up volunteering me to help out a Tekkie team with a project on the roof."

"Oh, that's just interstellar," I say, crossing my arms. "I'm here studying blueprints until my eyes bleed and you're taking cool side projects for extra credit."

"Extra credit?" Canter says, his mouth falling open. "I'm going to freeze my Inscriptions off in a spacesuit, trying to extend the electrical pathways into their stupid new design while you're wandering around the nice, warm, grav-controlled hallways. Did you at least find the vents that lead to the garden?"

"Yes," I say, giving the hallway a quick scan to make sure no one is around, then pointing my pendant at the wall, projecting the blueprints onto it. "I found about twelve."

Canter squints at the plans. "How can you even tell which ones might?"

I spout off some calculations and angle equations, pointing to this duct and that, while he stares at me with a glazed look.

"Are you sure you don't have any Number Whisperer

magic?" he finally asks. "I don't even know what language you were speaking."

"That's all just theory. The point is, I don't know how to tell which of these leads inside, and it's going to be hard enough to check even one of them out."

"So, what do we do?"

I stare up at the ceiling and sigh. *If only there was a way to use my Botan magic to figure out which is the right access point.*

Eyes wide, I whip my head toward Canter. "I've got an idea."

"Are you sure you're doing it right?" he asks, brow furrowing.

"Of course I'm not sure," I snap, and press my hand back to the wall. It's the tenth location we've checked with zero luck. "Lila said Mender magic has to do with your feelings. The first time I found the moongarden, I thought the classroom wall outside felt warm, but I don't think that was right. I think it was the garden calling to me. Telling me how to get inside."

"That . . . doesn't really make sense," Canter says slowly.

I sear him with a glare.

"But as long as it makes sense to you, give it a shot," he quickly adds.

"It doesn't make sense to me. That's the problem." I have no idea if this will work, but it's all we've got. If the plants can't send me some sort of signal where to go, we might never find a new entrance.

"Maybe you're too far away from the vent?" Canter says.

"Maybe." I close my eyes and wait. For what, I'm not sure. When nothing happens, I push off the wall with a frustrated groan. "I can't really explain it, but the garden . . . it always had a sort of sound to me. It wasn't exactly noise. More like—"

"—a pulse running through it."

"Exactly." I study him for a moment. "You hear it, too, then?"

He glances around and activates the blueprint projection. "A little. I can't really tell if I'm picking up on the plant's electricity or the garden's magic, though. My Elector powers are still stronger. I can feel electricity humming through the walls, flowing through wires. It's almost like a static crackle, but the sound is in my brain rather than my ears. It's different with the plants. For me, anyway."

I nod slowly, then turn back to the projection. "There are only a few more places to check."

"Let's try this one," he says, pointing to a duct a couple corridors over from the moongarden classroom. I nod, and we head off toward our new target.

As we approach the familiar hall, I cringe and will my

feet forward. We turn the corner, and I skid to a stop. "Um, hi, Ms. Curie."

She jumps at the sound of her name, her hands jolting from where she'd had them pressed against the wall— exactly where the door to Fiona's classroom used to be. "What are you two doing here?" she snaps. "It's almost curfew."

Canter and I exchange a confused look. "I was just telling Myra about that project I'm going to be doing with the Tekkies. I was showing her the site."

Ms. Curie's eyes narrow. "You mean the project on the *roof*?"

"Yeah." Canter shifts his weight. "We were heading to the supply closet first. To get a repulsor lift."

"And I remembered your office was nearby," I add, "so we thought we'd come ask you to approve it."

"I see."

Footsteps echo from around the corner and we all freeze before an older woman in Rep overalls shuffles timidly into the hallway. Canter and I both breathe a sigh of relief, but Ms. Curie looks tenser than ever.

"These students need to sign out a repulsor lift from the supply closet," she says to the woman. "You can put me down as approving the request." The woman nods and disappears down the hall. Ms. Curie turns back to us. "Be careful," she finally says after a tense moment, her gaze shifting from Canter's face to mine. "You both need to be careful."

"Uh, we will, Ms. Curie," Canter says.

She stares at us a beat longer, then without another word, turns and leaves, her steps echoing as she disappears down the hall.

"What was that about?" I murmur. Canter shakes his head.

A few minutes later, the Rep woman returns, guiding a repulsor lift in front of her.

"Thank you," I say as she pushes it toward us.

When the woman's gone from view, Canter and I exchange a look, and some of the strain of the past hour melts away.

"On to duct eleven?" he asks.

"Maybe eleven is our lucky number," I say hopefully. "Because we're running out of options."

We walk quickly down the hall, around the corner, and down the next. In no time, I'm hovering on the repulsor lift six feet in the air. There's a charging station in the hall beneath the access vent in the ceiling. I hold on to it with one hand to steady myself as I trail my fingers over the seams cut deep into the metal. Immediately, I can tell that something is different. The air seems to ripple and shift around me, like I'm moving in water. Tilting myself up, I press my ear to the vent. There's no audible sound, and yet I hear something. A lot of somethings. Like a silent symphony.

"This is it," I whisper.

Canter's eyes flutter shut, and after a minute, he nods. "I feel it, too."

I pull the lever and the lift swoops toward the ground. Canter squeezes on, and I fly us carefully back up. "How are we going to get the cover off?"

"I can handle that," Canter says, pointing an index finger at one of the bolts holding the grate in place. A zap and then a whirring sound follow, and the bolt drops into his palm.

"How'd you do that?" I ask, not even trying to filter the awe out of my voice.

His eyes sparkle as his cheeks flush pink. "I used my electricity to activate the bolt sensors so they'd spin, same as a hydrodrill would. I just had to give it the same charge."

"That was pretty cool."

Canter tilts his head in a mock bow. "Thank you, thank you. I'm here all week."

I bump his shoulder with mine. "All right, hotshot. We'll both be here all week if you don't get moving."

I keep watch while Canter zaps the remaining bolts, and then together we gently raise the cover and climb inside the duct, pulling the lift in behind us. Canter gives the hallway a quick scan before clicking the cover shut.

"Let's go," I say, then start crawling, Canter close on my heels. The farther we go, the stronger the energy buzzes in my head. "We're getting close." After several minutes, we come to some sort of intersection. The duct continues on in six different directions.

"Oh no," I whisper.

"Can you tell which way to go?" Canter asks. "I feel like the pulsing is everywhere."

"We're too close to the garden. I hear the humming all around, too. It's . . . it's too loud." I slowly twist my body in the tight space, turning back to face Canter. "Maybe if we look at the blueprint again, I can figure out where some of these ducts lead."

"But you said we're close. We could be at the garden for all we know. It could be right below us." He rubs his hands over his face. "We might not even be able to see this intersection. The center of the school is just open space on the blueprints. We need to find another access point to know for sure."

"We don't have time to check every direction," I insist. "Not today, anyway. If either of us gets caught breaking curfew again, we'll be on house arrest for sure."

"We must be really, really close," Canter murmurs. "Why don't you, I don't know, ask the plants for help?"

"What do you—*oh!*" I stifle all the questions and processes and theories shuffling through my brain, and simply do what Canter suggests: I *ask*. Something inside me reaches outward. The feeling reminds me of when I wrote all those messages to Hannah. I'd hover over the Send button and immediately my chest would ache, longing for a reply. A message. Anything.

My hand drifts up as I think of the garden somewhere below us, and a familiar pang strikes me as I remember what it felt like to be inside the garden. I miss it. It's almost as painful as when I think of Bernie.

With a start, I recall all the times my magic worked. It was always tied to how I was feeling. That couldn't have been a coincidence.

My heart aching for the garden, I reach my hand out as if to brush against the plants . . . and something grabs ahold of it. My eyes fly open as I stifle a scream.

"Crashing comets!" Canter says with a gasp.

A vine winds its way up my arm, the other end disappearing down one of the small tunnels ahead—leading us back to the garden.

I grin and look over my shoulder at Canter. "We're in."

We crawl along the duct, guided by the vine, until we make a turn around a bend and are greeted by a wall. The vine disappears through a mesh panel like the one in the hallway. It takes us a few awkward minutes of twisting and turning past each other before Canter and I manage to switch places.

In practically a nanosecond, he has the bolts off. He lifts the cover and peers down. Even with my obstructed view, I can see plants sprawling out beneath us. We're on the very edge of the garden. A delicious aroma greets me, an exhilarating blend of perfume and soil. I inhale deeply and can practically feel the balmy air cleansing me from head to toe. Canter climbs out first, and we slide carefully down using branches to ease our way to the ground.

"*Weee-oooo, weeee-oooo.*" A blaring siren cuts through the silence. Something bursts out of the brush, spinning in circles around our feet.

"Bin-ro!" I exclaim. "We're excited to see you, too, but can you choose a sound that doesn't sound like an alarm system next time?"

He whistles and twirls a few more times. Then his beeping shuts off and the garden is silent. Too silent. It takes a few seconds for the reason to sink in.

"This is the first time we've been back here since—" I blink furiously, trying to fight off tears.

"Bernie," Canter finishes, his own eyes glassy.

"He would have wanted us to do this," I say. "I mean, he would have tried to talk us out of it, but deep down, it's what he would have wanted." Swiping my sleeve across my face, I try to reboot my features into a look of determination. "It's what he and your mom were working toward before . . . before whatever happened."

Canter nods, then drifts to where the half-assembled broadcaster lies in a heap. A few feet away, a rake rests on the ground. He bends and picks it up, propping it carefully against a nearby tree. "We'll do it," he says after a while. "We'll show the galaxy. For both of them."

I nod and make my way over to a small bush a dingy shade of sepia. Mustiness hangs heavy in the air around it, hints of decay wafting toward me as I settle onto a patch of moss and lay my palm against its base, as if checking its temperature. The leaves are so dry, they scrape together when I touch them, flaking off and fluttering to the ground. I close my eyes and imagine how the shrub looked a few weeks ago—lush and green and healthy. Love for the tiny plant rushes through me, followed by a wave of happiness. When I open my eyes, the bush glows as golden as the sun, and then all the brown disappears, transforming into a vibrant emerald.

Canter reaches a hand out to me, and I slap my palm to his.

"You channel your new magic," he says, kneeling down beside the pile of parts, "and I'll use my old one."

"Deal," I say, and we both set to work.

CHAPTER THIRTY-NINE

A WEEK LATER, CANTER AND I PEER AROUND the corner of the Elector hallway, making sure the coast is clear. Most kids are in class now. We've been working in the moongarden every day between the end of afternoon classes and curfew, but now we've reached a dead end. A temporary one, anyway.

"We're not going to get a much better shot," Canter whispers, eyeing the door at the far side of the hall. "Still, if anyone walks by, we're going to have a hard time explaining what we're doing messing around in the supply closet without a teacher."

"You just overload the lock with a power surge, and then walk away," I say firmly. "I'll take care of the rest."

Canter frowns. "But if anyone sees you—"

"I'm getting kicked out of here in a few weeks anyway,

unless we get this broadcaster built. You're an Elector. You belong here."

"You do, too," he replies, shaking his head. "There's got to be a way around your Creer test."

"There is. Broadcasting the garden to the galaxy and proving plants aren't bad so I can stay at S.L.A.M. as a Botan."

"You'll still need a teacher," Canter reminds me.

"There've got to be more Botans out there. Once we prove our garden is safe and show the galaxy that a couple of Novice Botans just saved the food cloning process, loads more will pop up. I know it."

"That's a tall order," he says with a sigh, "but I'm not letting you get booted out of here."

"So bust the lock and *go!*"

Canter rolls his eyes. "See, this is why you can't leave. What am I going to do without you bossing me around?"

"You'll get a lot less done, that's for sure." I scan the hallway again. "You know, like right now. Curie is probably going to blow a circuit that I'm skipping again. And here we are, just chitchatting the period away."

"All right, I'm going." Canter darts into the hall, while I keep watch. He reaches the closet door, pausing briefly in front of it, before laying his hands on the access panel. An instant later, he nods at me, then disappears down the next corridor.

I step out into the hallway and retrace his steps. I hit the key, and the panel slides open. Then, I rummage around, snagging the parts and tools Canter had described, stuffing them into my bag.

"Ahem!" A familiar-sounding fake cough echoes from down the next hall and I quickly close my bag and shut myself inside the closet, thanking my lucky constellations that Canter decided to hang back instead of leaving like I told him to.

"Mr. Weathers, shouldn't you be in class?" Ms. Goble's voice sends a chill down my spine. If she catches me cutting, her cascading decimals will chase me straight to Director Weathers's office.

"I . . . was headed to the bathroom but then I . . . uh . . . got lost," Canter replies weakly.

"Amateur," I mutter. An array of questions, admonishments, and detention details echo down the hallway as Ms. Goble unleashes her wrath on Canter. I hold my breath and wait.

The scolding fades, and then clicking footsteps are coming closer and closer. I squeeze my eyes shut, asking all the powers of the universe to keep Goble from opening the supply closet. The footsteps sound right outside the door. . . .

I wince, waiting for the door to fly open. It doesn't, but a new patter of footsteps echo through the hall.

"Sandra!" Ms. Goble calls, and my stomach drops to my shoes. "I was hoping to catch you. I thought you had class."

"Just first-year theory," comes Ms. Curie's muffled reply. "They're working on an assignment. I have my Elector-tracks trying to power on a light bulb, and the room's not very bright, if you know what I mean."

"They're just first-years, Sandra," Ms. Goble scolds. I can practically see her looking down her nose at Ms. Curie as she says it.

"First-years who will be taking their Creer test in a few weeks," Ms. Curie responds, her voice tense. "So what are you doing in Elector territory?"

"I need a battery for my messenger dock, but I don't have access to this supply closet."

"I think I can help you there," Curie replies.

I whip my head around, looking for something, any-thing, to hide me from view. There's nothing. I cringe, waiting for the inevitable.

"Wait," Curie says, the door still shut. "What sort of battery?"

"A T2-mini."

"Oh! I have one in my pocket."

Ms. Goble chuckles, and I think I might pass out from the tension.

"Yup, here it is," Curie replies.

"I can always count on you to have an Elector-supply closet's stock of resources on you at all times, ever since we were kids."

Curie snorts a laugh. "That's why Fiona nicknamed me *Pockets*, remember?"

"I do." Goble's reply is so soft I barely catch it through the panel.

"Don't do that," Ms. Curie says sharply, and I jump. "Don't get all misty. You know I can't stand it."

"Sandra, calm down," Ms. Goble says. "You've been one spark away from an explosion since her classroom was sealed."

"Fiona's gone, and now her classroom's gone, too." She laughs coldly. "All thanks to me."

My eyes bulge. *What's thanks to her? Fiona being gone, the classroom, or both?*

"The director told me you requested the garden be sealed off," Ms. Goble says carefully.

"Of course he did," Ms. Curie sneers. "Did he tell you why?"

"He said you were convinced someone was accessing the . . . room's hidden features."

My hands tighten around my bag.

"Not *someone*, Val. His son. I told our *dear director* that Canter was headed down the exact same path as his mother, and he'd better nip it in the bud, if you'll excuse the expression. That boy will end up the same as her if he's not careful."

"You're being dramatic." Goble's voice is tinged with worry. "And how do you even know it's Canter? Robert mentioned a girl to me."

"Oh, yes. A girl. A Rep. It's a big plant conspiracy."

"Keep your voice down," Ms. Goble hisses.

"Why? I'm the one causing all the trouble, remember? What does it matter if someone else overhears?"

"Sandra." Ms. Goble's voice is deadly serious. "You need to let this go."

"You know I can't. I'm too entwined. I have a pretty clear idea what Canter and the girl have planned, and I'll stop them if it's the last thing I do."

"It's sealed now," Ms. Goble reminders her. "It's over. They won't be able to get back inside."

"This is Fiona's son we're talking about," Ms. Curie says grimly. "Not to mention Claire and Joe Hodger's kid. Stubbornness and craftiness united in one goal. If anyone can figure out a scheme to get back inside, they will."

"Myra Hodger is wrapped up in this, too?" Ms. Goble says, and I tense inside the closet. "That's very interesting. I'll have to keep a closer eye on her."

"Don't bother. I've put some things in motion that

should alert me if they find another way back in. Robert's got his head buried in moondust, so I have to be the one to handle this."

"Your obligations with that garden ended when the shuttle exploded."

"No," Ms. Curie says quietly. "That's when they really began. I'm sorry. I've got to get back to my class."

"Sandra, wait," Goble calls, her voice drowned out by Curie's retreating steps.

"I've got to go, Val."

For a moment, there's silence. Ms. Goble must still be standing outside the door in the empty hall. Maybe she's turning Ms. Curie's words over in her mind, just like I am.

Finally, her footsteps click slowly away. To be safe, I count to a hundred before easing open the closet door and slipping back into the empty hallway, shifting my heavy backpack on my shoulders. The contents may only be a jumble of bolts, surge connectors, and converters, but right now, they're the most valuable thing on the Moon. Without them, there's no broadcaster. And without the broadcaster, Curie will succeed in silencing the garden for good.

CHAPTER FORTY

LATER THAT DAY, WHILE THE REST OF THE school is at dinner, Canter and I plan to meet in the modulab. While I wait, I use Mom's log-in to access her university network, looking for any new updates on the food cloning problems or articles from the university now that they've implemented the MFI menu.

The students do not disappoint. Half the articles on the school website are about the new food. Apparently, some Chemic students conducted experiments on it, and they concluded that the new food has no nutritional value. "If we're eating only the imitation products," one Chemic student observed, "we'll starve."

Another headline catches my eye: "Lunar University Students Organize Protest Over New School Food. Colleges on Mars and Venus Settlements Plan Protests for

Next Week." My eyes bulge. The shortages are spreading across the solar system.

"What's up?" Canter asks, making me jump. He chuckles as he settles into the putty-lounger next to mine, stretching it out like a hammock. I hand him the computer, watching his eyes widen as he reads. "This is not good."

"It's spreading everywhere. Of course, Mr. Melfin's trying to convince the Settlements that everything's fine. That it's just hotheaded kids complaining about every little thing, like they have for centuries. He even tried to say S.L.A.M. endorsed his nutritional junk."

Canter's knuckles go white as he clutches the screen. "'"The director of the Scientific Lunar Academy of Magic, Robert Weathers, has reported that his students are thrilled with the new menu," said Mr. Melfin, CEO of MFI. "Perhaps these college students are under the misguided illusion that the attention they're receiving from their amateur experiments will increase their career prospects following graduation. Or they're simply trying to find a way to get out of class."'" He winces. "My dad will not like being quoted in this."

"It gets worse. Look." I point to another tab. "Here it says MFI will be rolling out their food to grocery stores next week."

"So the food cloning isn't fixed, and the stockpiles of real food are gone."

"Basically." I chew my lip. "Or Mr. Melfin is trying to use the publicity as an excuse to sell more of his fake food."

"Either way, looks like we need to hurry up," Canter says grimly.

"And there's more bad news," I say, filling him in on the conversation between Curie and Goble. By the time I've finished, Canter looks as pale as a white dwarf star.

"So Curie definitely knows about the garden, probably knows what we're planning, and has made it her mission to stop us?"

"Pretty much."

"Why does she even care?"

I shrug. "She and your mom were friends. Maybe she's trying to protect you since your mom can't."

"The plants didn't lasso my mom's shuttle and crash it. What does the garden have to do with what happened to her?"

"I don't know . . . but Curie was definitely connecting what happened to your mom with the garden."

"Now you sound like a conspiracy theorist."

I shove his putty lounger so hard, it nearly dumps him onto the floor. "I'm just repeating what I heard! I guess it doesn't matter, so long as we get the broadcaster finished before Curie finds out we found a way back inside."

"Sounds like she might already know." He nods at the

computer, where shapes and lines fill the screen like a web. "Good thing the broadcaster is almost finished, and now we have a way to use it."

"What is that?" I ask, leaning closer.

"The public network," Canter explains, his voice full of wonder. "I hacked into it."

I gasp. "You're kidding. How?"

"Doesn't matter. The point is, we're in. If we go to the garden before curfew, we can stay there all night, finish the broadcaster, and have the garden vid-streaming by the morning."

"The moongarden's ready, too. All the new crops Bernie planted are ripe." Excitement fizzes inside me. After everything, we're almost ready to show the garden to the galaxy. "Even if Curie knows we're inside, there's no way she's crawling through the ducts. How's she going to get to us?"

"She can't," Canter says slowly. "Not if we stay until we're streaming."

We pack up and leave the modulab. Canter heads to the garden while I swing by my room to grab my bag full of stolen parts.

I scan my pendant on the door and scramble inside. Lila's hunched over her computer, working. The others must still be at dinner.

"Hey, Myra," Lila says, her eyes still fixed on her screen. "How was dinner?"

"Didn't go," I say, scooping up my bulging backpack and turning toward the door. "Got to run. Sorry."

Lila looks up. "Are you going to the garden?" she whispers.

I nod and pause. "I think tonight's the night," I say breathlessly, and her eyes go wide.

"It's done?"

"Almost. And just in time." I tell her about the articles from the Lunar University network and the protests across the galaxy. "So we may be there a while."

"I'll cover for you if I can," Lila says, deep in thought. "I can say you're in the Mender wing with a stomach bug."

"Perfect! Thanks a lot, Lila."

"No problem." She beams up at me. "Need me to touch up your Inscriptions before you go?"

"No time," I say. Hopefully by tomorrow, I'll never have to display fake Inscriptions again. "But tha—"

Pounding on the door makes us both jump. We exchange a terrified look, then Lila leaps off her chair and pushes me behind a dresser, blocking me from view. "Stay there," she whispers.

She hurries across the room, sliding the door open.

"Is Myra here?" Canter asks frantically, and I pop out from behind the dresser.

"What's wrong?"

He looks nervously at Lila. "It's fine," I assure him. "She's the good one."

"Oh, phew. Hey, Lila," he says, shooting her a quick smile. But his expression turns back to panic as he runs his hands through his hair. "The repulsor lift is gone. Someone must have found it. And I can't ask Ms. Curie for another one. She'll—"

"The Mender wing has them," Lila interrupts. "They have a bunch for people to use if they get injured or sick."

"That could work," I say.

"You couldn't sneak one out, though," says Lila. "You'd have to get by too many people But if you *needed* one, they'd just give it to you."

"But what reason can we give for needing one?" Canter asks. "It's not like I can lie and say I'm injured. They'll know."

I pace the room, the wheels in my head spinning. "Lila, do your powers work in reverse?" I ask suddenly.

She cocks an eyebrow at me. "What do you mean?"

"I know you can heal injuries, but can you create them?"

"I've never tried, but maybe?" she says slowly, her gaze flicking between Canter and me. "It won't be fun, though."

A few minutes later, I'm limping down the hall, my swollen ankle throbbing with every step. "You. Owe. Me." I grip Canter's elbow, grinding my teeth against the pain. Lila hurries along at my other side.

"I told you I would do it," Canter snaps back, sweat beading at his temples as he helps support my weight.

"Your dad is here. If you show up in the Mender wing injured, they're a lot more likely to call him than they will be to call my parents."

"The Mender on duty will reverse it as soon as you get there," Lila says apologetically. "But it'll take a little while for it to feel totally back to normal. That's why we have the lifts. The magic works, but it's not instantaneous."

"I wish the injuring part wasn't instantaneous, either."

"I didn't even know I could create a sprain," Lila says thoughtfully. "I've never tried, obviously."

"Well, I think you're a pro," I grind out. "Okay, you two hang back while I go in and get the lift. The fewer questions we get, the better."

I limp the rest of the way. Five minutes later, I zip back out, seated on the repulsor lift in slightly less pain.

"Good to go?" Lila asks.

"Definitely better," I tell her. "Thanks, Lila. For everything."

"Good luck," she says. "I call the first tour of the garden once the galaxy knows about it."

"You got it," I say, whizzing by her down the hall, Canter jogging to keep up.

The corridors are deserted, thankfully, except for a man

cleaning the floor. As we pass, he looks up and catches my eye. I nod, but he doesn't react, which isn't unusual for a Rep. What is strange is that he also doesn't look away.

I zip up to the vent, sending the lift back down to Canter. Once we're inside the garden, we get straight to work on the broadcaster. Canter does most of the heavy lifting, while I hobble around handing him tools and checking on the plants.

"Almost showtime," I whisper to them, excitement bubbling up in my chest.

"Nearly there," Canter says with a grunt, tossing a tool behind him into the dust. "Just got to—"

A loud grinding sound somewhere behind the far wall drowns out the rest of his sentence. We stare at each other wide-eyed.

"Is that Bin-ro?" Canter asks anxiously.

The little robot scoots out from the bushes, sharp beeps accenting a clear *no*.

"It's her," Canter whispers.

"Hide," I bark, jumping to my feet. We scramble into some dense shrubs, crouching down and peeking through the leaves and branches.

Crunching and shuffling drift from near the chute connecting to the lab. A man in Rep overalls trudges out of the brush before disappearing into another part of the garden—it's the same one I saw cleaning the hallway. I grab

Canter's hand and he squeezes back hard enough to turn his knuckles white.

Before I can react—before I can even think about how to react—a stern voice rises above the noise of the man's footsteps.

"Curie! Where are you? I know you're in here."

Director Weathers pushes through a tangle of branches, emerging into the center of the moongarden like a spider surveying its web, calculated and commanding. He pauses, steadying himself against a thick tree trunk, then shakes his head and pushes off, cutting a quick path through the garden and straight toward us.

CHAPTER FORTY-ONE

DIRECTOR WEATHERS KICKS AT THE PLANTS and flowers, and I find myself wincing with every step he takes. My hands tingle, but I ball them into fists.

"Show yourself, Curie!" he bellows, his heel grinding a small rosebush into pulp. "I didn't have a Rep lasercut a new doorway into Fiona's classroom so you can hide out in this green mess. I will burn this place to the ground like I should have years ago. I know what you're trying to do. My son's already lost his mother to this place. I'm not letting you lure him here, too."

Should we show ourselves? I look at Canter and he just shakes his head, his jaw muscles dancing.

"Lure him?" A new voice drifts through the air, tinged by crackling static. "Have you listened to a single word I've been saying all year? He's already here!"

The director rotates on the spot, searching for the source of the voice.

"Is that Ms. Curie?" I whisper, my eyes frantically darting around. I don't see her anywhere.

"I think she's using the broadcaster," Canter hisses back to me.

"And I never *lured* Fiona here, either. She discovered who she truly was with this garden. I have a lot of regrets, Robert, but giving her those seeds isn't one of them."

"Where are you?" Director Weathers demands, approaching our mostly assembled broadcaster. A blue light flickers from somewhere inside it.

"Did you turn that on?" I ask.

Canter shakes his head, his eyes glued on his father.

Director Weathers bends down beside the broadcaster, tilting it to the side, before letting it drop back into the dust. "I knew you were tampering with the garden, Sandra," he says, his voice as hard and cold as Neptune's core.

"Only to figure out who else had found it, since you've been so determined to cast me as the villain in your life," her voice crackles back from somewhere inside the machine. "I told you something was going on in the garden. I told you I'd seen Canter, and then that friend of his, the Hodger girl, lurking around Fiona's old classroom. I told you I'd seen Fiona's pendant access the school network. And then, between the new surges of electricity and the parts missing from my supply closet, it wasn't hard to figure out who was responsible for the recent activity." There's a pause filled with more static. "I *told* you my suspicions, and all you did was seal up the garden. But I was right. Someone's been building a broadcaster. I should know: I helped Fiona design the original. I planted this transmitter in one of the parts I knew Canter would need and left it in my supply closet so I could listen in once he took it."

"I'm not playing this game," Director Weathers growls. "You blame me for what happened to Fiona, but you played your part. There wasn't anything either of us could have done to save her."

"You keep telling yourself that, Robert," Curie snarls. "At least *I* tried."

"That shuttle didn't blow itself up. And don't you dare tell me I didn't try to save Fi. . . . Is that what this is all about? Revenge? You're trying to drag Canter here to implicate me. Have me sent away, too."

Canter stands and steps out from our hiding spot. "Sent away?"

Director Weathers blinks at his son, his mouth hanging open. "Canter, what—"

The speaker crackles again. "I tried to warn you, Robert," Curie says quietly, resigned. Then the static cuts out, and she's gone.

"Sent away where?" Canter's face is red and his hands are balled into fists at his sides.

"You can't be here," Director Weathers snaps. "You've got to go."

"What happened to my mother?" Canter yells. "She's not dead, is she?"

"She may as well be!" Director Weathers bellows. "She's gone, and she's never coming back. All because of her *dear friend* and these—these *things*." He stomps on a flower and I flinch, tucking myself deeper into my hiding place.

"You had Mom sent away," Canter says slowly, "for being what she was. For being a *Botan*."

"*Don't say that!* Don't call her that, that *word*! Where did you even— How did you—"

"How did I find out that you've been lying to me about my mom my entire life?" Canter asks, his eyes blazing. "And why wouldn't I call her a Botan? That's what she was—what she is. And you got rid of her because of it!"

"Canter, how could you be so foolish! Of course I didn't have your mother sent away."

"THEN WHERE IS SHE?" Canter bellows.

Director Weathers sets his jaw and looks his son firmly in the eye, like a judge about to deliver a sentence. "In the Mercurian Mines with the rest of the plant offenders and criminals," he replies coldly.

"She's alive," Canter whispers, shaking his head. "She's still alive."

"It was easier this way," his father says, rubbing at his temple. "It's . . . what she wanted."

"Easier for who? FOR YOU?" Canter's yelling again, his words echoing through the garden. *So you didn't have to tell me the truth? That you let her be shipped off to Mercury?*

"She was caught by a Council member in possession of seeds. I didn't have a choice. Don't you know what happens to the families of people caught with plants? We were fortunate that my connections on the Council helped me keep it quiet, using the shuttle crash as a diversion." He sweeps his arm around. "And it's lucky they never found out about this—this *monstrosity*. The Council assumed she'd tried to grow a few plants. If they'd known about all *this*, they may have locked us all away on Mercury."

"At least we'd have been together," Canter says quietly, eyeing his dad like he's a stranger.

"You've completely lost your mind if you believe that could have been a viable solution," Director Weathers spits back. "Who knows how long you've been coming here, doing Pluto knows what. But no more." He shakes his head, then moves toward the exit. "I'm going to destroy this place once and for all. I should have done it years ago."

I bolt out of my hiding spot, cutting off the director's path. "You can't!"

"What are you— What is going on here?" the director sputters. "I guess Curie was telling the truth."

I close the distance between us, my sprained ankle twinging painfully with every step, but I'm too desperate to pay it much mind. "This garden could do so much good," I plead. "It could change everything. You've got to see that."

"That's what I thought once, too. But I was young and foolish," he says, his eyes glazing over as he looks out over the browns and greens and golds. I know he's not seeing the garden as it is now. He must be remembering what it was like with Fiona. "We had big plans for this place. We were going to prove to the galaxy that the plants were safe. That they could help the Settlements." His eyes darken as they snap back to focus on me and Canter. "But that was a ridiculous idea. Even if they are safe, it would never work. The public won't ever accept a garden."

"They might if they knew all the food codes were broken," I press.

An ember of fear sparks in Director Weathers's eyes. "We had a deal, Miss Hodger. You were to forget that conversation, and I would forget your repeated absences." His mouth forms a hard line. "As you should have read in our school handbook, a pattern of truancy may lead to expulsion."

"Myra, don't," Canter warns.

I rip up my sleeve. "Expulsion is kind of the least of my worries now, Director Weathers."

But he isn't looking at me anymore. His focus is fixed on Canter. Canter, who's stepped in front of me and pulled up his own sleeves. His are the only set of Botan Inscriptions reflecting in his father's eyes.

"You may be ashamed of this place. Ashamed of my mother. Of who she was and what she accomplished. But I'm not. I'm proud of her. And I'm proud to be like her. She was a Botan, and I am, too."

CHAPTER FORTY-TWO

DIRECTOR WEATHERS STARES AT HIS SON'S arms, unmoving, before he eventually sinks to the ground and puts his head in his hands.

He couldn't turn his back on his own son, could he?

Canter looms over him, glaring down with a fury I've never seen before. "How could you keep all this a secret? Mom's life's work! People should know about this. She'd be in textbooks."

"You think people would praise her for this—this *abomination?*"

Canter recoils, but doesn't say anything more. I tug my sleeve back down so the hem reaches past my knuckles.

If the director can condemn his own son, what will he do to me?

"She'd be ridiculed," Weathers continues. "All she accomplished, even as a non-Creer, discredited."

"She's not a non-Creer," Canter growls.

"That would be better than her being a Botan," spits Director Weathers. "This garden is dangerous, even if it's not poisonous."

"So why'd you leave it intact?" I swallow hard. "Why not destroy it back then?"

"It meant so much to her. I had to protect it. Just like I always promised her I'd protect that Rep, and look how that turned out. . . ."

"I knew it," Canter says, his voice like ice. "I saw it all over your face when I mentioned Bernie. I knew you were the one who terminated his cycle."

"He was due to be retired anyway."

I feel all the air leave my lungs but somehow manage to still choke out a few words. "It was you in the hall."

"I told that Rep in no uncertain terms that if he so much as *breathed* the word *garden* again, he was vapor. The only reason I spared him in the first place was because Fiona made me swear I'd look out for him. She said he could be trusted. Well, she was wrong about a lot of things. I heard him shooting off his mouth about the garden in the middle of a school hallway. For Pluto's sake, he was probably the one who brought you kids here!"

"It wasn't Ms. Curie, and it wasn't Bernie, either. *I* found the garden." I take a step closer. "It was me. *I* shared it with Canter, and *I* made Bernie help me." Tears are streaming down my cheeks, but I don't care.

Director Weathers's voice is grim when he says, "None of that matters anymore. This place has brought me nothing but misery, and now that misery is infecting more people." He juts his chin at us, glaring at the green markings on Canter's arms. "Without the plants, your Elector Inscriptions will overtake the—the *other* ones. No one need ever know."

And what about mine?

"What if I don't want them to?" Canter demands.

"I don't recall asking what you wanted." The director nods at something behind us. I'd forgotten all about the Rep man. He's been standing silently in the corner this entire time, awaiting orders. At Director Weathers's signal, he starts ripping down the mesh we'd hung on the wall for the plants to climb and throwing the panels into a pile. Next, he grabs Bernie's rake from where it's still leaning against the wall and tosses it onto the heap before continuing ripping up the garden.

"Stop it!" I shriek, rushing toward him.

Director Weathers grabs me by the arm, holding me in place.

"I'll tell *everyone* about this place if you destroy it!" I hiss. "And the broken food formulas and how you and Jake Melfin are covering them up. I'll tell everyone that Canter's a Botan, and Fiona, too. And I'll tell them that you helped create the garden and then kept it a secret."

"And who will believe you?" The rage simmering beneath his voice is clear.

I shrug. "They might; they might not. I guess you'll find out."

We stare at each other in silence, locked in a perfect stalemate. I don't know how Canter and I can win, but I don't see how Director Weathers can, either.

He paces, tucking his hands into his pockets. It seems to go on forever, until he turns and points at us. "I will seal the garden, and I mean *seal* it. That entry"—he gestures toward the chute leading back to the lab—"will be blocked for good. And if I hear one word, one *whisper*, that you've told anyone about this place, or that you are anywhere near this side of the school, I will implode this entire wing. Or bury it. Or send it off into space. Anything to destroy it. I don't care what questions it raises. Am I clear?"

We both nod, and he gestures us toward the chute. It's a win, but it doesn't feel that way. We're leaving the garden—leaving forever—and I know he won't even allow us a minute to say goodbye. I hesitate, turning back to gaze at the moongarden, *my* moongarden, one last time.

"Wait!" My eyes scan the ground frantically. "Bin-ro!"

"Let's go." Director Weathers stands at the bottom of the chute, his arms crossed over his chest. "No more nonsen—"

His voice is cut off by a frantic beeping as Bin-ro shoots out from the greenery in a blur of silver. Canter scoops him up as he turns away.

At least we saved Bin-ro. Still cradled in Canter's arm, a light on the little robot's shell glows a melancholy blue. *But who will take care of the flowers with Bin-ro gone?*

With no more ideas or solutions, I trudge past Director Weathers and climb into the mouth of the chute leading back to the lab. He turns to follow me, opening his jacket to reveal an assortment of tiny vials, jars, and bottles. He selects a few, removing the lids, and, using his Chemic magic, mixes the contents midair. The silver, grainy substance flutters to the ground like snow. When it hits the floor of the tunnel, it fizzes and foams, and from the solution, thick, impenetrable glass rises. The clear wall bubbles higher and higher. In a few seconds, it's nearly sealed the entire opening into the garden. Just before it does, Director Weathers tucks his hand back into his jacket pocket, digs something else out, and hurls it back into the green.

CHAPTER FORTY-THREE

THROUGH THE MAGICAL GLASS, I WATCH AS A vial explodes against the ground and purple liquid spills out, then rises into the air, spraying like shrapnel across the room. From the corner of my eye, I watch Director Weathers's hands extend, directing the chemicals into position. The purple droplets sizzle in the air, transforming into a purplish-gray smoke.

Choking back a scream, I fling my arms out in front of me. Golden bubbles emerge from my palms and pass through the glass into the garden.

As if in slow motion, the second vial sails through the room, bounces off a branch, a shrub, and then tumbles toward the ground. I know that when the solution in the second vial mixes with the first, the plants will be destroyed. My protective bubbles drift lazily across the room, shielding the plants one by one. Even so, there's no way I can save them all in time.

I wince, waiting for the inevitable. But before the second vial smashes, Canter steps forward, thrusting out a hand and curling it into a fist. A vine of ivy shoots upward, catches the vial, and winds itself around it.

The whole scene spans a pair of heartbeats.

Director Weathers whips around to face me. "What are you— What are you doing?"

"Protecting them," I say softly. I look him in the eye and think of Fiona imprisoned on Mercury and all of the Botans who were left to die on the Old World. No one tried to protect them. No one helped them. I can't change that, but I can honor their memory. "Protecting your wife's work. Like you should be doing."

"That's— This is impossible," he sputters, desperately shifting his attention between the glowing bubbles surrounding the flowers and me.

"It's not, actually." I roll up my sleeve and hold out my arm for him to see.

His eyes widen, and he snatches my wrist in an iron grip. "You don't have any other Inscriptions?"

Ripping my arm away from him, I toss my hair over my shoulder and plant my hands on my hips. "I'm a *Botan*. I don't need any other Inscriptions."

He hisses, like I've said something vile. "But your parents—"

"Are very smart Number Whisperers, I know. I'm not like them."

"No." He shakes his head. "No, you're not."

The purple fog slowly fills the room. Canter's ivy is still curled around the second vial. The red contents inside it boils, but the vine holds the cap in place. My protective bubbles are glowing around every stem and leaf and bud.

We can't stay like this forever.

A cough from nearby, *inside* the garden, makes us all jump.

"There's someone in there!" Canter steps closer to the glass.

I press my nose up to the newly made wall, my breath fogging the surface. I can just make out the gray overalls of a Rep uniform through the purple fog. The man is still inside the moongarden, trapped.

I turn to face the director. "You've got to let him out of there!" Director Weathers looks smug, like he's just won a point in an argument. He doesn't even glance toward the glass. *He doesn't care.*

"Drop the defenses and let the vial go, and I'll open the door." He glances at his wrist. "You'd better hurry. That gas is toxic, and it's almost reached lethal levels."

"You'd really let him die in there?" Canter yells. "Over some *plants*?"

Director Weathers turns calmly to face his son. "What do you think?"

Canter and I lock eyes, quickly and silently coming to the only decision we can. With tears in my eyes, I jab a finger into the air, and all at once, the shimmering bubbles burst. At the same moment, Canter opens his fist and the second vial crashes to the ground with the tinkle of breaking glass. It's a tiny sound, but it echoes in my head like an explosion.

"Open it!" Canter shouts.

Director Weathers presses his hand to the glass. Around his palm, spiraling bigger and bigger, the glass streaks a cloudy white. When the foggy section grows large enough, he beckons the man forward. He stumbles in, passing through the transformed glass, and falls to his knees, hacking and struggling for breath. Director Weathers lifts his hand again and the glass is clear and solid once more. Canter and I throw out our arms, golden bubbles blooming back into the room.

They drift lazily through the air, trying to wrap the plants in their glittering protection, but this time, they burst the second they make contact. It's too late. The plants are already dying. The smoke shifts from purple to black, and the plants fade, too, from brown to black, then an ashy gray.

Before long, all that remains of the bubbles is a golden mist, and then even that is consumed by the black smoke. New protective bubbles emerge from our palms only to sputter and burst a second later. The plants are gone, and without them, so is our Botan magic.

"Let's go," Director Weathers says for a second time.

Like a zombie, Canter turns and climbs up the tunnel, his face twisted with rage and grief. Bin-ro follows close on his heels, beeping softly.

The director pauses, glancing back at the room where the garden used to be. He drops his eyes as if apologizing, then turns and begins to clamber up the tunnel.

Alone, I stare through the glass. "I'm sorry," I whisper. I can see the whole room without the leaves and branches in the way. It looks so small and hollow. "I'm sorry I couldn't save you."

The gray ashes of my garden—of *my friends*—mix with the gray, gravelly ground, until it's hard to tell one from the other.

And then a small spot of color catches my eye—a blip of yellow in a sea of nothing. My eyes widen as a daffodil pushes itself free of the ash and dust. It stands tall for a moment, proud, beautiful, and pristine. A perfect flower. But then I see the edges of the petals blacken, the wobble in the stem.

The bloom turns toward me, bending forward so dramatically I think it must have fallen to the black fog, too. But then it rises again, fluttering peacefully like a breeze is flowing through the room. My cheeks wet, I smile and give a small curtsy in return. "You're welcome," I whisper.

The flower stands defiantly for a moment before the black decay swallows its sunshine like ink soaking through paper. The perfect daffodil finally wilts, then crumples, then crumbles into dust.

I turn from the barren room and numbly walk away for the last time.

Director Weathers and Canter are waiting for me in the lab. The director raises an eyebrow. "So, *Miss Botan,* what exactly are we going to do with you now?"

CHAPTER FORTY-FOUR

"MYRA, WHY ARE YOU CALLING SO LATE? IS everything okay? Who's that behind you?"

My mother's normally perfect hair is rumpled and frizzy. Dad rubs at his eyes and yawns.

Director Weathers pushes his chair into the frame.

"Robert?" Dad's yawn snaps into a frown. "Myra, what's going on?"

I fiddle with the edge of the table, flipping buttons and shutters open and closed, forcing myself to hold their gaze. Tossing my own messy hair over my shoulder, I will my swollen eyes to dry. Director Weathers didn't even give me time to clean up after our little *chat* and visit to one of the Chemic classrooms. After he proved his theory right, he insisted we inform my parents immediately, as if he's afraid I'll change my mind.

How could I? Like Canter said, there aren't any options left.

"I'm not taking the Number Whisperer exam," I say so softly, it's a wonder they hear me at all.

Two sets of eyes blink back at me. My parents open their mouths to object, but their words overlap in an incoherent jumble.

Director Weathers raises his hand, and surprisingly, they both fall silent. "Let her finish."

I take a deep breath, like I'm about to plunge underwater. *I hope I don't drown.*

"I don't have Number Whispering magic."

They stare at me, mouths hanging open, a storm of emotion on their faces: Shock. Disappointment. Denial. Outrage. A few of them I'm used to; others sting more than I'd like to admit.

Mom recovers first. "But you—"

I shake my head. "I've never had any Numbers magic. Never heard a trace of a whisper."

Dad blinks his way out of his comatose state. "But your—"

"The placement test scores aren't always right," I say, reciting the words as if they're lines from a play.

"Myra, how could you not tell us?" Mom looks genuinely hurt.

I lean forward toward the camera. "How could you not notice?"

"That's not fair. I never—" Mom stops and resets, her forehead creasing into a *V*. "You kept all this from us for— How long have you known?"

"I was good at math, but I never liked it," I reply, my voice low. Little flickers shine on Mom's cheeks as tears cross with the light from the screen. "The magic never came, and what was I supposed to say? *So sorry to disappoint you, but I won't be following in your Whispering footsteps.*"

"Myra, I don't care about that! I care that you kept this to yourself, all this time!" Mom swipes at her eyes with her sleeve. "So what happens now? Are you being sent home?"

"We can start looking at the very best non-magical Lunar schools," Dad says, his gaze already distant, probably computing how many acceptable non-Creer schools there are in the vicinity.

Director Weathers shakes his head. "She doesn't need to leave S.L.A.M."

So you can keep a close eye on me. But I don't argue. I want to stay, and if this is the only way I can, I'll go along with it.

"But how?" Mom asks.

"I'm going to be a Chemic."

But I'm not a Chemic, not really. I just have a little Chemic magic. Director Weathers thought I might. Fiona had done some research . . . but that's not important.

Dad blinks. "A Chemic?"

"Myra, you've never had *any* affinity for Chemic theory," Mom says. "None. It's your worst subject."

"I'd be happy to have her do a Chemic magic demonstration," Director Weathers says smoothly. "You'll see she *does* actually—"

Mom holds her hand up, cutting him off. "I know my own daughter, Robert. Even if I have been a bit distracted." She shoots me an apologetic glance. "And I know she's not a Chemic. So what is really going on?"

Director Weathers looks at me expectantly.

"I'm a Chemic," I repeat robotically, twisting my hands together.

"What are those?" Dad points to the bottom of the screen. "On your wrist."

I turn, wide-eyed, to Director Weathers. After everything that's happened tonight, I'd forgotten to be careful about my sleeves. A glance down tells me that the night has resulted in some new Botan Inscriptions, too. An emerald vine curls around my wrist like a bracelet, tendrils dotted with golden leaves sprouting off it like glittering jewels.

"They are Chemic Inscriptions," Director Weathers says quickly. "See, I told you—"

"I've never seen green Chemic Inscriptions before," Mom interrupts, leaning closer to the screen. "Myra, what is really going on?"

"I've told you—" Director Weathers starts.

Mom's eyes flash with a fire I've never seen, not even when she was debating number theory at an intersettlement conference. "I'm asking my daughter, Robert. And if I have to come down there to find out, I will be on the next train." She turns back to me, her gaze softening. "Myra?"

I roll up my sleeves and show my arms to the camera. "I don't have any Chemic Inscriptions. Only these."

Director Weathers pushes my arm back down, out of sight of the camera. "I think it's best we keep those hidden."

Dad's eyes bulge. "Are those what I think they are?"

I nod.

"How is that possible?" Mom asks.

"I found this garden," I begin.

"I'm sorry, what?" Dad asks, his mouth hanging open.

Director Weathers shifts beside me. "That's a long story, and not a particularly important one. The garden is gone." He glances pointedly in my direction. "For good."

Mom and Dad exchange a look, and a whole conversation must pass within the one glance. "We could have dealt with you being a . . . a Chemic." Dad puts his arm around Mom's shoulders. "We could have helped you . . . figure things out. I'm disappointed that you thought you had to hide all this from us."

"I'm *not* a Chemic! I'm a—"

"*Chemic*," Director Weathers cuts in. "You're a Chemic, or you're on your way to Mercury."

"Don't you *dare* threaten my daughter!" Dad growls.

"There will be no problem, Joe, so long as Miss Hodger keeps to her word," Director Weathers replies icily.

"Myra, is this what you want?" Mom folds her hands on the table in front of her, looking at me for what seems like the first time ever.

I want to go back to the moongarden. I want to be a Botan. I want to learn more Botan magic. But most of all, I want to stay. Because staying as a Chemic is better than leaving as a Botan.

"Yes."

Staying means there's hope.

"Then she stays. As a Chemic. I hope I've made myself clear." Director Weathers locks eyes with both my parents, and then turns to me, searching for confirmation. I nod, and he seems satisfied. "It's settled, then." Director Weathers sits back in his chair. "I can't have you take the Chemic exam, obviously. You wouldn't be able to pass the full practical, just the areas that deal with the elements derived from the Old World plants. . . . I'll work out the arrangements."

Dad nods. Mom just stares at me.

Director Weathers spouts off a long list of instructions—something about what classes I'll attend and which professors will know what—and then moves to end the call.

Mom raises her hand to stop him.

"Myra." She leans forward, her face filling the screen. "Myra, I'm sorry. About everything."

I try to roll my eyes—to come up with something sarcastic to snap at her—but instead, I hear myself saying, "Me, too."

She ends the call.

I hover outside the classroom door. From this angle, I can see my seat in the back. It's empty, but so are the rest. Class won't start for another twenty minutes, but I was hoping to catch Ms. Goble before the other kids got there. She's working at her desk, but my feet seem to be stuck in the hall.

I don't have to be here. Director Weathers said he already talked to Ms. Goble and made all the arrangements. But I have a question for her.

I pluck my feet from the floor and hurtle through the doorway.

Ms. Goble glances up, then returns her attention to her computer screen. "Miss Hodger, don't tell me you're here to turn in that research paper on non-Creer jobs I assigned you."

I never even started that thing. "Er, no." I take a breath. "I came to ask you about Fiona Weathers."

She looks up sharply, then powers her screen off. "We

started here the same year," she says matter-of-factly, as if I'd asked her about the weather. "We hit it off right away, long before she opted to leave to attend a non-Creer school." The ghost of a smile plays across Ms. Goble's face. "She came back to visit often. First to see me and Ms. Curie, and later to see Robert—Director Weathers, too." Ms. Goble steeples her hands and touches them to her chin. "Fiona was a lovely person, and a good friend."

I rock on my heels, turning thoughts over and over. "Do you know who turned her in to the Council?"

"The Chemic representative, Bradford Melfin, apparently caught her with seeds."

My eyes must flash with recognition at the name, because she adds, "His son, Jake, serves on the Council with your father."

I fight back a smirk. Pretty soon, the whole galaxy will know Jake Melfin's name.

"It was lucky that Director Weathers was friendly with Jake. Things can be very difficult for the families of those caught with plant paraphernalia. Prejudices left over from Old World days . . ." She waves a hand as if she can brush away the thought. "Luckily, Director Weathers was able to work out a deal that kept Fiona's imprisonment quiet."

"The crashed shuttle."

Ms. Goble nods. "Ms. Curie was very much against the idea. I thought there was a good chance Director Weathers would leave the room a human lightning bolt when they explained the plan to us. But in the end, Fiona was able to convince her to help."

"If it's what Fiona wanted, then why do they hate each other so much?"

"Ms. Curie felt they should have gone public with the garden as they'd planned. She thought Director Weathers should have fought harder to convince Fiona to try it. And I think Director Weathers grew to despise the plants. He blames them for what happened to his wife. And he blames Ms. Curie for giving Fiona the seeds in the first place."

"But the seeds helped her." I pause. I don't know how much Ms. Goble knows about Fiona and the seeds and how exactly she got the garden to grow as well as it did. "The seeds helped her discover who she was," I try.

Ms. Goble nods slowly, locking her gaze with mine. "Yes, that's true."

She doesn't say anything more, and she doesn't need to. I see it all there in her eyes. Certain things can't be spoken aloud, not even now. Some secrets have to stay secrets.

"Where did Ms. Curie get the seeds?" I ask instead, changing the subject.

Ms. Goble smiles softly and shakes her head. "That's not my story to tell."

"Okay, I'll ask Ms. Curie."

The smile drops off Ms. Goble's face like a Moon rock.

"I'm afraid that won't be possible. Ms. Curie no longer teaches at S.L.A.M."

My mouth falls open. "Where did she go?"

"She's accepted a position on the Venus Settlement. She left yesterday morning."

Neither of us says anything for a few moments. After a while, Ms. Goble resumes her work, and I walk toward the door.

"So, a Chemic."

I turn back around. Ms. Goble hasn't looked up from her screen. I shrug anyway. "It was a surprise to me, too."

"You never struck me as a Chemic."

"The director told me that our Creers know us better than we know ourselves. They choose us for our affinities, even if we don't know what they are yet."

"Did he, now?" She glances up at me. "I'd have to agree with that."

She looks back at her work, and I turn to leave again.

"I'm very interested to see the type of Chemic you bloom into, Miss Hodger."

CHAPTER FORTY-FIVE

TWO WEEKS LATER, I SIGH AT THE BLOBS OF purple now stored in my closet. Chemic jumpsuits—five of them—hang in a neat row. I press a button and the door slides shut.

"You'll get used to it," Lila says with an encouraging smile. She's already wearing her white Mender jumpsuit, proudly smoothing out the perfectly unwrinkled sleeves. "Purple will look nice on you."

"Green would look better," I mutter. I'm convinced that if Botans were still an accepted Creer, their jumpsuits would be green. I filled Lila in on *everything* after the showdown in the moongarden. I half expected her to ditch me, or at least start acting weird and awkward, but she didn't seem at all bothered by the fact that her roommate's a secret Botan. I guess growing up with a non-Creer dad made her pretty tolerant of people off the Creer map.

"Green would be nice, too," she admits, flopping onto my bed. I plop down next to her. "At least you don't have to wear the purple ones until next year if you don't want to."

With the Creer tests behind us and classes over for the year, we only have a few days to pack before we head home for break. *That's going to be a long two months.* I glance toward my closet door. *Especially with what's in there.*

"How's it going, Mixture Myra?" Canter pops his head into our room and leans against the doorframe. Bin-ro scoots in from behind him, whistling a greeting. We agreed it would be easier for Canter to keep him in his quarters. We already have enough people living in my dorm room.

I fight back a grin and stoop to pat the little robot. (He still likes me best, even if he *is* Canter's roommate now.) "Stop calling me that!"

"Hey, I thought you'd be happy to have a place in society and all."

Lila laughs as he walks in and jumps onto the bed.

"It's not really what I had in mind. And don't encourage him," I add, glaring at Lila.

"Being a Chemic is a respectable position."

"It's also a boring one." I nod toward my closet full of purple. "Plus, I'm not a *real* Chemic. My powers only work on plant-related solvents."

"It's enough to keep you here," Lila reminds me.

I shrug and stare into the hallway. For half a second, my heart stops. I think I see Bernie. But when I blink again, it's just a younger man in a Rep uniform. I've never seen him before. He does a funny little sidestep that reminds me of Bernie dancing with the sunflower, before he disappears down the hall. I stifle a sigh and turn back to Canter.

"Any luck with the research?" I ask, raising my eyebrows.

"Some."

Without the threat of expulsion looming on the horizon or the garden to tend to, we've thrown ourselves into finding out as much as we can about what happened to Bernie. Director Weathers refused to tell us anything, and from what I gather, he and Canter aren't talking about much of anything lately, except for his Elector studies. He's got Canter reading Elector theory and practicing his electrical magic every spare moment, trying to coax his Elector Inscriptions to cover over his Botan ones.

Thankfully, it's been slow going. As I know all too well, magic and Inscriptions take passion as well as knowledge, and now that Canter's discovered his other talents, it's dulled his love of Elector magic, for better or worse.

"What'd you find?" Lila asks, leaning forward on her elbows. "Anything on your Rep friend?"

"Bernie," Canter corrects. "And not exactly. I kind of stumbled across something when I was doing a general search on Rep life cycles. There wasn't a lot out there."

"Of course there wasn't."

"Quiet, Myra. Let me finish. I found some posts on some weird thread. They were kind of intense."

I swivel to face him. "Intense how?"

"Just . . . strange. Talking about Rep rights. How they're humans and shouldn't be tied to the choices their originals made generations before them, and how . . . how if someone *flips the switch*, the whole system could crumble."

Lila fidgets. "What does that mean? Flip the switch?"

Canter leans toward us. "I didn't get it, either, so I asked one of my Tekkie friends about it, and he said that Reps have some sort of implant injected into them that suppresses their magic."

Lila's eyes widen. "Their magic?"

I turn this over in my mind. "Reps are human. Literally perfect copies of humans. But I've never heard of a Rep having magic. How could they not, though? Unless something *was* stopping them from accessing it?"

A shriek in the doorway makes us all jump. For half a second, I catch a flash of a blond-haired form wrapped in a fuzzy pink bathrobe with green blotches all over her face, followed by slapping footsteps echoing down the hall.

"What the— What was that?" Canter asks.

"Bethany," Lila replies with a smirk. "She was running

her mouth about how bad the Chem wing smells, and some fifth-year Chemics heard her. They decided to test out some of their experiments on her. She's been trying to scrub the green off since *yesterday*."

I crack a smile, but my mind's still on the posts Canter found. "Who controls the implants? Do you think Bernie had one, too?" If anyone should have had Botan magic, it's Bernie.

Canter shrugs. "Probably? And I don't know who controls them."

"What do they mean about the whole system crumbling?" I ask.

He sighs. "I don't know. Maybe it's just some weird person ranting."

Weird's not sounding so bad these days.

"What about your dad's passwords?" Lila asks. "Any luck cracking the new ones?"

"No," Canter says, "but I haven't had a good try at it yet, either. With all that extra Elector work he has filling my every waking hour, I was lucky to sneak in all the research I did. But I was thinking of taking a Tekkie course over the break. It's all about programming computer systems and databases. Maybe it'll help me figure something out, and Dad shouldn't suspect anything."

He'd better not. There's no way I'm letting Bernie just fade into space dust. How many other Reps have walked this Moon, just to vanish into oblivion? How many more will? Plus, if these implant things are real . . .

And what about the Botans? If there are more people like Canter and me out there, more *Botans* hiding or . . . wherever they are, I need to find them. *Before anyone else does.*

I pick up my messenger and glance at the note glowing on the screen, taking in the message I've written and rewritten more times than I can possibly count.

Dear Hannah,

I'm writing to say I'm sorry. I'm sorry about everything. I'm the last person you probably want to hear from right now, and I have absolutely zero right to ask you anything, especially a favor, but here I am. I need to talk to you about something—I can't write it here—it has to do with that thing we fought about. I'll understand if you don't reply, but it's important. Really important. I hope you write back. And I hope you like your new school and the Venus Settlement.

Your very sorry friend,
Myra

I take a breath and hit Send. Based on everything I've learned, I can't pretend that the story Hannah told me was made up. Not anymore. I'm sure something happened to make Hannah and her family move, and all I can do now is try and set things right.

Staring off into the distance, I wonder if she saw the message yet. If she's typing a reply, or just hitting Delete. Probably the latter. But response or not, the apology at least was the right thing to do.

I tap over to my Sent folder, scrolling down to the message below the one I just sent. This one's time stamped a week earlier, though, and I have no doubts it was read. Read by quite a few people, actually.

"What are you smiling about, Mixture Myra?" Canter asks. "Find a new recipe?"

"No." Lila laughs. "She's been giggling about her little news story all day."

"Let me enjoy my small victory!"

"Not that small," Lila says, grinning.

Canter flops over with a groan. "I don't know how you two are so chipper about the whole thing. I, for one, am not excited to eat slime squares forever."

Hopefully, not forever. I swipe over to the school network and tap the first headline on the *Lunar Chronicle* news site: "Food Cloning Formulas Broken. Council's Chemic Representative Resigns as a Result of Cover-Up."

"The article says they were tipped off by an anonymous source," I reply, still smirking.

Canter's eyebrows draw together. "You know my dad knows it was you, right? That was pretty risky."

I shrug. "I've got too much on him for him to expel me. Besides, people have a right to know." *And maybe, just maybe, it'll make the galaxy a little less freaked out by the idea of a garden. One day.*

There's a window in the hall opposite our door. I imagine a flower curling its way through the dusty gravel, like the first time I saw a flower bud unfold with Bernie. "I miss him," I say softly. "And them."

"Me, too," Canter replies. "But we'll see them again. Soon. Maybe you will, too, Lila."

I whirl around so fast I almost topple off the bed. "What do you mean?"

He shrugs, his eyes sparkling. "I got you an end-of-the-year present. Or better yet, a *you-didn't-get-expelled* present."

My mouth hangs open as he digs in his pocket, then pulls his hand back, holding his fist out toward me. He slowly uncurls his fingers. Resting in his palm are a half-dozen seeds.

A grin stretches my face so much it hurts. I force it away and shrug. "Is that it?"

Canter's excited expression fades. "Are you serious? Do you know how lucky it is that I stuck these in my pocket while we were working that day?"

"Myra." Lila gasps. "You know what this means, right? You can grow more plants!"

I shrug again, fighting back my grin. "Won't be much of a garden with only six seeds."

Canter looks seriously wounded.

I can't keep this up much longer.

Rising from the bed, I cross to the closet, then dig around, looking for something. When I emerge, I have an old pair of green socks balled up in my hand. I toss the bundle onto Canter's lap. "Check those out."

Canter grimaces. "I don't want to touch your dirty socks," he grumbles. His face looks like a Crawler ran over Bin-ro.

"They're clean, and they were the best option I had to— Oh, just unroll them already!"

He carefully unfolds them, his eyes focusing on the bulge in the toe. He peers inside and gasps.

"What?" Lila asks, leaning in.

Wordless, Canter holds the green sock upside down over her palms. A cascade of seeds of all sizes and colors pours out. Hundreds of them.

I smirk. "I *am* glad you had those seeds in your pocket. Accidentally. I don't think I snagged any of those kinds." I sit back down beside them. "But I am *super* glad I decided to start stockpiling seeds months ago."

Canter grins and shakes his head. "I guess that was a pretty smart move."

I nudge him with my shoulder. "*Highly* intelligent, I'd say."

He nudges me back. "You're right. I may consider giving you some sort of position of authority in our new garden. *If* you're nice to me between now and then. Maybe Head Moongarden Janitor?"

I shove him, and then bound off the bed, grabbing him and Lila by the arm. "I've already been scouting the school for places we could hide a garden. Not a big one, but big enough." Bin-ro whistles and scoots into the hall ahead of us. "C'mon! I'll show you."

ACKNOWLEDGMENTS

For over a decade, I've been daydreaming about writing the acknowledgments for my book. It feels very surreal to be sitting here right now and attempting to draft them. To that end, I'd like to first acknowledge and thank the greater writing community. Reading about the daily successes, obstacles, anecdotes, and celebrations of my fellow writers fueled, inspired, and motivated me more than I can say. Thank you for sharing your journeys with the rest of us. And to all of you in the query trenches, please keep going. You never know what happy surprise could land in your inbox tomorrow.

To my incredible agent, Moe Ferrara, there aren't enough pages in all the libraries of the world to fully express my gratitude and appreciation for all that you do. From taking a chance on me and *Moongarden*, to the support, guidance, and interstellar meme-game you have provided along the way, I can never thank you enough. This book has become infinitely more special to me through all you've brought to it.

And to the rest of the BookEnds Literary Agency team, thank you for everything you do for the agency's clients. I am proud and honored to count myself among them.

I feel like I hit the Jupiter Jackpot to land at such an exceptional publisher as Pixel+Ink, and a large part of that good fortune is getting to work with the brilliant superhero of an editor, Alison Weiss, whose insights, guidance, and vision are out of this universe. Thank you for bringing your magic to *Moongarden*.

To Derek Stordahl, Bethany Buck, and the rest of the Pixel+Ink team—Terry Borzumato-Greenberg, Aleah Gornbein, Darby

Guinn, K Dishmon, Michelle Montague, Miriam Miller, Erin Mathis, Annie Rosenbladt, Mary Joyce Perry, Melissa See, Elyse Vincenty, Alison Tarnofsky, Sara DiSalvo, Carmena Jarrett, Melanie McMahon Ives, Courtney Hood, Jamie Evans, Raina Putter, Melissa Kavonic, Regina M. Castillo, Jay Colvin, and Arlene Goldberg—you have my endless gratitude for turning this story into a real book.

To *Moongarden*'s cover artist, Sarah Coleman (aka Inkymole), and cover designer, Sammy Yuen, I'm not sure which lucky star granted me the honor of having you both bring *Moongarden* to life through your artistic visions, but the cover is absolutely a wish come true.

If I never published a single word, this journey would have been worth it for the friends I have made along the way.

To Tracy Townsend and Maura Jortner, my first writing friends who have become some of my most treasured all-around friends: Your writing inspired me to want to become a better writer, and your friendship allowed me to survive in the query trenches long enough to become one. I remain awed by your stories and forever grateful for your friendship. *Moongarden* would not exist without both of you.

Thank you to all the readers of the many, many versions of *Moongarden* over the years, but most especially to Jen Griswell for your endless support, read-throughs, and encouragement. I feel so lucky to call you a friend. And to *Moongarden*'s first kiddo beta readers, Felicity Jortner and Corwin Townsend, thank you for your perspective and insights. They are ingrained in the fibers of this story.

To my oldest friends, Deyonne, Kate, and Mikaela, I appreciate and love you all more than I can say. And a special thanks to Christina and Sarah for celebrating my book news when it was still in the super-secret phase, and to Melissa, for our coffee-shop writing sprints that helped keep me on track for Book 2. I cannot wait to see your stories on a bookshelf someday!

I have a very large family, and these acknowledgments are already turning into the book version of my family's usual "Italian goodbye" (IYKYK), but I have to call out a few folks in particular. To my sister, Carrie, my sister-in-law, Rachel, and Linda Mazzoni, thank you for always checking in on my book news, for cheering me on, and for the laughs (and book recs!). And especially to Julie (aka "Auntie"), who has been a pillar of goodness in my life for as long as I can remember.

They say cousins are your first friends, and that's certainly true, but I count myself lucky that mine are also some of my best friends.

To Victoria, thank you for your constant support, sound advice, and endless patience with my random questions. Your talent is an inspiration and your friendship a treasure. To Kimberly, thank you for all your encouragement over the past many years and for always being there for me. I appreciate you more than you know. And to Corinne—tag, you're it! Now it's your turn. ☺

To my mom, thank you for always bringing me to the library and never complaining about the towering stack of books I would lug out the door, for reading to me endlessly, and for always believing in me. And to my dad, thank you for instilling in me the rewards of hard work and for being a shining example of what it means to give things your all. I would never have finished one page of one book without the work ethic you personified.

And finally, to my husband and children, thank you for forgiving my late nights and early mornings, for celebrating the victories, large and small, and for believing in me. I love you to the moon and back, and I hope you know that I believe in your dreams, too, always.